OTHER WORLDS,
OTHER GODS

OTHER WORLDS, OTHER GODS

Adventures in Religious Science Fiction

Edited by

MAYO MOHS

1971
Doubleday & Company, Inc., Garden City, New York

"The Cunning of the Beast" by Nelson Bond. Copyright 1942, 1954 by Nelson Bond. Reprinted by permission of the author.

"A Cross of Centuries" by Henry Kuttner. Copyright © 1958 by Ballantine Books, Inc. Reprinted by permission of Harold Matson Company, Inc.

"Soul Mate" by Lee Sutton. Copyright © 1958 by Mercury Press, Inc. Reprinted by permission of the author and the author's agent, Robert P. Mills, Ltd.

"The Word to Space" by Winston P. Sanders. Copyright © 1960 by Mercury Press, Inc. Reprinted by permission of the author and his agents, Scott Meredith Literary Agency, Inc., 580 Fifth Avenue, New York, N.Y. 10036.

"Prometheus" by Philip José Farmer. Copyright © 1961 by Mercury Press, Inc. Reprinted by permission of the author and his agents, Scott Meredith Literary Agency, Inc., 580 Fifth Avenue, New York, N.Y. 10036.

"The Nine Billion Names of God" by Arthur C. Clarke. Copyright 1953 by Ballantine Books. Reprinted by permission of the author and his agents, Scott Meredith Literary Agency, Inc., 580 Fifth Avenue, New York, N.Y. 10036.

"The Vitanuls" by John Brunner. Copyright © 1967 by Mercury Press, Inc. Reprinted by permission of the author and his agents, Scott Meredith Literary Agency, Inc., 580 Fifth Avenue, New York, N.Y. 10036.

"Judas" by John Brunner. Copyright © 1967, 1969 by Harlan Ellison. Reprinted by permission of the author and his agents, Scott Meredith Literary Agency, Inc., 580 Fifth Avenue, New York, N.Y. 10036.

"The Quest for Saint Aquin" by Anthony Boucher. Copyright 1951 by Phyllis White. Reprinted by permission of Collins-Knowlton-Wing, Inc.

"Balaam" by Anthony Boucher. Copyright 1954 by Henry Holt and Company, Inc. Reprinted by permission of Collins-Knowlton-Wing.

"Evensong" by Lester del Rey. Copyright © 1967 by Harlan Ellison. Reprinted by permission of the author and his agents, Scott Meredith Literary Agency, Inc., 580 Fifth Avenue, New York, N.Y. 10036.

"Shall the Dust Praise Thee?" by Damon Knight. Copyright © 1967 by Harlan Ellison. Reprinted from *Dangerous Visions* by permission of the author.

"Christus Apollo" (selection) by Ray Bradbury. Copyright © 1969 by Ray Bradbury. Reprinted by permission of Harold Matson Company, Inc.

And a special word of acknowledgment to Edward L. Ferman and Robert P. Mills, present and past editors of the magazine *Fantasy and Science Fiction*, whose generous assistance in finding some of these stories was invaluable.

For my Mother and Father,
  who endured that early wonder

For Fred Nolan,
  who shared it

For Father Walter Reger,
  who blessed it

And for Patty,
  who helped bring it back to life.

CONTENTS

Introduction: Science Fiction and the World
   of Religion   11

The Cunning of the Beast—Nelson Bond   19

A Cross of Centuries—Henry Kuttner   44

Soul Mate—Lee Sutton   61

The Word to Space—Winston P. Sanders   80

Prometheus—Philip José Farmer   100

The Nine Billion Names of God—Arthur C.
   Clarke   162

The Vitanuls—John Brunner   171

Judas—John Brunner   196

The Quest for Saint Aquin—Anthony Boucher   206

Balaam—Anthony Boucher   230

Evensong—Lester del Rey   249

Shall the Dust Praise Thee?—Damon Knight   256

Christus Apollo—Ray Bradbury   261

OTHER WORLDS, OTHER GODS

INTRODUCTION

Science Fiction and the World of Religion

"All names belong in the hat, Ben. Man is so built that he cannot imagine his own death. This leads to endless invention of religions. While this conviction by no means proves immortality to be a fact, questions generated by it are overwhelmingly important. The nature of life, how ego hooks into the body, the problem of ego itself and why each ego *seems* to be the center of the universe, the purpose of life, the purpose of the universe—these are paramount questions, Ben; they can never be trivial. Science hasn't solved them, and who am I to sneer at religion for *trying?*"

—Jubal Harshaw, in Robert Heinlein's *Stranger in a Strange Land.*

These are paramount questions. The words are those of a character in a novel, but they may explain why that novel —a science-fiction work now nearly a decade old—has gone through ten paperback printings in the past two years and become an underground best seller, especially among the young. The words may explain, too, why Stanley Kubrick's *2001: A Space Odyssey* has attracted such wide and devoted attention that even a book on its making is a brisk-selling success. Beyond Kubrick's gadgetry and Heinlein's potboiling style, both efforts are ultimately concerned with questions that in Jubal Harshaw's phrase "can never be trivial."

Science fiction, that onetime realm of voluptuous maidens and bug-eyed monsters, has rediscovered an element in life that mainstream literature, in recent years, has largely ignored. Science fiction has found religion—or at the very least, a new sense of the infinite that no star drive can conquer. The encounter, as the stories in this book may at least partly demonstrate, has been fascinating.

The phenomenon is not exactly new, but it has been slow in the building. There are twelve stories and one poem in this book, the earliest dating from 1942, the latest from 1969. All, in one way or another, have to do with religion, religious myth, conscience or that inestimable beyondness about life that we call the transcendental. Doubtless there are earlier examples, but most of early science fiction was largely innocent—or ignorant—about religion. Jules Verne's wondrous voyages displayed a concern with religion about on par with that of the technological prophets of the nineteenth century: very little. Verne's machines were splendid, but his characters—even the haunted Captain Nemo—seemed to place their faith only in those machines, as if the technological, rather than the transcendent, was the ultimate answer to man's problems. Traditional spiritual awe was reflected principally in fantasy, or in such rare (and genuine) pieces of science fiction as Ambrose Bierce's "The Damned Thing."

Later, a different kind of attitude influenced science fiction. For H. G. Wells, an outspoken atheist, the world of the future was a world where any notion of the spiritual should have disappeared. Other science-fiction writers, many of them optimistic technocrats or at least rebels against the religions of their day, followed suit. When religion appeared in their fiction at all, it was esoteric or primeval. Writers fell into the sort of "South Seas" syndrome that infected Hollywood movies in the thirties. The gods of Flash Gordon, Buck Rogers, and *Amazing Stories* —when there were gods—were mostly demeaning caricatures of oriental religions and primitive pagan cults. James Churchward's reconstructed religion of Mu was perhaps a more serious attempt (indeed, one might charitably note that it was not intended as science fiction), but it was nonetheless so outlandish as to appeal only to *aficionados*.

Perhaps World War II helped effect a change, for science, it became consummately clear, did not have every answer after all. But perhaps some of the change still derived from continuing attempts to solve ancient riddles, a la *Mu*. Remember Immanuel Velikovsky's *Worlds in Collision*, that fascinating effort to explain the parting of the Red Sea and the stationary sun over Jericho (among other ancient myths and miracles) by postulating a close brush with another planet? That sort of pseudoscholarly venture is still with us. Just last year, a Swiss hotelman named Erich von Däniken published *Chariots of the Gods*, which argues that highly intelligent space travelers visited earth during man's early history and became the prototypes of the "gods" of various ancient mythologies. A Russian philologist has proposed that Jesus Christ was a cosmonaut and the Star of Bethlehem his rocket. Jesus, says the Russian, was quite explicit: "My Kingdom is not of this world."

Däniken also dredges some of his examples out of the Bible. Ezekiel's famous fiery wheel, he says, was a flying saucer. Genesis 6 ("there were giants in the earth in those days") describes the mating of the "sons of God" with the "daughters of men"—a reference, argues Däniken, to the visiting spacemen's couplings with earthlings. For my own part, I prefer the straightforward fable-telling of Nelson Bond, whose reconstruction of Genesis in "The Cunning

of the Beast"—the first story in this collection—begins
from a similar hypothesis. Yet Bond develops this into an
observation about mankind that the old Hebrew Scripture
writers themselves would hardly fault.

I have considerable affection for Bond's story because it
was, in my fourteenth summer, my first experience with
science fiction that had anything to do with religious
symbols I myself held dear. I was then a very conscientious
young Roman Catholic, and Bond's poignant fable disturbed my traditionalist view of the Genesis account. I
took it to a wise priest, more a friend than a counselor,
and asked him whether I should (as I did) enjoy such
stories. His considered reply was that the story was a fine
allegory. That judgment may or may not be accurate, but
at that moment Father Walter Reger demonstrated that my
faith had plenty of room for a sense of wonder—and it
does still.

Indeed, some of the most imaginative of religious science
fiction, if that is the term, has been built on the very rock
of orthodoxy. For C. S. Lewis, the worlds of fantasy and
science fiction were not at all incompatible with deep and
conservative Christian faith—a contention he demonstrated
handsomely in his literate trilogy, *Out of the Silent Planet*,
Perelandra, and *That Hideous Strength*. His Perelandrans,
for instance, were simply creatures who had not fallen
from primordial grace and thus retained special powers
(Thomas Aquinas called them "preternatural gifts") which
sinful humans had lost with Eden.

More recently, science-fiction novelists who like to
dwell on mankind's nature and future have been extrapolating destinies for the race that seem to owe more to
humanistic or oriental philosophies. In Arthur Clarke's
Against the Fall of Night, man finds it necessary to create
his own gods—pure intelligences—to rule and serve his
universe. In Clarke's *Childhood's End*, on the other hand,

a mysterious race of "Overlords" raises mankind from "childhood" to the next evolutionary step—but in an arbitrary way that suggests the contemptuous gods of ancient paganism. *Starchild*, by Jack Williamson and Frederick Pohl, suggests a Buddhist view of life. Men become a part of the omnipotent (and omnivorous) Starchild—a part of "god," as it were—achieving a kind of secular nirvana. One of the stories in this collection, Clarke's "Nine Billion Names of God," finds its inspiration in the strange mission of a Tibetan monastery—and its horror in the fate of those who exploit belief.

In one sense, such authors are playing on safe ground: Their predictions are not likely to be outdistanced by events. Authors who deal with more contemporary religious ideas and institutions, no matter how insightfully, may find themselves quickly overtaken. No finer "future history" of the pre-Vatican II Roman Catholic Church exists than Walter Miller's marvelous 1959 epic, *A Canticle for Leibowitz*. But the Church he defines so carefully—the monasteries, the confessionals, the omnipresent Latin prayers—is already changed, and his "future history" (though still well worth reading) seems somehow curiously, if affectionately, dated.

Robert Heinlein has similar problems in his 1951 novel, *The Day After Tomorrow*. In it, Heinlein tells how a U.S. resistance movement defeats the nation's Asian conquerors by creating a phony church as the upperground infrastructure for the subversive network. It is still a rousing tale, but the Catholic priests in it (once again, hard at work in the confessional) are clearly pre-Vatican II. By contrast, the Heinlein of *Stranger in a Strange Land* (1961) seems positively prophetic. Years before they became commonplace, he describes Esalen-type psychodynamic sessions, the spiritual benefits of liberated sex, and communal "families" where partners are warmly and

regularly exchanged. Yet the novel's distinctively modern
tone does not detract from the surely intentional resemblance of Valentine Michael Smith, the hero, to Jesus
Christ—nor from the resemblance of his followers to primitive Christians. The hero is joyously martyred, the followers are winsomely zealous, and the sage of the novel,
a hack writer named Jubal Harshaw, is clearly on his way,
at its end, to becoming Smith's first evangelist-biographer.

At least some of the best works in religious science
fiction are such novels, and detailed structures like Heinlein's and Clarke's may well require the length of a novel.
Our business here, however, is with short stories, in which
the same considerations of life and death, conscience and
destiny have increasingly become the concerns of the
genre's best authors. Ray Bradbury, I would propose, is
the artistic dean in this shorter medium, and it is only with
great regret (but I hope good reason) that only an excerpt
of a poem is included here: Nearly all his work is readily
available in print. Yet his short story, "The Man," is still
the best variation I have seen on two old Christian themes:
the search for the historical Jesus and the speculation that
Christ might repeat his mission to other beings on other
planets. "The Fire Balloons" (like "The Man," part of *The
Illustrated Man* anthology) is one of the best—and gentlest
—stories of encounters between humans and aliens, in
which two Episcopalian missionaries on Mars discover
spheres of blue fire that are intelligent beings. More recently, Bradbury explores the eternally repeating Christ
again, in a long, lyrical "cantata," "Christus Apollo,"
which is reprinted, in part, in this volume.

Repetition of themes hardly dulls them, for the possible religious permutations seem endless. Poul Anderson's
"Kyrie" (currently available in *The Farthest Reaches*)
postulates an intelligent creature of pure electromagnetism,
and manages to evoke a huge sadness for the creature

when it sacrifices itself to save a ship full of humans from a supernova firestorm. The encounter theme (of which "Kyrie" is just one variation) is in fact loaded with theological implications. Suppose one discovers that God has made a new covenant with another race—but yet has to fight that race? Lester del Rey, in his novelette "For I Am a Jealous People," explores just that proposition—and mankind's angry reply. A similar situation—and a different reply—are the subject of Anthony Boucher's fine and ironic story in this volume, "Balaam." Philip José Farmer examines an encounter of another kind, when a space-traveling monk meets a race of intelligent, birdlike creatures. Do they have souls? And what should they be told about God?

Religious science fiction turns on such questions. Can robots have souls? The late Anthony Boucher suggests how one can even achieve sainthood in his classic "The Quest for Saint Aquin," reprinted in these pages. Could a robot become a god? John Brunner explores that terrible possibility in "Judas." Could God, perchance, run out of souls to distribute to an ever-burgeoning mankind? Brunner ponders that thought—not so whimsically if you believe in reincarnation—in his warm vignette of a famed physician turned holy man, "The Vitanuls." Will pragmatism—or situation ethics—take the edge off human guilt? Or will the human conscience survive to haunt the mind of the sinner? Two of the most memorable stories in this vein came from the late Henry Kuttner: "Two-Handed Engine" and "A Cross of Centuries," the latter included here.

The inclusion of a Kuttner story pleases me for a special reason. Much of this book was conceived and put together in New York, where my wife, Patty, and I now make our home, but I write this introduction in a more appropriate place: a rambling, quasi-Spanish ranch house on a hill high above the Pacific shore in southern California, a home I onced lived in and in a sense have never really left. Almost from the spot where I write now, the sunset glinting off the blue-gray water, the late science-fiction master Henry Kuttner also wrote. We shared this house a decade apart, but as I write, looking out over the same timeless sea, I feel he might just as well be at my elbow.

Whatever his private thoughts about mankind's collective and individual destiny, Kuttner seemed publicly convinced that there was more to life, in Robert Heinlein's phrase, than "a bunch of amino acids bumping together." Since our focus in this volume is on that conviction, the presence of Henry Kuttner's spirit seems most fitting.

—MAYO MOHS

Pacific Palisades, California
June 1970

THE CUNNING
OF THE BEAST
Nelson Bond

There is no reason, I suppose, to search for anything more in Nelson Bond's pleasant fable than meets the eye. Of the many science-fiction stories that have found their inspiration in Genesis, I still think it is perhaps the cleverest—but it wears its moral on its sleeve. One need not complain that the image of God writ here is so anthropomorphic as to be positively fallible: the writers of Genesis, after all, themselves pictured the Lord walking casually in the Garden. What is more interesting is the considerable bias Bond seems to share with those writers—a bias perhaps shaped by the fact that the story was first published in 1942, when men were generally busy with "the flame which explodes, the fire that destroys." Man's primordial sin, suggests Bond, was not so much curiosity as a perverse attraction to the technology of violence—a remarkable prefiguring of the theology of Jacques Ellul. That the proposition seems fully as valid today is sad, if not unexpectable. As the ancient authors would surely agree, that is simply the nature of the animal.

There has been much disagreeable comment on the case of our late brother, the Yawa Eloem, and we number amongst us many who feel that the punishment meted out to him, severe as it was, still did not exact complete retribution for the evil he loosed in our midst.

It is with these vengeful ones I should like to take issue.

Now, let it not be thought that I view with approval the experiments of the learned and unhappy Doctor Eloem. The reverse is true; being one of his oldest friends and earliest confidants, I was perhaps the first to warn him against doing that which he did. This warning I delivered on the night the Yawa conceived his staggering ambition.

But to those who contend that his intention was to overthrow our great civilization, destroy our culture, and turn the rulership of our beloved homeland into the hands of barbarian monstrosities, I feel I should present the true facts.

Doctor Eloem is more to be pitied than scorned. His was the sad fate of one who, delving into secrets better left unlearned, suceeded only in creating a monster mightier than its maker . . .

Well I remember the night the Yawa's dream was born. It was the Night of Utter Black which occurs but once in each twelve revolutions of Kios. Both suns were set, and all nine moons were vanished from the sky. No doubt the burning stars shone true in the encircling jet vault of space, but from our Refuge they could not be seen. Great clouds hung thickly to our shielding Dome; against its transparent hemisphere, torrents of corrosive rain lashed in unending fury.

Though our shelters were warmed and kept dry for just such times as these, my body creaked and groaned when I tried to move; one limb was so stiffened in its socket that I could scarcely will it to function. Eloem was in better condition, having but recently completed a re-habilitation at the Clinic, but the condensation affected his vision, and time and again as we huddled there in misery he wiped the moisture from his visor.

Dimly we heard the thud of running feet, and peering

fearfully into the mists we saw our friend Nesro, who had been caught in the deadly storm and was belatedly racing to shelter. But even before we could call him to our Dome he fell prey to the cursed climate. His footsteps faltered; his joints locked; he stumbled and fell headlong.

A horror gripped us. For a Kiosian to lie for more than minutes on that drenched ground meant certain ending. But we were helpless. To attempt a rescue without shedders would only put us in the same plight.

Eloem lurched to his feet, and what he cried should convince his enemies that, whatever else his faults, he was no coward.

"Courage, Nesro," he cried. "We are coming."

But in answer to his words came a cry from the fallen Nesro.

"No, comrades! It is better *one* should end than many." His voice was feeble. "Open the Refuge. I shall try to make it without my carrier."

We screamed in unison then, "No, Nesro—no! You can't possibly make it! The pelting death—"

But our pleas were vain. Desperately Nesro scurried from the rain-glistening cover of his carrier, flashed toward us flaming like a pillar of crimson in the darkness. For an instant it seemed his madness might be crowned with success—but only for an instant. Then the raw and dreadful poison of the rain seeped through his feeble shield. A high, thin scream of pain rent our nerves, and where Nesro had been, briefly there blossomed in the night a white incandescence unbearable to look at. Then—nothing.

So ended Nesro. I was moved, but my emotion was as naught compared to that of my friend, the learned Yawa Eloem. He moaned, and there in our tiny Refuge cursed aloud, speaking Names which I dare not repeat.

"Now, woe and despair," he cried terribly, "upon the

mocking gods who made us the weaklings we are! For we are at once masters of a world and cringing servants to that world's every element. What matter that our intellect has built for us an empire, or that with wit and wisdom we have plumbed the secrets of a universe? Our minds are living glories, but we hobble about our kingdom like cripples, poorest of all we hold in fee. Even those wild, breathing beasts who grub for worms beneath the stones dare face the forces which strike us low. Even such miserable clods as *that*—"

And he pointed a shaking hand toward the rain-soaked carrier abandoned by Nesro. It lay face down in a wind-lashed rivulet, motionless, rusting, ruined beyond repair. As we watched, there scampered from the woods a small air-breather. The furry creature sniffed hopefully about the carrier. Then, scenting nothing wherewith to sate its revolting appetite, it shuffled off, rain dripping from its pelt.

I shuddered and asked reasonably, "But surely, Eloem, you would not barter your soul for the brute body of such a beast? True, the gods have ordained that we must pay a price for our mastery. We lack the physical stamina of those lower animals. But is not our superior intellect compensation enough?

"And as for form and substance, we have made great progress. Our forefathers knew not how to build themselves tangible bodies. Today we encase ourselves in cleverly wrought metal carriers which perform all physical functions for us."

"Bah!" spat the Yawa savagely. "Carriers which but accentuate our impotence. We garb ourselves in shells of forged metal, and fancy we have gained mobility. But is this true? No! We have succeeded only in making ourselves slaves to the bodies we have wrought—" He laughed hollowly, mocking the chatter of the Clinic specialists—

"Grease here—grease there—a drop of oil in the knee-joint. Replace lens—replace digits—repair rusted plate in frontal lobe—"

"Still," I protested, "our metal bodies *do* enable us to get about more easily, perform tasks otherwise impossible."

"And under what handicap?" he thundered. "In cold weather we shiver and tremble in our metal homes; in hot, our yielding rivets warp and melt. In dry weather our joints lock with grating sand. In wet—" he paused and stared bitterly at the empty carrier of Nesro—"we perish."

I said resignedly, "What you say is true. But there is nothing to be done about it. I, for one, am content—"

"But *I* am not! There must be *some* way of living other than huddling pitifully caged in a metal carcass. There must be *some* other form of servant—"

He stopped abruptly, and I stared at him curiously. "Yes?"

"Servant," he repeated. "Yes, that's it! Another kind of servant. One which does not melt in the heat and freeze in the cold, shrivel in the drouth and rot in the rain. A servant by Nature adapted to combat Nature's terrors. *That* is what our race needs—what we must have—*will* have!"

"But where will you find such a servant?"

The Yawa Eloem pointed a creaking arm to the mist-shrouded forest. "Out there, my brother."

"In the forest? You mean—"

"Yes. The creatures of flesh. The air-breathers."

I laughed. Despite my pain and misery, I laughed. It was too ridiculous, the concept of training those tiny furry beasts to perform for us our manual tasks.

"Oh, come now, Eloem, you can't be serious! Those miserable, dwarfed weaklings?"

"Bear within them," he said slowly, shrewdly, "the seed

of animate life. That is all that matters, my friend. The germ of life. Their size, their form—such things are unimportant. These I will mold to meet our requirements. I will raise them from all fours, refashion their brute brains to give them intellect. Yes, even this, I, the Yawa Eloem, shall do. And I so pledge unto the gods."

A strange uneasiness filled me, I knew not quite why. I said thoughtfully, "Have a care, O Yawa, lest these same gods take offense at your intent. I am no metaphysician, but it seems to me there are certain limits beyond which one may not go without too greatly daring. The altering of form, the giving of wisdom, these are feats which only the gods may accomplish with impunity. It is not for ones like thee and me—"

But I fear the Yawa did not hear my words. Too intent was he on the vision that had come to him. There in the wet and the darkness beside me he stirred, and his voice was rapt and strident with a dream.

"Yes, this shall I do," he proclaimed. "I shall build a new race, a race of servants obedient to us, their masters."

Many time-periods passed ere next I saw the Yawa Eloem. We of Kios are a recluse race, separate by nature and individual in our working habits, and I was busy with duties of my own. The Grand Council had commissioned me to perfect a form of craft wherein our colonists might hurtle the darkness of space to the yet unconquered planets of our double sun. With this tremendous labor was I occupied.

So the moons waxed and waned. Thrice changed the seasons, warm and cold, and wet and dry and wet again. And in the privacy of his own domed laboratory the Yawa Eloem pursued his secret labors in solitude.

And then one double twilight, when the crimson rays of the smaller sun sinking in the north merged weird shadows with the pale green luminescence of the greater sun's southern setting, there came to me in my workshop the Yawa.

Excitement was strong within him, and he cried without preface of formal greeting, "My friend, would you behold a marvel to strike awe into the boldest heart?"

"Why, who would not?" I laughed.

"Then come!" cried the Yawa intently. "Then come with me and wonder and behold!"

And he led the way to his own Dome. . . .

Let me say that never dwelt a scientist amidst such great refinement as that with which Eloem had surrounded himself. His Dome comprised no single chamber, as is the case with most of us; his was a mighty structure subdivided into numerous rooms and niches, each dedicated to its own purpose.

Once we passed through a chemical laboratory, its shelf-lined walls aglisten with innumerable rows of vials and beakers; again we crossed a library whose musty tomes spanned the whole range of living knowledge; elsewhere sprawled chambers filled with electrical apparatus, surgical equipment and curious machines of which I could not even guess the purpose. I yet recall traversing a steaming room wherein was sunk a hydroponic tank whence emanated an oddly noisome scent. I cannot speak with surety of what this tank contained, but I do recall that as we passed, from its oily depths there flopped a strange, amorphous something which scrabbled with nail-less paws at the walls of its prison and bubbled piteous plaints in a voice of tongueless horror.

But past all these, his chambers of experiment, the Yawa led me swiftly until we came at last to the furthermost door. Before this he paused for an instant dramatically. And then:

"Here," he proclaimed, "is my final testing chamber. Here the fulfillment of my great invention."

He flung open the door and bade me enter.

Well might the Yawa glory in what he here had wrought. For frankly do I confess that my eyes, following the motion of his hand, widened in astonishment at what they beheld.

This was no mere room. It was a vast Dome-covered acreage, formed to the semblance of a veritable living forest. Nay, more than forest; say rather a garden spot, a paradise. For its growth was as various as any wrought by Nature. Yet with such thought had the Yawa Eloem conceived and carried out its purpose that here he had brought into being a landscape more beautiful than ever was sown by Nature's heedless hand.

Here a high grove cast towering green spires upward. There, through mossy banks bedecked with fragrant flowers, purled a tiny crystal brooklet; elsewhere, rimmed by lush meadows, sprawled lazy hills and flatlands ripe with grain. Small beasts stirred in the forests, their restless murmurings a balm to weary spirits; fish flashed and rippled in the eddies of the stream; and from some distant grove came the thrilling cadence of birdsong raised in joy.

I stared at Eloem, stunned with wonderment. "It is," I cried aloud, "it is indeed a miracle you have created here, wise Yawa! What beauty and what charm! The Grand Council will be astonished."

"You think so?" he asked, pleased at my praise. "You really think so?"

"How could they be otherwise? By the gods, Eloem, would that the whole of our planet were as delightful as this small niche you have created beneath your laboratory Dome. What joy would be ours, what wonderful existence, if all Kios were such a garden spot as this; a shielded wonderland wherein we might dwell without fear of the natural terrors which beset us—heat and cold, drouth and murderous rainfall.

"You said you would awe me, my friend. You have succeeded beyond your wildest imaginings. I humble myself before a master artist who has created perfection."

"But," said the Yawa, "you have not seen all."

"There is *more* to see?"

"Much more. Not yet have you seen the greatest of my accomplishments. Come."

And he led the way down a tiny path curving through the wilderness. As we neared a grove deep-nestled in the rolling hills he called in gentle tones, "My son! My son! Where art thou, child of my making?"

And before I could question this strange salutation a movement broke the silence of the glade. Branches parted, and from a leafy bower stepped a vision which stunned and left me speechless.

It was a living creature, an animal of flesh and blood, an air-breather walking upright on its two hind limbs. Truly had Eloem boasted he would mold a creation in his own image. So closely did its shape resemble that of the carriers which we of Kios build for our own usage that for an instant I believed it a gigantic hoax. I thought Eloem to amuse me had coated the carrier of a friend or assistant with pigment.

Then I saw this monster's body was not forged of sturdy metals like our own, but was soft, pulsating, resilient. The curious dark growth of fur which covered its head, its breast and its limbs grew naturally, it seemed, from its very flesh. It breathed with great gulping motions of the chest, and its wide, natural optics were not sensitive visors such as those through which *we* see, but were the natural eyes of animals!

These now shifted from one to the other of us in mute

appraisal as the sensate beast asked, "Yes, my lord? You called me?"

Eloem, his voice benevolent and warm as that of a parent, asked, "Where hast thou been, my son?"

The creature replied quietly, "I wandered through the fields, my nostrils savoring the fragrance of the flowers. I walked amongst the trees and touched them, marveling at their strong, rough firmness. Beside the brook I knelt and drank of its waters. I tasted the berries of the vines and the fruit of the trees, and gave thanks unto thee, O my lord, who brought these things into being and myself unto this paradise."

"And art thou happy, my son?"

"Happy?" The beast's blank stare questioned the very meaning of the word.

"Lack you anything for which your heart hungers?"

"Nay, nothing, lord. Save perhaps—"

The Yawa's creation hesitated. His voice stopped, his eyes fell, as if he were abashed at his own temerity in questioning the perfection of this garden.

Eloem demanded, "Then there *is* something, my child?"

"There is—one small thing, my lord. It is scarce worth mentioning, but—" The creature shuffled in embarrassment. "I am lonely, O Yawa. I walk at evening in the cool of the garden, seeing about me the bright-colored birds, the rustling insects and the beasts of the fields, and lo! for each of these there is one to be companion. Only I, of all the creatures who inhabit this paradise, am mateless."

"But—" frowned Eloem.

"I question not thy bounty, O great Yawa," said the creature hastily. "In thy infinite wisdom thou knowest best what shall be given thy servant. Still—"

He faltered to silence, head bowed servilely before the pondering Yawa. But I could not help noticing that

THE CUNNING OF THE BEAST

his glance darted swiftly up from beneath shyly lowered lashes.

I said, with a touch of pique, I am afraid, "This is a strange being you have created, Eloem. Though he dwells in paradise, still he dares question the perfection thereof."

But Eloem said gently, slowly, "Nevertheless, there is wisdom in what he suggests. It was much effort to create this being, my friend. It were folly to attempt the creation of scores, hundreds, thousands of others like him in my laboratory. Perhaps in his innocent demanding he has offered the proper solution to this problem. A mate? But yes, of course! I need but create for him a mate and then—in the fullness of time—he and she shall produce for Kios the race of servants for which they were conceived.

"Very well, my son." He turned again to the waiting creature. "It shall be as you ask. On the morrow come to the room where first thou awakened. There, out of thy substance and my wisdom, shall I create a second like thyself, but of another sex. And now—farewell."

So left I Eloem's garden. But this time I did not allow so long a time to pass ere my returning. My curiosity was stirred, not only as to how the Yawa's magnificent experiment would turn out, but also as to what form of creature he would create to be his beast's companion. Moreover, when it was bruited about that I, alone of all Kios, had been invited to visit Eloem's laboratory, great interest was aroused and I was summoned before the Grand Council, there to report on that which I had seen.

In glowing terms I told them of the wonders he had wrought, and greatly did they marvel. Great Kron, who heads our Council, mused, "Intelligent life in fleshly form? But yes! That *is* the answer to our problem! The Yawa

Eloem is a sage spirit, and mighty is this thing he seeks to accomplish."

Another cried rapturously, "Now dawns the long-dreamed-of liberation of our race! When this new herd of servants has been bred, then will we of Kios be free to rid ourselves once and for all of the metal carriers in which we house ourselves. Secure beneath great Domes we may rest ourselves in easeful pursuit of pleasure and knowledge, while our servants, not sensitive as we to climatic conditions, carry out our instructions."

But still another, older than the rest, spoke dubiously.

"I do not know," he said. "This is, in truth, a mighty thing the Yawa has attempted. Perhaps it is *too* mighty. The gods in their omnipotence frown upon our seeking to delve too deeply into certain mysteries. And methinks already Eloem has tampered with a secret and occult lore—the creation of living souls."

"Souls?" laughed one of our younger councilors. "But how can there be souls in bestial bodies?"

"Where life alone exists, perhaps the soul is absent. But our brother has told us that this creature of Eloem's not only moves and obeys, but voices his own thoughts. That bespeaks intelligence. And where exists intelligence may also be a soul. If this be true—"

The speaker shook his head gravely. But the rest of us laughed. As we all knew, old Saddryn was ever a pessimist and a crier-of-woe.

Yet Kron in his infinite wisdom took heed of even this gloomy warning, and bade me continue my visits to Eloem's laboratory that I might keep the Council informed as to the progress of the experiment.

Thus it was that some short time later once again I strolled with the Yawa through his delightful garden.

As we neared the glade wherein it was the creature's custom to lurk, I sensed a subtle change. What it was

I could not at first detect, whether of sight or sound or simply atmosphere. Then suddenly and with a sense of resharpened curiosity I realized what was different. When first I had strode this pathway, a part of its beauty had been in its fresh, untrammeled wildness of growth— the helter-skelter confusion of vines and trees and bushes, the lavish abundance with which bright flowers sprang from unexpected places, the haphazard delight of natural beauties seen amidst natural surroundings.

But now all that was changed. The pathway upon which we walked no longer twisted aimlessly beneath arboreal bowers. It had been carefully scraped and straightened; the rank brush flanking it had been trimmed to a semblance of order; the low and overhanging boughs had been cut back to allow the wanderer headroom. Beauty was still present, but no longer was it the clean, unspoiled improvisation of Nature; it was a neat and regimented orthodoxy, pleasing to the eye but somehow strangely stifling to the senses.

I commented on this to Eloem, and he smiled quietly.

"That," he said, "is the doing of the She. An orderly creature, that one!" And he shook his head with almost reluctant admiration.

"*Her* doing? Then you have finished her?"

"Oh, yes. As a matter of fact, I finished two of them. The first one dwelt here with him for a while, but I had to"—he sighed—"remove her. She was too much like the He. Carefree, adventurous, enamored of gay wanderings and pleasant sloth, rather than earnestly intent upon her duties. They were more companions than mates. They laughed and played together throughout the livelong day and accomplished nothing. So I was forced to create another She, one with instincts and desires unlike his own."

"But I should think," I demurred, "this would not be

to his liking? After all, a companion is what he asked for."

The Yawa chuckled.

"What he *asked* for, but not what he really wanted. You should study psychology, my friend, to realize that in nature, even as in the electrical art, it is opposites which attract. This second She is so unlike him that he is drawn to her as by a magnet. She baffles and confuses him—and brings him running. She commands and he obeys; she demands and he fulfills. With a motion of a finger she exacts from him the most arduous labor. She is a bother to him, I fear, and a source of vexing trouble—but for her rare words of praise he has done more actual work than ever since I placed him in this garden."

"Then," I said, comprehending, "you followed the example of the insect? Made her larger than him and stronger that she might enforce her demands?"

"On the contrary," denied Eloem, "I made her—but see for yourself." And he called, "My children!"

The bower parted, and into its opening strode his twain creatures.

In a glance I saw it was as he said. The male beast was oddly changed. There was a new assurance in his features, a confidence which might have been born of his newfound capabilities. But there was at the same time a—a something else I could not quite decipher. It was a reserve, a furtiveness which had not been present when first I saw him. But more than this at first glance I saw not, for my attention was drawn and riveted to the creature's new companion. And strange as it may seem, coming from one uncorporeal as myself, I must confess that even *I* was fascinated by this, the Yawa Eloem's latest creation.

For he had combined in her not only the sturdiness and the nobility of the male, but something subtler still; a grace, a charm, a winsomeness and allurement far out of proportion to the small physique with which he had endowed her.

Shorter by half a head was she than her mate, slighter boned and more fragile, whiter of skin. One could tell at a glance that hers was strength not built of sinew but of purpose. She bore herself lightly, walking on the balls of her feet with lissom grace, and she seemed all sweet docility. Yet, curiously, she spoke for both.

"You called, my lord?" she asked. "What would you of us?"

"Naught," said the Yawa Eloem. "I wished but to see you, show you to my friend. You are happy here, my children?"

"Yes, my lord," said the She. "Of course, there are a few things—"

"Yes?" asked Eloem.

The male spoke querulously.

"She wants the stream-bed widened that we may swim therein. She thinks, too, that I should transplant berry bushes nearer to our glade that we need not hunt so far for provender. And we have talked—" he cast a dubious glance at his mate—"that is, *she* has talked much of our building some sort of dwelling."

"She?" laughed Eloem. "Always she? What is *your* desire in these matters, my first-made?"

"Well—" said the male hesitantly.

"I have pointed out to him," interrupted the She in sweet and lilting tones, "that only by doing these things can we prove to the lesser beasts that we are their superiors and their rightful masters. It is true, my lord, is it not, that we *are* their masters?"

I asked impatiently, "Since when do beasts rule beasts?" but the Yawa silenced me with a gesture.

"There is logic to that. It is right and proper that one animal should exercise dominion over its inferiors. If your mate wants these things, I see no harm in your providing them for her."

"Oh, very well," said the male petulantly. "But it is wearisome work, which I like not. When the *other* She was here we roamed where we would for berries, swam at chance when we found a widening of the stream; we laughed and played and found no need of stifling shelter."

"Like," laughed the second-made gayly and, I thought, perhaps a bit tauntingly, "like two happy and carefree children. All day they played, then in the dark of night they curled apart, each to his own soft nest of ferns, and slumbered in cool companionship. Of course—" And she laughed again, flexing her muscles smoothly, languorously; until that moment I had not realized how strong was the animal within her. "Of course, if *that* is what you want, the master can no doubt bring back the other She—"

But a swift light, warm and hungry, brightened in the male's eyes, and he shook his head.

"No," he decided, "I shall do as she asks, my lord."

"Very well," said Eloem, "it is your decision to make. And now farewell, my children. We must go."

But even as we turned the She addressed us, humble as ever and sweetly supplicating, but with a cunning determination nonetheless.

"Master—"

"Yes, my daughter?"

"There is another thing—another trifling thing. We are humble creatures, ignorant and unworthy of your attentions. We would not trouble you for counsel and advice on every tiny thing we wish to do. Is it not possible that when need arises we may be allowed to enter into the chamber wherein are stored the books of knowledge and learning? If we could but do this, we need not waste time and effort learning to do things wrongly, but may build and create in proper fashion."

"No!" said the Yawa Eloem. "No, my daughter, that is one thing you may *not* do. All this wide garden is open unto you; its hills and valleys, glades and rivulets. But there is one door through which you may not pass: that which leads to my private laboratory. This is the Law, and the only Law I have laid down unto you."

"But—" pouted the She enticingly.

"Let us speak of it no more," cried Eloem sternly. "You have heard my word. And now, good-bye."

So we left them standing there, he shrugging and resigned, she with head lowered. Yet as we left, I felt her eyes upon us, shrewd and bold beneath their lowered lashes.

You may wonder, my brothers, why waste I so much wordage on the telling of this. Believe me, it is but to demonstrate that *never* did the Yawa Eloem—as he has been accused by his detractors—conspire against our own race for the overthrow of our empire. Who says so speaks untruth. The Yawa came near to bringing disaster upon us, true; but only because, being the soul of righteousness himself, he could not comprehend the cunning of the beasts he had created. . . .

From this point on, you are familiar with the facts of the case. You know how on the Night of the Four Moons it was strangely noted that the laboratory Dome of Eloem glowed with the reflection of a ruddy flame throughout the evening. It is unfortunate that no investigation was made of this at the time, but it is understandable. We of Kios are a recluse of race, self-sufficient and solitary by nature. None knew that the Yawa was not in his laboratory, but visiting afar in search of new equipment with which to stock his depleted stores.

All those of us, including myself, who maintain residence within sight of our brother's laboratory remember well the subsequent series of incidents emanating from that spot. Once the sounds of explosion. Still another time the clamorous pounding of metal upon metal as if a dozen of us, carrier-clad, vied in games of strength.

But none knew, or guessed, the import of these sights and sounds.

Knowledge of dawning peril came to us only when one morn we wakened to discover the Dome of our neighbor Lato smashed and in smoldering ruins. When startled friends braved the wreckage to learn Lato's fate they were grieved to find Lato's carrier lying amidst the wreckage. When the headpiece was forced open, it was found that Lato himself was ended. His volatile energy had been expended in a single gigantic burst of flame which fused the metal wherein he had maintained residence.

Even after this disaster no suspicion attached to Eloem's labors. And certainly none dreamed that his creations were in any way responsible. Not even when a few nights later the nearby Dome of the councilor Palimon was found to be rudely split and flooded with poisonous oxide of hydrogen was it guessed that the animals could be responsible for such a brutal attack upon their overlords.

Palimon was, of course, ended. His spirit seared and shriveled by the lethal liquid, he could tell us nothing. What dreadful tale of agony he might have related is better left unguessed.

And then, at fearful last, came revelation as to the cause of these disasters. This occasion was, as you will remember, the destruction of the Dome of the Grand Council itself. Like the other events, it occurred in the dark of night when no Kiosian dares venture forth, and horrible was its accomplishment.

First came, as had before, a violent explosion. Then in its wake rose a fearful sea of flame, sweeping the council-hall and slaying all who dwelt beneath the Dome.

And when blistering fire had gutted the ruined hemisphere, then came the dank night wind, bearing with it lethal rains to destroy such life as might remain within the halls.

It is by sheer chance that on this night scarce half the Council was foregathered, else might a blow have been struck from which our empire might never have recovered. But as it was, great Kron and half his Councilors had been in my Dome inspecting my new and nearly complete spacecraft. Shedder-garbed against the night mists, they were returning to their dwelling when the explosion trembled the ground beneath their feet. As they spurred their carriers to top speed, they—or I should say we, for I was with them—reached the scene in time to see outlined against the flickering flames two bodies. These, like our own, were carrier-clad; and at the sight of them Kron burst forth with a terrible cry.

"Traitors!" he roared. "Two of our own people—traitors! Now the gods forfend that I should have lived to see this awful day! Then the other explosions were *not* accidents; they were deliberate murder! Woe upon Kios that has spawned such vermin—"

Then I stopped him with a shrill, excited cry. For upon sight of us the two marauders had turned and raced away. And though the taller of these could not be told from one of our own brethren, by the pace and motion of the other—an awkward, gliding run—I instantly recognized and knew the nature of our enemy.

"Nay, these are no children of Kios, O Kron," I cried, "but the beasts—the beasts of the Yawa Eloem, turned like serpents against their masters!"

Great Kron cried loud in his thunderous rage; then turned he to the royal messenger. "Gavril!" he ordered. "Sound now your trumpet over all the land. Bid Eloem here instantly. Mikel, arouse your troops!"

And then I knew the fury of great Kron, for not in

a score of centuries had the gleaming troops of Mikel
been ordered into action. But without a word the commander of our armed forces turned and sped toward the
armory wherein were carefully stored against the hour
of need those dreadful weapons which our race holds
ever in reserve.

What happened next you know. The Yawa, being summoned, came immediately. Nor waited he even upon the
slow movements of his mechanical carrier. Risking the
night mists and the dark, with the speed of light he
flashed from the other end of the land in his natural form.
We saw him approach from afar, a pillar of flame in
the darkness.

When he learned what had befallen, a cry of pain
and anguish broke from him. Like a patient parent he
might have denied the evil intent of his children were
not the proof of their mischief a smoldering wreckage
before him.

Then said Kron, "Now great is the evil your creations
have wrought, O Yawa. But greater still shall be their
punishment. For even now our warriors sweep forth to
destroy them."

But the Yawa pleaded, "Wait, O Kron! Stay yet your
hand till I have learned what lust inspired this evil. Let
me go to my children and learn from their lips the
reason for this deed."

And Kron nodded.

"So be it. But be swift."

Eloem turned to me beseechingly.

"You, my friend? Will you come with me?"

So, for the last time, together went we two into the
paradise which the Yawa had created within his Dome.
Within, the paths were cool, the grottoes shadowed, and
the soft brook purled through mossy silences. No songbird
sang, but from the thicket came the soft and lazy cadences

of restless insects. Together but alone, unspeaking, we trod the paths marked out by the He and She. And as we neared the glade wherein it was the creatures' wont to dwell, the Yawa Eloem raised his voice in stern command—but in sadness, too, I thought.

It is perhaps meaningful that in this hour of sorrow he should have called only to the first of his creations.

"My son!" he called. "My son! Where art thou, O child of mine own making?"

There came no answer but the rippling of the breeze through the boughs, the rustling of a frightened thing in the high grass.

"My son," cried Eloem again. "Where art thou? Know you not the voice of your lord and maker?"

And then suddenly, a dim whiteness in the shadows, rose the crouching figure of the He from the brush before us. And I saw with sick horror that he was not, as ever before, clad only in his own fleshly raiment, but that his body was shielded within the greaved and bucklered harness of a carrier such as we ourselves wear.

He spoke, and his voice was meek.

"You called, my lord?"

The Yawa's voice was stricken.

"My son, my son!" he grieved. "Wherefore hast thou donned this raiment?"

The male's voice was a thick mumbling in the darkness. He spoke in half apology, half defiance.

"It was the She, my lord. She told me I was naked and a weakling, and I was ashamed. Together we built these garments that we might be strong and mighty."

"Built?" repeated Eloem. "Built those garments? But where, O creature of little knowledge, learned you the secret of such things?" Then in a tone of sudden understanding, "You learned this not in the garden, my son, but—elsewhere."

The beast bowed miserably. "It was the She, my lord," he whined. "It was the She who—"

Then cried the Yawa in a terrible voice:

"Let the She stand forth!"

And suddenly she was there, rising from the thicket beside her mate. She too was garbed in a metal carrier, but her headpiece was removed, and never thought I to see such boldness in the eyes of a creature bred to serfdom. On her features was scorn; on her lips pride, anger, and rebellion.

And she cried defiantly, "Yea, even I, my lord. It was I who showed the He how to build the garments. I, too, who read the books and learned the secret of making the flame which explodes, the fire that destroys, of smashing the Masters' Domes, that the night-waters might seep in and end them."

"These things," said the Yawa in awful tones, "you could learn in but one place. In my library, which was forbidden to you. But how entered you there? The door was locked and bolted."

The male creature shifted nervously.

"There was a grill in the door, O Master," he explained. "Through this the She sent our friend the serpent with instructions to unlock the portal to us."

The Yawa trembled with an awesome rage, and his voice was like the rolling of great thunders.

"Now cursed be you!" he cried. "For you have defied my commands, and in opening the forbidden gate tasted the fruits of evil knowledge I forbade you! And cursed be the serpent who aided your rebellion. May he be eyed with endless loathing by all who spring from your loins in countless generations to come! For surely I say unto you, never shall it be forgotten what you have this night done—neither by yourselves, nor by your children, nor by your children's children's children unto the end of time.

"Here"—and his voice broke with the intensity of his passion—"here did I build for you a garden of wondrous beauty, a paradise wherein was all for which your hearts might hunger. But it was not enough. You would escape its walls and set yourselves up as masters even over those who created you. Henceforth I rid my heart of you. You are a broken reed, an experiment which failed. I disclaim myself of you and your beast-born ambitions.

"Mikel!" And he called to the warrior captain who now, with gleaming sword held high, had appeared at the gate of the garden. "Do what you must, Mikel!"

But Mikel said quietly and with a great sorrow, "My orders have been changed, O brother Eloem."

"Changed?"

"Yes. Kron has decided that mere ending is not a fitting punishment for that which these creatures have done."

"But," I gasped, "if not ending, then what?"

It was Kron himself who answered.

"According to our laws, O Yawa Eloem, it is forbidden that any living creature with a soul be brought by our hands to mortal ending. And in council sage have we decided that by their very rebellion have these creatures proven the existence of their souls.

"Yet since we must rid ourselves of their evil presence, there is one solution. They shall be placed in the spacecraft recently completed by our friend here, and transported across the everlasting darkness of space to such bourne as may be farthest removed from our own planet. Where this journey may end I cannot say nor guess, but somewhere may be another planet where you and your ill-spawned experiments can exist beyond our ken and finding until the gods, in the fullness of their mercy, see fit to rule otherwise."

The Yawa Eloém whispered shakily, "Not only they, but—myself?"

And said great Kron sadly, "Even so. For was it not you, O Yawa, who brought them into being?"

Thus ended the matter of the Yawa Eloem and those beasts which, in the great folly of his wisdom, he undertook to remold as fleshly servants in the image of himself. It is a sad and disheartening tale, and one I would not tell save that some critics have seen fit to cast aspersions upon the truly noble character of our exiled brother.

So ended, too—so far as our knowledge extends—the existence of the Yawa and his creations. As had been commanded, they were placed within my spacecraft, therein forever banished from fair Kios. Where, when, and how their journey ended, or if ever, I know not. Perhaps they wander still, their craft a tiny mote in the vastness of all-swaddling space. Perhaps somewhere they met cruel ending in the flaming heart of a star. Perhaps—and this I hope—they found somewhere a planet and upon it made a new home.

However this may be, I cannot say. But this I know: those do great harm who criticize the Yawa Eloem, naming him fiend and traitor. Never lived a nobler soul, nor one with greater ambition for the welfare of his own race. That he sinned is undeniable, but his sin was only that of tampering with forces too great for him. For as all know, there are limits beyond which one is forbidden to probe. And they who seek to know, with the gods, the secret of the creation of life are ever doomed to failure.

It was a wondrous dream the Yawa Eloem dreamed. But there was one thing he failed to take into consideration: the animal nature of those he tried to endow with intelligence. Never, never—though they raised themselves from all fours to walk like beings—could they slough off those animal instincts. It was that which the Yawa could not foresee, and that which caused his downfall.

So—they are gone, the Yawa Eloem and they whom he created: the male to whom he gave the name Adam and the she who was called Eve. Yet mourn I my exiled brother, and ever is my soul sick within me when I think on that which overthrew him—

—On the cunning—the dreadful, dreadful cunning of the beasts. . . .

A CROSS OF CENTURIES
Henry Kuttner

If Nelson Bond is convinced that violence has infected man since his beginnings, Henry Kuttner is no more sanguine about any disappearance of violence in man's future. It is one of several themes he touches upon in this story of the far future, when the world, long at peace, worships a new and immortal Messiah. How and why violence re-emerges is Kuttner's tale, and with it one more look at an eternal paradox. Though Kuttner wrote the story shortly before his own tragic death in 1958, some of what he says may speak rather pointedly to the revolutionaries of our own day. The quest for peace, Kuttner seems to agree, has its grim necessities. Peace, seemingly, can only be secured through power, and power through— There's the rub. The price, as Kuttner assesses it, is high. In the end, the unforgetting human conscience will exact it in full: slow and patient in the process, but a remorseless Shylock all the same.

They called him Christ. But he was not the Man Who had toiled up the long road to Golgotha five thousand years before. They called him Buddha and Mohammed; they called him the Lamb, and the Blessed of God. They called him the Prince of Peace and the Immortal One.

His name was Tyrell.

He had come up another road now, the steep path that led to the monastery on the mountain, and he stood for a moment blinking against the bright sunlight. His white robe was stained with the ritual black.

The girl beside him touched his arm and urged him gently forward. He stepped into the shadow of the gateway.

Then he hesitated and looked back. The road had led up to a level mountain meadow where the monastery stood, and the meadow was dazzling green with early spring. Faintly, far away, he felt a wrenching sorrow at the thought of leaving all this brightness, but he sensed that things would be better very soon. And the brightness was far away. It was not quite real any more. The girl touched his arm again and he nodded obediently and moved forward, feeling the troubling touch of approaching loss that his tired mind could not understand now.

I am very old, he thought.

In the courtyard the priests bowed before him. Mons, the leader, was standing at the other end of a broad pool that sent back the bottomless blue of the sky. Now and again the water was ruffled by a cool, soft breeze.

Old habits sent their messages along his nerves. Tyrell raised his hand and blessed them all.

His voice spoke the remembered phrases quietly.

"Let there be peace. On all the troubled earth, on all the worlds and in God's blessed sky between, let there be peace. The powers of—of——" his hand wavered; then he remembered—"the powers of darkness have no strength against God's love and understanding. I bring you God's word. It is love; it is understanding; it is peace."

They waited till he had finished. It was the wrong time and the wrong ritual. But that did not matter, since he was the Messiah.

Mons, at the other end of the pool, signaled. The girl beside Tyrell put her hands gently on the shoulders of his robe.

Mons cried, "Immortal, will you cast off your stained garment and with it the sins of time?"

Tyrell looked vaguely across the pool.

"Will you bless the worlds with another century of your holy presence?"

Tyrell remembered some words.

"I leave in peace; I return in peace," he said.

The girl gently pulled off the white robe, knelt, and removed Tyrell's sandals. Naked, he stood at the pool's edge.

He looked like a boy of twenty. He was two thousand years old.

Some deep trouble touched him. Mons had lifted his arm, summoning, but Tyrell looked around confusedly and met the girl's gray eyes.

"Nerina?" he murmured.

"Go in the pool," she whispered. "Swim across it."

He put out his hand and touched hers. She felt that wonderful current of gentleness that was his indomitable strength. She pressed his hand tightly, trying to reach through the clouds in his mind, trying to make him know that it would be all right again, that she would be waiting —as she had waited for his resurrection three times already now, in the last three hundred years.

She was much younger than Tyrell, but she was immortal too.

For an instant the mists cleared from his blue eyes.

"Wait for me, Nerina," he said. Then, with a return of his old skill, he went into the pool with a clean dive.

She watched him swim across, surely and steadily. There was nothing wrong with his body; there never was, no matter how old he grew. It was only his mind that stiffened, grooved deeper into the iron ruts of time, lost its friction with the present, so that his memory would fragment away little by little. But the oldest memories went last, and the automatic memories last of all.

She was conscious of her own body, young and strong and beautiful, as it would always be. Her mind . . . there was an answer to that too. She was watching the answer.

I am greatly blessed, she thought. *Of all women on all the worlds, I am the Bride of Tryell, and the only other immortal ever born.*

Lovingly and with reverence she watched him swim. At her feet his discarded robe lay, stained with the memories of a hundred years.

It did not seem so long ago. She could remember it very clearly, the last time she had watched Tyrell swim across the pool. And there had been one time before that—and that had been the first. For her; not for Tyrell.

He came dripping out of the water and hesitated. She felt a strong pang at the change in him from strong sureness to bewildered questioning. But Mons was ready. He reached out and took Tyrell's hand. He led the Messiah toward a door in the high monastery wall and through it. She thought that Tyrell looked back at her, with the tenderness that was always there in his deep, wonderful calm.

A priest picked up the stained robe from her feet and carried it away. It would be washed clean now and placed on the altar, the spherical tabernacle shaped like the mother world. Dazzling white again, its folds would hang softly about the earth.

It would be washed clean, as Tyrell's mind would be washed clean too, rinsed of the clogging deposit of memories that a century had brought.

The priests were filing away. She glanced back, beyond the open gateway, to the sharply beautiful green of the mountain meadow, spring grass sensuously reaching to the sun after the winter's snow. *Immortal*, she thought, lifting her arms high, feeling the eternal blood, ichor of gods, singing in deep rhythm through her body. *Tyrell was the one who suffered. I have no price to pay for this —wonder.*

Twenty centuries.

And the first century must have been utter horror.

Her mind turned from the hidden mists of history that was legend now, seeing only a glimpse of the calm White Christ moving through that chaos of roaring evil when the earth was blackened, when it ran scarlet with hate and anguish. Ragnarok, Armageddon, Hour of the Anti-christ—two thousand years ago!

Scourged, steadfast, preaching his word of love and peace, the White Messiah had walked like light through earth's descent into hell.

And he had lived, and the forces of evil had destroyed themselves, and the worlds had found peace now—had found peace so long ago that the Hour of the Anti-christ was lost to memory; it was legend.

Lost, even to Tyrell's memory. She was glad of that. It would have been terrible to remember. She turned chill at the thought of what martyrdom he must have endured.

But it was the Day of the Messiah now, and Nerina, the only other immortal ever born, looked with rever-ence and love at the empty doorway through which Tyrell had gone.

She glanced down at the blue pool. A cool wind ruffled its surface; a cloud moved lightly past the sun, shadowing all the bright day.

It would be seventy years before she would swim the pool again. And when she did, when she woke, she would find Tyrell's blue eyes watching her, his hand closing lightly over hers, raising her to join him in the youth that was the springtime where they lived forever.

Her gray eyes watched him; her hand touched his as he lay on the couch. But still he did not waken.

She glanced up anxiously at Mons.

He nodded reassuringly.

She felt the slightest movement against her hand.

His eyelids trembled. Slowly they lifted. The calm, deep certainty was still there in the blue eyes that had seen so much, in the mind that had forgotten so much. Tyrell looked at her for a moment. Then he smiled.

Nerina said shakily, "Each time I'm afraid that you'll forget me."

Mons said, "We always give him back his memories of you, Blessed of God. We always will." He leaned over Tyrell. "Immortal, have you truly wakened?"

"Yes," Tyrell said, and thrust himself upright, swinging his legs over the edge of the couch, rising to his feet in a swift, sure motion. He glanced around, saw the new robe ready, pure white, and drew it on. Both Nerina and Mons saw that there was no more hesitancy in his actions. Beyond the eternal body, the mind was young and sure and unclouded again.

Mons knelt, and Nerina knelt too. The priest said softly, "We thank God that a new Incarnation is permitted. May peace reign in this cycle, and in all the cycles beyond."

Tyrell lifted Nerina to her feet. He reached down and drew Mons upright too.

"Mons, Mons," he said, almost chidingly. "Every century I'm treated less like a man and more like a god. If you'd been alive a few hundred years ago—well, they still prayed when I woke, but they didn't kneel. I'm a man, Mons. Don't forget that."

Mons said, "You brought peace to the worlds."

"Then may I have something to eat, in return?"

Mons bowed and went out. Tyrell turned quickly to Nerina. The strong gentleness of his arms drew her close.

"If I never woke, sometime—" he said. "You'd be the hardest thing of all to give up. I didn't know how lonely I was till I found another immortal."

"We have a week here in the monastery," she said. "A week's retreat, before we go home. I like being here with you best of all."

"Wait a while," he said. "A few more centuries and you'll lose that attitude of reverence. I wish you would. Love's better—and who else can I love this way?"

She thought of the centuries of loneliness he had had, and her whole body ached with love and compassion.

After the kiss, she drew back and looked at him thoughtfully.

"You've changed again," she said. "It's still you, but—"

"But what?"

"You're gentler, somehow."

Tyrell laughed.

"Each time, they wash out my mind and give me a new set of memories. Oh, most of the old ones, but the total's a little different. It always is. Things are more peaceful now than they were a century ago. So my mind is tailored to fit the times. Otherwise I'd gradually become an anachronism." He frowned slightly. "Who's that?"

She glanced at the door.

"Mons? No. It's no one."

"Oh? Well . . . yes, we'll have a week's retreat. Time to think and integrate my retailored personality. And the past—" He hesitated again.

She said, "I wish I'd been born earlier. I could have been with you—"

"No," he said quickly. "At least—not too far back."

"Was it so bad?"

He shrugged.

"I don't know how true my memories are any more. I'm glad I don't remember more than I do. But I remember enough. The legends are right." His face shadowed with sorrow. "The big wars . . . hell was loosed. Hell was omnipotent! The Antichrist walked in the noonday sun, and men feared that which is high. . . ." His gaze lifted to the pale low ceiling of the room, seeing beyond it. "Men had turned into beasts. Into devils. I spoke of peace to them, and they tried to kill me. I bore it. I was immortal, by God's grace. Yet they could have killed me. I am vulnerable to weapons." He drew a deep, long breath. "Immortality was not enough. God's will preserved me, so that I could go on preaching peace until, little by little, the maimed beasts remembered their souls and reached up out of hell. . . ."

She had never heard him talk like this.

Gently she touched his hand.

He came back to her.

"It's over," he said. "The past is dead. We have today."

From the distance the priests chanted a paean of joy and gratitude.

The next afternoon she saw him at the end of a corridor leaning over something huddled and dark. She ran forward. He was bent down beside the body of a priest, and when Nerina called out, he shivered and stood up, his face white and appalled.

She looked down and her face, too, went white.

The priest was dead. There were blue marks on his throat, and his neck was broken, his head twisted monstrously.

Tyrell moved to shield the body from her gaze.

"G-get Mons," he said, unsure as though he had reached the end of the hundred years. "Quick. This . . . *get him.*"

Mons came, looked at the body, and stood aghast. He met Tyrell's blue gaze.

"How many centuries, Messiah?" he asked, in a shaken voice.

Tyrell said, "Since there was violence? Eight centuries or more. Mons, no one—no one is capable of this."

Mons said, "Yes. There is no more violence. It has been bred out of the race." He dropped suddenly to his knees. "Messiah, bring peace again! The dragon has risen from the past!"

Tyrell straightened, a figure of strong humility in his white robe.

He lifted his eyes and prayed.

Nerina knelt, her horror slowly washed away in the burning power of Tyrell's prayer.

The whisper breathed through the monastery and shuddered back from the blue, clear air beyond. None knew who had closed deadly hands about the priest's throat. No one, no human, was capable any longer of killing; as Mons had said, the ability to hate, to destroy, had been bred out of the race.

The whisper did not go beyond the monastery. Here the battle must be fought in secret, no hint of it escaping to trouble the long peace of the worlds.

No human.

But another whisper grew: *The Antichrist is born again.*

They turned to Tyrell, to the Messiah, for comfort.

Peace, he said, *peace—meet evil with humility, bow your heads in prayer, remember the love that saved man when hell was loosed on the worlds two thousand years ago.*

At night, beside Nerina, he moaned in his sleep and struck out at an invisible enemy.

"Devil!" he cried—and woke, shuddering.

She held him, with proud humility, till he slept again.

She came with Mons one day to Tyrell's room, to tell him of the new horror. A priest had been found dead, savagely hacked by a sharp knife. They pushed open the door and saw Tyrell sitting facing them at a low table. He was praying while he watched, in sick fascination, the bloody knife that lay on the table before him.

"Tyrell—" she said, and suddenly Mons drew in a quick, shuddering breath and swung around sharply. He pushed her back across the threshold.

"Wait!" he said, with violent urgency. "Wait for me here!" Before she could speak he was beyond the closing door, and she heard it lock.

She stood there, not thinking, for a long time.

Then Mons came out and closed the door softly behind him. He looked at her.

"It's all right," he said. "But . . . you must listen to me now." Then he was silent.

He tried again.

"Blessed of God—" Again he drew that difficult breath. "Nerina. I—" He laughed oddly. "That's strange. I can't talk unless I call you Nerina."

"What is it? Let me go to Tyrell!"

"No—no. He'll be all right. Nerina, he's—sick."

She shut her eyes, trying to concentrate. She heard his voice, unsure but growing stronger.

"Those killings. Tyrell did them."

"Now you lie," she said. "That is a lie!"

Mons said almost sharply, "Open your eyes. Listen to me. Tyrell is—a man. A very great man, a very good man, but no god. He is immortal. Unless he is struck down, he will live forever—as you will. He has already lived more than twenty centuries."

"Why tell me this? I know it!"

Mons said, "You must help, you must understand. Immortality is an accident of the genes. A mutation. Once in a thousand years, perhaps, or ten thousand, a human is born immortal. His body renews itself; he does not age. Neither does his brain. But his mind ages—"

She said desperately, "Tyrell swam the pool of rebirth only three days ago. Not for another century will his mind age again. Is he—*he's not dying?*"

"No—no. Nerina, the pool of rebirth is only a symbol. You know that."

"Yes. The real rebirth comes afterward, when you put us in that machine. I remember."

Mons said, "The machine. If it were not used each century, you and Tryell would have become senile and helpless a long time ago. The mind is not immortal, Nerina. After a while it cannot carry the weight of knowledge, learning, habits. It loses flexibility, it clouds with stiff old age. The machine clears the mind, Nerina, as we can clear a computer of its units of memory. Then we replace some memories, not all, we put the necessary memories in a fresh, clear mind, so it can grow and learn for another hundred years."

"But I know all that—"

"Those new memories form a new personality, Nerina."

"A new—? But Tyrell is still the same."

"Not quite. Each century he changes a little, as life grows better, as the worlds grow happier. Each century the new mind, the fresh personality of Tyrell is different —more in tune with the new century than the one just past. You have been reborn in mind three times, Nerina. You are not the same as you were the first time. But you cannot remember that. You do not have all the old memories you once had."

"But—but what—"

Mons said, "I do not know. I have talked to Tyrell. I think this is what has happened. Each century when the mind of Tyrell was cleansed—erased—it left a blank mind, and we built a new Tyrell on that. Not much changed. Only a little, each time. But more than twenty times? His mind must have been very different twenty centuries ago. And—"

"How different?"

"I don't know. We've assumed that when the mind was erased, the pattern of personality—vanished. I think now that it didn't vanish. It was buried. Suppressed, driven so deeply into the mind that it could not emerge. It became unconscious. Century after century this has happened. And now more than twenty personalities of Tyrell are buried in his mind, a multiple personality that can no longer stay in balance. From the graves in his mind, there has been a resurrection."

"The White Christ was never a killer!"

"No. In reality, even his first personality, twenty-odd centuries ago, must have been very great and good to bring peace to the worlds—in that time of Antichrist. But sometimes, in the burial of the mind, a change may happen. Those buried personalities, some of them, may have changed to—to something less good than they were originally. And now they have broken loose."

Nerina turned to the door.

Mons said, "We must be very sure. But we can save the Messiah. We can clear his brain, probe deep, deep, root out the evil spirit. . . . We can save him and make him whole again. We must start at once. Nerina—pray for him."

He gave her a long, troubled look, turned, and went

swiftly along the corridor. Nerina waited, not even thinking. After a while she heard a slight sound. At one end
of the corridor were two priests standing motionless; at
the other end, two others.

She opened the door and went in to Tyrell.

The first thing she saw was the blood-stained knife on the
table. Then she saw the dark silhouette at the window,
against the aching intensity of blue sky.

"Tyrell," she said hesitantly.

He turned.

"Nerina. Oh, Nerina!"

His voice was still gentle with that deep power of calm.
She went swiftly into his arms.

"I was praying," he said, bending his head to rest on her
shoulder. "Mons told me. . . . I was praying. What have I
done?"

"You are the Messiah," she said steadily. "You saved the
world from evil and the Antichrist. You've done that."

"But the rest! This devil in my mind! This seed that has
grown there, hidden from God's sunlight—what has it
grown into? They say I *killed!*"

After a long pause she whispered, "Did you?"

"No," he said, with absolute certainty. "How could I?
I, who have lived by love—more than two thousand years
—I could not harm a living thing."

"I knew that," she said. "You are the White Christ."

"The White Christ," he said softly. "I wanted no such
name. I am only a man, Nerina. I was never more than that.
But . . . something saved me, something kept me alive
through the Hour of the Antichrist. It was God. It was
His hand. God—*help me now!*"

She held him tightly and looked past him through the
window, bright sky, green meadow, tall mountains with
the clouds rimming their peaks. God was here, as he was

out beyond the blue, on all the worlds and in the gulfs between them, and God meant peace and love.

"He will help you," she said steadily. "He walked with you two thousand years ago. He hasn't gone away."

"Yes," Tyrell whispered. "Mons must be wrong. The way it was . . . I remember. Men like beasts. The sky was burning fire. There was blood . . . there was blood. More than a hundred years of blood that ran from the beast-men as they fought."

She felt the sudden stiffness in him, a trembling rigor, a new sharp straining.

He lifted his head and looked into her eyes.

She thought of ice and fire, blue ice, blue fire.

"The big wars," he said, his voice stiff, rusty.

Then he put his hand over his eyes.

"*Christ!*" The word burst from his tight throat. "*God, God—*"

"Tyrell!" She screamed his name.

"Back!" he croaked, and she stumbled away, but he was not talking to her. "Back, devil!" He clawed at his head, grinding it between his palms, bowing till he was half crouched before her.

"Tyrell!" she cried. "Messiah! You are the White Christ—"

The bowed body snapped erect. She looked at the new face and felt an abysmal horror and loathing.

Tyrell stood looking at her. Then, appallingly, he gave her a strutting, derisive bow.

She felt the edge of the table behind her. She groped back and touched the heavy thickness of dried blood on the knife-blade. It was part of the nightmare. She moved her hand to the haft, knowing she could die by steel, letting her thought move ahead of the glittering steel's point into her breast.

The voice she heard was touched with laughter.

"Is it sharp?" he asked. "Is it still sharp, my love? Or did I dull it on the priest? Will you use it on me? Will you try? Other women have tried!" Thick laughter choked in his throat.

"Messiah," she whispered.

"Messiah!" he mocked. "A White Christ! Prince of Peace! Bringing the word of love, walking unharmed through the bloodiest wars that ever wrecked a world . . . oh yes, a legend, my love, twenty centuries old and more. And a lie. They've forgotten! They've all forgotten what it was really like then!"

All she could do was shake her head in helpless denial.

"Oh yes," he said. "You weren't alive then. No one was. Except me, Tyrell. Butchery! I survived. But not by preaching peace. Do you know what happened to the men who preached love? They died—but I didn't die. I survived, not by preaching."

He pranced, laughing.

"Tyrell the Butcher," he cried. "I was the bloodiest of them all. All they could understand was fear. And they weren't easily frightened then—not the men like beasts. But they were afraid of *me*."

He lifted his clawed hands, his muscles straining in an ecstasy of ghastly memory.

"The Red Christ," he said. "They might have called me that. But they didn't. Not after I'd proved what I had to prove. They had a name for me then. They knew my name. And now—" He grinned at her. "Now that the worlds are at peace, now I'm worshiped as the Messiah. What can Tyrell the Butcher do today?"

His laughter came slow, horrible and complacent.

He took three steps and swept his arms around her. Her flesh shrank from the grip of that evil.

And then, suddenly, strangely, she felt the evil leave him. The hard arms shuddered, drew away, and then tightened again, with frantic tenderness, while he bent his head and she felt the sudden hotness of tears.

He could not speak for a while. Cold as stone, she held him.

Somehow she was sitting on a couch and he was kneeling before her, his face buried in her lap.

She could not make out many of his choking words.

"Remember . . . I remember . . . the old memories . . . I can't stand it, I can't look back . . . or ahead . . . they—they had a name for me. I remember now. . . ."

She laid one hand on his head. His hair was cold and damp.

"They called me Antichrist!"

He lifted his face and looked at her.

"Help me!" he cried in anguish. "Help me, help me!"

Then his head bowed again and he pressed his fists against his temples, whispering wordlessly.

She remembered what was in her right hand, and she lifted the knife and drove it down as hard as she could, to give him the help he needed.

She stood at the window, her back to the room and the dead immortal.

She waited for the priest Mons to return. He would know what to do next. Probably the secret would have to be kept, somehow.

They would not harm her, she knew that. The reverence that had surrounded Tyrell enfolded her too. She would live on, the only immortal now, born in a time of peace, living forever and alone in the worlds of peace. Some day, some time, another immortal might be born, but she did not want to think of that now. She could think only of Tyrell and her loneliness.

She looked through the window at the bright blue and green, the pure day of God, washed clean now of the last red stain of man's bloody past. She knew that Tyrell would be glad if he could see this cleanness, this purity that could go on forever.

She would see it go on. She was part of it, as Tyrell had not been. And even in the loneliness she already felt, there was a feeling of compensation, somehow. She was dedicated to the centuries of man that were to come.

She reached beyond her sorrow and love. From far away she could hear the solemn chanting of the priests. It was part of the rightness that had come to the worlds now, at last, after the long and bloody path to the new Golgotha. But it was the last Golgotha, and she would go on now as she must, dedicated and sure.

Immortal.

She lifted her head and looked steadily at the blue. She would look forward into the future. The past was forgotten. And the past, to her, meant no bloody heritage, no deep corruption that would work unseen in the black hell of the mind's abyss until the monstrous seed reached up to destroy God's peace and love.

Quite suddenly, she remembered that she had committed murder. Her arm thrilled again with the violence of the blow; her hand tingled with the splash of shed blood.

Very quickly she closed her thoughts against the memory. She looked up at the sky, holding hard against the closed gateway of her mind as though the assault battered already against the fragile bars.

SOUL MATE

Lee Sutton

The possibility of telepathy is one of science fiction's favorite themes, and one that opens endless moral and religious considerations. I have spoken in the Introduction of Poul Anderson's poignant "Kyrie," but Lee Sutton here presents us with a far different kind of psychic match, between a pleasantly promiscuous but sentimentally religious young girl and a cool, rational man of the world, who is totally horrified by both the messy life style and pious beliefs of his "soul mate." What he does about it is author Sutton's to reveal. I do think Sutton is perhaps too harsh with the girl in assessing her fate, but that quibble aside, the denouement does offer us something that is rare enough in any literature, sacred or profane: A poetic, believable evocation of what some Christian philosophers like to call the Beatific Vision—the presence of God in Heaven—and what it means to lose it.

The church was a jumbled disorder of towers, false buttresses and arches, reaching irrationally into nothing—but achieving peace. Quincy Summerfield rushed by it, down the stairs to the subway, intent only on his own kind of peace. He picked his way quickly through the crowds, avoiding the eyes that followed him. The chaos of people was an agony, but, because of the rain, he could have missed his train waiting for a taxi.

He settled himself behind a pillar near the tracks, looking cool and contained in his perfectly tailored covert coat and dark-blue homburg, but inside he was trembling. He had had these periods before, when every set of human eyes seemed to open into agony and even the order and control of his office could not allay his sense of disorder in the presence of his staff. Seven interviews in a row had done it today. He had played seven men like instruments and had hired the five best for his company at fifty thousand dollars a year less than any other personnel man could have gotten them for. It was for this that he was paid. But now he would need a day or so of isolation. It might even be better to send away Charlotte, the wife whom he had schooled into order and control.

Just then a girl's rich laugh floated to him down the tunnel and he glanced around the pillar. A girl with a long black pony-tail squatted just past the turnstiles, art portfolios propped against her legs. With distaste he noticed the full breasts thrust out against an overbright blouse under an open, dirty trench coat. Her full mouth was deeply curved with laughter as she gathered up the miscellany of a spilled handbag; and she seemed to Quincy Summerfield the very essence of disorder.

He pulled his eyes away from her. He had to force his eyes away from her. He was seized with the shocking conviction that he had known her all his life; yet another part of his mind knew that he had never seen her before. She was like a fragment of a nightmare that had wandered into daylight. He prayed she wouldn't be on the same car with him. She was not; as he went through the sliding doors, he saw her enter the car ahead of him.

Inside the car, Quincy looked quickly around him, and sensing her monumental calm, sat down beside a gray-haired woman with light brown skin. Out of the crowd of the ramp he felt a little better. He seemed almost the embodiment of dignity as he sat there, erect, his long slender face, with its clipped graying mustache, composed and calm. The effect was achieved, however, only by considerable effort.

A guard pushed open the sliding door at the end of the car. The girl in the trench coat teetered through, rich lips in a teeth-flashing smile. Her sloppy good humor seemed to reach out to everyone in the car. For a moment even the guard's sullen face came alive. She sank gratefully into the seat directly opposite from Quincy Summerfield, dropping her load of portfolios helter-skelter.

Quincy Summerfield looked down, staring at the dull rain marks on his well-polished shoes. He felt her eyes on him. He began to shake inside again, and looked up. He looked deliberately away from her, as if in an attempt to ignore her so obviously she could not fail to notice the slight.

The sense of her presence was just too great. Even across the car he could feel the scent of her heavy perfume; it was deep with musk. His eyes were slowly drawn toward her: the pile of portfolios in disorder around her knees; the foolish, soaked ballet slippers on tiny feet. A squiggle of modernist jewelry, tied with a leather throng, nestled in the hollow of her throat. It was a distorted crucifix. All this messiness and the messiness of religion, too, he thought. But his eyes were drawn up to the curve of her lips. He was trembling even more; for no reason his feet ached with cold.

Then he met her clear, deep brown eyes; *lambent the word is. Such cool, gray eyes.*

He moved his feet. They were very cold. *That damned bra is much too tight* . . . His hand pushed up against his breasts. A drip from the homburg fell cool and sharp onto her nose. His breasts actually hurt. *A hot shower if the heater is fixed* . . . *Then I'll tell everyone about selling the picture* . . . *Charlotte will make me a warm drink* . . .

God, I'm feeling funny. I wonder if Arthur—would he believe? That's a distinguished disgusting-looking girl how aristocratic homburg mustache low class slut.

My seeing's all wrong. That's me and there's no mirror. Who's Charlotte, Arthur, Quincy? I'm Quincy. I'm . . . That man. That girl. Jesus, Jesus. I'm thinking his her thoughts. Let me out. Let me out!

"Let me out!" The girl's rising scream brought everyone in the car to his feet. She stood there a moment, her eyes rolling and wild, then collapsed to the concrete floor in a faint.

Quincy Summerfield was shaking from head to foot, his hands over his face, fingers digging into his eyes. He had been conscious of the lifting of a great weight as the world had whirled into darkness and the girl collapsed onto the floor. She was going to throw up. He knew. He could feel every sensation she had as she lay there in the half faint. He could feel his own gorge rising. People were lifting her up. He felt her eyelids flutter. The mirror, mirror, mirror of her being conscious of his being conscious of her being conscious of the colored woman with the sculptured calm taking her into her arms. Then the girl threw up horribly and his throat ached with the agony of her embarrassment.

The train came screeching to a stop. Quincy jumped up and ran blindly headlong through the sliding door. He all but knocked down an old lady entering. She hit after him with her umbrella.

"Young pup!" The words followed him down the ramp as he ran, his leather heels echoing through the noisy underground. His face was wild. People stopped in their tracks and stared after him, but he did not care. His hat fell off. He stumbled, almost fell. His head was awhirl with her seeing and his seeing, her thoughts and his thoughts. The turnstiles were just ahead. Soon he would be away, outside, away from all the people, away from the girl, into the open air.

The colored woman—she'll help me. She was picking up his pictures.

He pushed down a scream, and plunged through the tangled vision. He hardly knew how he got there, but finally, hatless, his trousers torn from a fall on the stairs, he was standing out in the street, flailing his arm at taxis.

Blessedly one stopped.

"Where to, buster?"

"Grand Central. Hurry, for God's sake!"

Through images of her seeing, he looked at his watch. He had smashed the crystal in some way and his wrist was numb. He sank back into the slick upholstery, breathing hard. Exhausted, he closed his eyes and gave himself up to single vision.

His bra was too tight; he reached around, letting out the hooks and eyes and breathed more easily.

"Now, honey," a soft voice was saying, "you be fine. You just got something now to tell your husband." The brown face was smiling. "You do got a husband?"

"But I'm not pregnant!" He burst out, speaking as the girl spoke.

"What's that, buster?" the taxi driver tossed over his shoulder. "You're not what?"

Quincy Summerfield opened his eyes and sat bolt upright. "Just thinking over some dialogue for a radio play," he said desperately.

With a grunt, the taxi driver went on driving.

Summerfield looked around him. It was a taxi, like any taxi. A small sign announced the driver was Barney Cohen. Outside it was raining. People leaned into the rain as they always did. He tried to push away the other images.

But he could not.

When he closed his eyes, he was in a dirty white, tiled

lavatory, a vague stench of vomit and the scent of a musky perfume surrounding him. A women's lavatory. He was looking into the mirror at his white, shaking face, a woman's face with frightened brown eyes. He was putting on lipstick. *SHE is putting on lipstick*, he forced his mind to say. She shook her head and closed her eyes.

You're still here, she thought.

Yes.

What's happened, for God's sake? There was the same desperate fear in her mind that he felt in his.

Fear. They shared their fear for a long moment.

Then he fought to bring his thoughts into order again. *Nothing to fear. Nothing. Just the same as I always was. Just the same. She, you just the same. She. Me. Just the same.*

Christ, Christ her mind intruded. *Our Father . . .* The prayer distorted into a jumble of religious images.

The depth of her superstitious outcry shocked him into steel-bright control, and he fought for domination. *There is nothing to fear.* He forced the thought through the images. *I am just the same. You are just the same. Somehow . . .* and for a second he slid out of control . . . *we have made total mental contact. I know what you think, feel what you feel, and you know my thoughts, my feelings.*

Under his controlling throught she calmed and contemplated his ideas for a moment. He could feel her mind reach out for the sensations of his body, his male body and he allowed himself to become fully conscious of hers, the femaleness of her.

A deep wave of erotic feeling took them both: him in the taxi, her a quarter of a mile away before the mirror. He could feel her breath quicken.

"But fabulous," she breathed aloud as her images of Arthur and Fred interlaced with his imaged memories of Charlotte.

Revulsion. He stamped down on the images as if they were pale, dangerous worms.

"Stop it!" he shouted.

"For Christ's sake, buster, we got three blocks yet," the taxi driver growled, but swung toward the curb.

"Sorry. Thinking aloud again."

"Nuts," the taxi driver muttered. "A stooge for nuts, that's all I am," and cut back into traffic.

You're a cold, terrible man, thought the girl, swept by feelings of shame and hurt that were alien to her. *Things were just getting* . . . she searched for a word which meant good, but which would not betray her to his disapproval.

You're a slut, he thought savagely. He was deeply shaken, as by a nightmare. *I've wandered into a nightmare. Just like the nightmares I started having at fourteen. Are they connected? Were they reflections out of the mind of this terrible slut of a girl?*

Christ, you're a prig! the girl thought. She was very angry at him and at herself. Very deliberately she brought up an image of Arthur, a hairy young man with . . .

Setting his teeth, Quincy tried to force her thoughts away from the image forming in her mind and thus in his, but it was like trying to push back water—a deluge that was sweeping over him. He opened his eyes, almost to the breaking point, almost ready to scream. His mental pain hurt her into submission.

All right, all right, I'll stop. But you'll have to stop being nasty, too. After all, I didn't do this. I didn't try to bring us together this way. She was trembling with his pain.

"Okay, buster. Grand Central."

Summerfield thrust a five-dollar bill into the man's hand and rushed off into the crowd.

Five dollars! You gave that man five dollars! Why . . . ?

Couldn't wait. Got to get my train. Get away. Far away. Then maybe I'll be rid of you.

Pushing through the people, her thoughts went on steadily through his mind. *Am I so terrible?* they came, touched with wistfulness.

Yes, he thought. *You are so terrible. Everything I cannot stand. Wretchedly superstitious. Involved in a messy affair with two men. Disorderly.*

Images of her apartment flashed into his mind: modern pictures askew, undusted. Garbage in the sink. *Everything I cannot stand.*

Then, for the first time, he really knew her deep hurt as his own, as if he were committing violence upon himself. It was as if some rich and various part of himself, long suppressed, were alive again and in pain. For a fraction of a moment his mind reached out hesitantly toward her with compassion.

In spite of everything, she thought, *I rather admire you. Why, now we're practically soul mates.*

His revulsion at the idea was too deep to be stopped by any consideration of her or of himself.

I hope I can get rid of you, she thought, trying desperately to withdraw from him as from the violent touch of cruel hands.

But I'm afraid. I'm afraid. Those ESP men at Duke . . . Her mind sought wildly for a shadowy memory. *Didn't they shield their people with lead, separate them miles and miles?* And he got tangled pictures of men in white robes, separating "sensitive" people, shielding them in a variety of ways, but with no effect on their abilities to read each other's minds. He let his contempt slap at her at believing such nonsense.

But she was right. The edges of perception sharpened; they did not fade. There was no shutting her off. And there was always the continuing and horrible sense of familiarity. It was almost as if the eyes of his mind were being drawn against his will toward a disgusting part of himself held up in a mirror.

Going down the walk to his home he was conscious of her in her apartment. But he concentrated on holding his own line of thought. His home, its barbered lawns and well-trimmed hedges, the whiteness and neatness of it, the pattern of twigs in the single tree was bringing him, momentarily, a pool of quiet.

Spare . . . bare . . . such crude design. The house was suddenly mirrored back at him from her mind. Suddenly he saw: *Petty bourgeois cheapness. All richness and complexity sacrificed to achieve a banal balance.*

Damn you.

Sorry. I didn't mean to hurt. But her laughter and scorn were still there under the surface.

And he couldn't help being infected by her thoughts. The landscape he owned and loved: *Poor stuff. Deliberately manufactured by a second-rate artist for people with third-rate taste.*

And Charlotte, so calm and sweet. Suddenly he saw how lost she was, the lines of frustration around her mouth.

Poor thing, the girl thought. *No children. No love.* Then came more than scorn. *You needed release and you've used her—just like the men you work with. You—*

There was no escaping her. Her scorn or shame or teasing laughter was omnipresent.

He didn't dare go back to work, for his confusion would have been noticed, and that was something he could not have borne. Luckily his post was high enough that he could make his own schedule, and could remain at home for a few days.

But the days were torture. There was not one flicker of his thought, one twinge of emotion the girl did not reflect.

Worse, he caught all of hers. Not one of his her secret
shabbinesses she he did not know. The tangled days ended
only in nights where their tangled dreams were all nightmares to him. It was as if his whole life were being im-
mersed in deep deep seas where nothing swam but strangeness which came echoing and re-echoing through caverns
of mirrors.

He lasted three days at home. During those three days
he sought desperately for some reasonable explanation of
the sudden, shocking contact that they had made. He half-
believed now that the knowledge of her had always been
there, just below the surface, fended off, forcing itself up
to his attention only when his defenses were down in sleep
—the source of his strange nightmares. That day on the
subway his defenses had been all but worn away by his
work; and her defenses, were they ever up? Besides, she
had just sold one of her silly pictures and was in love with
the entire world of people. By the most fantastic of bad
luck they had to meet just at that time. It was their eyes
meeting that finally pierced the thin shells holding them
apart. Maybe there was something to the old wives' tales
about the magic meeting of eyes, windows of souls. But all
that was superstitious nonsense; he couldn't believe it.

He sought out one of the books by Rhine, but couldn't
believe that either. He would have rather believed he was
insane. Particularly he wouldn't believe that distance
would make no difference. He decided to put a continent
between them to see if that couldn't break the contact. He
had Charlotte drive him to La Guardia field and he took
the first plane west.

It was a bad mistake, for on the plane there were no
distractions, and her presence remained as clear as it had
always been. He could not move around. He found he
could not force himself to concentrate on a book. Having
been lucky enough to find a seat to himself, he couldn't
engage anyone in conversation. There was nothing to do

but lean back and close his eyes and live her life with her. That evening on the plane he became convinced that since he could not get rid of her, he must dominate her.

It was her peculiar religious notions which finally convinced him. She was walking through a tiny park at evening; it was spring and the trees were just beginning to bud. She paused before one tree, her stomach growling a little with hunger, sensing the city smells, the roar, the silence of the trees. *The tree reaches. Steely, reaching up among the stones of the city. Each bud tingles, leaves opening like angels' wings. Root tips reach down, tender in the dark. The smooth reach up of the branches. Like you, Quincy. Like the feel of your body, Quincy.*

And her eyes traced each line of the branches, following the angles, the twists. And as she reached the very tip of the tree, she felt something very terrible to him—a kind of ecstatic union with the life of the tree. And she glanced down then to where a pair of lovers were strolling, hand by hand, along the littered walk, her artist's mind stripping away their clothes, seeing their bodies almost as she had seen the tree. *The bodies are juicy, longing for one another, sweet muscles running along the bones. Aren't they lovely, Quincy?* she thought. *Look at the girl's hip thrust, the man's thighs. What a sweet rolling they're going to have.*

Can't you think of anything else?

I won't let you spoil it. It's too lovely an evening. And she turned toward a shabby little church. He had no desire to continue in such an unprofitable direction, and tried to steer her away from the church by playing on her hunger. She caught his purpose immediately and carefully concentrated on her own. She ignored his disgust and intellectual scorn as she entered through the arched doorway. There in the dimness she bought a candle, genuflected, and placed it before the Virgin.

It was a wordless prayer. For protection, for understanding. As she glanced up at the rather crude piece of statuary, she ticketed it for what it was, but moved beyond it to an inflated vision of feminine richness and purity. Here was the woman, the full breast at which God tugged, utterly pure but female, bowels and womb, hunger and pain. *How she knows what I feel! So high, so beautiful, and yet she understands!*

Only after contemplating the Virgin did she turn to the crucifix. Here was all vigorous male sweetness, hanging from bloody nails. Quincy Summerfield tried to shy away, hold off this whole concept. He shaped an obscene word, but again the girl ignored him. Her feeling was too strong. The remoteness and terror and wonder and glory that were embodied in the tree and in the bones and blood of all men in their suffering, were richly present in the figure of the crucifix; *the timeless which betrayed itself into the agony of time out of compasssion for* me *and* my *weakness.* She knelt in a submission to unreason that made Quincy there in the plane writhe in protest. But she was too submissive. He felt the position of her body as she knelt, and knew that she was a trifle off balance. Abruptly he willed a sudden small twitch of her leg and she went sprawling forward on her face. Quincy winced with the bump but jeered at her none the less.

That's mean—trying to make me look foolish.

Not any more foolish than kneeling before a piece of plaster. Disgusting. All that nonsense you have in your head. All that untruth.

She was furious. She pushed herself to her feet and stared at her dirty hands, down at the dust on her spring dress. She thought of a bath and quick meal, and left the church hurriedly. She ignored him, but as she went up the stairs to the apartment which, under Quincy's prodding, she had brought into some kind of order, she was still numbly angry.

What you did there in the church was shameful, she thought. *I'll get even with you. It's not all nonsense. It's all true and you know it's true. Of all the people in the world, why did I have to get you?*

She stripped deliberately before a mirror and watched herself so he would see her. It was a good body, high and full in the breasts, slender of waist, flaring and tapering down to the dirty feet. She ran her hands over it, under it, between, concentrating on the sensations of her fingers, feeling his responses to them.

Then abruptly she stopped and went to the phone and called her friend Arthur. She was tingling with desire and Quincy felt his gorge rise, even as his loins tightened.

I'm feeling lonely, Arthur. Could you come right over? I'll be in the bathtub, but come on in. All right then, join me if you want to.

Fifteen minutes later, Quincy staggered to the rest room on the plane, locked himself in and sat down on the seat. With trembling fingers he took out his nail file and stripped back his coat sleeve. His jaw was tight, his eyes were a little mad. He looked for a place in the arm where it seemed large veins were not present. With one hard jab he stuck the nail file a half inch deep into his arm and forced himself to leave it there. Then he jiggled it slowly back and forth, letting the pain of it sweep over him in red waves, concentrating completely on the pain until the girl began to scream.

Get him out of there, he said through clenched teeth. *Get him out of there!*

And when, finally, a very bewildered Arthur was ejected from her apartment, as yet only half dressed, he pulled the nail file from his arm and let his head lean for a moment against the cool steel of the washbowl. He had learned how to control her. She could not stand his pain.

If it had not been for his own betrayal of himself,

if his own revulsion had not been weak, she would not
have been able to get as far as she had with Arthur.
Still, in the end, it was his mind, not the anarchy of his
body that had won out.

Lying there with his head against the steel, with his
arm still bloody, knowing she was lying across the bed
half-conscious with frustration and his pain, he took over
control completely for a moment and pushed her up to
a sitting position. She pushed herself up to a sitting position. She moaned slightly in protest, but allowed him to
move her toward her closet, make her reach for her
pajamas. He sensed that she almost enjoyed it. She enjoyed their complete rapport of feeling. And even with
the pain in his arm, he found there was a certain joy
in her emotion; and it was as if with his own mind
alone he thought of what wholeness an experience together could be.

It was a peculiar moment for something like that to
begin, but his steel-like control meshed together and held
the rush of her emotion and his pain. Her admiration for
his strength warmed him; she even shared in his triumph,
and suddenly both of them found the experience good—
not so much the experience itself but the perfect unity
of thought and feeling that followed it.

Quincy cleaned his arm and bound it with a hand-
kerchief, and when he went back to his seat the stewardess
brought him his dinner. In her apartment the girl, too,
ate, and their rapport persisted as they shared the savors
of each other's food. He was firmly in control of their
joint thought and feeling, but it was an experience richer
than he had ever known. As they moved west, the desire
for her physical presence grew and grew.

Wouldn't that magazine be shocked at our *together-
ness?* She thought; and at that moment Quincy shared in
her scorn of the bourgeois fetish.

They existed in that kind of rapport for the rest of the evening, he on the plane, she in the apartment, arranging it for his ultimate return. Even in sleep they remained almost joined into a single entity.

It was a strange period. Quincy got off the plane in San Francisco, and almost directly boarded another going nonstop back to New York. Less than twenty-four hours after he left New York, he had returned and was walking down her street toward her walkup.

But then things changed. The shabby Greenwich Village street was filled with her memories, and she began to take precedence. Everything around him now was a part of her. All of her life began to engulf him. Her terrible disordered memories surrounded him, memories he could not repress.

He paused by the ugly little church where she had gone at times to make agonized confessions—only to dive back into the tangled messiness of her life again.

Not any more. Not messy any more. We'll be married and then . . .

He felt a blind impulse to enter the church to pour out his agony there. And find peace. Her impulse or his? He wrenched away. *Not now. Not ever . . .*

Only a few steps now . . . past the place where Fred and Arthur had fought that night. *Can't you stop remembering?*

And up five flights of ill-lit stairway, his mind filling with her anticipation. His mind filled with all the times she had gone up those stairs. His heart pounding with his anticipation. Knowing she was lounging there on the bed sofa in her blue dressing gown. Knowing the cocktail shaker was filled with martinis as only he could make them, dry and cold.

As his foot touched the landing he knew she was moving languidly from her couch toward the door, and her hand was on the door. And it was open. And she was standing before him.

Like a sleepwalker he moved past her and into the room, sensing now the subtler perfume of her. And she closed the door and he looked around the room, utterly numbed.

Then feeling came back and he saw that the room was beautiful. The pictures in their wild excess were ordered into a subtle harmony by their arrangement. For all of the dirt ingrained in it, the furniture was better than his own expensive pieces. It was all fuller and richer and more harmonious than anything he had ever experienced.

And the girl standing there, her dark hair about her shoulders!

My God, you're beautiful. She was beautiful and his thought reflected back into her mind and she flushed with pleasure. And he sensed her admiration of his lean white face and gray mustache, and the strength of his mind, and hard, lean feel of his body. And he knew the beauty of the room was completed by the two of them standing poised and not touching. Even the crucifix in the corner blended with them into one harmonious whole.

And she he reached out to a bare touching of hands . . . pause . . . then a sweeping together in their arms. And he felt his chest against her breast, against her chest his breast. Her mouth against her mouth, her his mouth against . . .

Then the whole world went crashing out of control and there was nothing but the rawness of her passion and of his passion, her his—

Until his entire reason revolted and he could stand it no longer. The need to give way to the feel of his her mouth, this irrational disorder of giving and taking at the peak of sensation, this need he could not and would not meet. A fragment of himself broke away from the unity and grew, until the strongest part of his mind floated over the chaos of sensation and contemplated it with cold disgust. Not all of his mind, for part of himself was engulfed and protesting.

But part of him was icy and knew what to do almost as well as if he had planned it. He reached down into her memory and brought out her image of the purity of the Virgin draped sweetly in blue with the haloed babe in the crook of her arm. Deliberately he intensified the picture into an almost transcendent purity of spirit, vibrating with light and wonder. Instantly he wiped it out except for the blue robes, robes like her dressing gown, and filled them with the naked girl, her mouth agape in the throes of animal lust. Then back to the picture Virgin again, who moved slowly sorrowing, her eyes looking up.

The girl's eyes looked up and sought the crucifix in the corner of the room, and his mind expanded it before her eyes to the living man on the cross, straining in agony and in sorrow.

Quickly now. In complete control now of her whole mind and of his. *Passion—your passion.* He wiped away the Christ figure from her mind and mocked her with the writhing body of Arthur, and dissolved it into an image of his own face. And wiped that away to present the face of the suffering Christ. A gross female figure loomed, its mouth agape. *My mouth all horrible. No! No!! Me driving the phallic nails in those sweet palms! The bones making a crushing sound.*

The girl screamed, and broke away from Quincy Summerfield, his eyes wild.

That's what you are. That's what you know you are.

She covered her face with her hand, jerking this way and that, trying to get away from him. Trying to get away from his her acknowledgment of her naked self, while she he lashed herself with disgust.

It was enough. Quincy's mind contemplated her but did no more.

It was only herself now that turned and ran, a decision shaping in her mind. She shaped the decision for herself and Quincy exulted in it, knowing that by her own insane standards she was damning herself.

She rushed weeping to the French windows opening on her little sundeck. She flung them open and did not pause but plunged on and out and over the parapet . . .

The railing smashed at his knees and he curled up suddenly with the pain, waiting the greater pain. He closed his eyes and set his teeth. Buildings tumbled through her eyes. Shrill sinking in the belly. A face flashed up from the street. Whirl of cars in the street. The fire hydrant rushed up red at her. The street plunged up, up, up. *Oh Chri*——The smash of red pain, unendurable to breaking!

Then there was a great darkness, a slow diminution of unconscious sensation. Then she was gone.

Quincy Summerfield pulled himself to his feet, and staggered toward a window. Peering through the curtain he saw the limp, twisted, huddled body near the fire hydrant, people running toward it.

She couldn't even die without a mess! he thought.

He left unobserved. He took the back stairs and there was no one to say that he had been there. A few blocks from her apartment, he hailed a cab and went to a hotel. He was utterly safe.

Oh, the blessed peace of it. She was gone, gone for good. There was nothing left of her disorderly presence but the gray emptiness a man might feel if he had lost an arm. There was still that: the gray ghostly taint of her. It was sure to pass, though, and this night he would sleep, really sleep for the first time in days.

He didn't even want Charlotte that night. He only wanted to be alone—and sleep. He hadn't been in the hotel room five minutes before he was in bed, and dozing.

Dozing, not sleeping. It wasn't that he worried about the thing he had done. It had been reasonable and right. Her own disorderly weakness had betrayed her. But there was the lingering gray sense of her presence that was not yet going away. That, and the feeling that he had lost half of his life.

Lost?

No.

The sense of her presence was sharpening into a live reality. He was wide awake . . . or was it nightmare again?

No—she was there. She paid no attention to him. This was frightening.

She was focused unwaveringly upon a distant light, a light that grew, that became brilliant, with a searching intensity that she had never known before. And through it all, there was a sense of the wonder of longing changed into beauty that was all but unbearable.

And his mind was filled with a sense of richness and variety and order that he had never believed could exist.

But the searching light went on, and suddenly all her life burned through him in the flicker of a dream. And his life. And then out of the center of that purity of light there was a sorrowing, and she was moving away from the light. Away from the light, and he felt her whimpering like a child afraid of the dark. Away from the light . . .

Quincy Summerfield woke. Sat straight up in bed and screamed. The throat-tearing scream of a full-grown man in an agony of terror.

For the channel was wide open to the absolute chaos of her eternity.

THE WORD TO SPACE
Winston P. Sanders

The clergy in religious science fiction seem often to fare as badly as the clergy in mainstream fiction, emerging most frequently as pleasant caricatures. Such, I'm afraid, is the fate of Father James Moriarty, S.J., the Jesuit geologist who here sets out to do a bit of ingenious (and insidious) missionary work in interstellar communications. Author Winston Sanders, moreover—like most of his colleagues—seems to have had a bit more trouble extrapolating the Roman Catholic Church than other aspects of his future society; some assumptions ("a Jesuit couldn't transfer himself casually") already seem almost anachronistic. Yet Sanders' tale is not only engaging but reasonably credible. Just what does one do when the first interstellar radio contact inundates the circuit with alien religious broadcasts? Among other things, as Sanders effectively demonstrates, one might consult a Jesuit.

"'—begat Manod, who reigned over the People for 99 years. And in his day lawlessness went abroad in the land, wherefore the Quaternary One smote the People with ordseem (Apparently a disease—Tr.) and they were sore afflicted. And the preacher Jilbmish called a great prayer meeting. And when the People were assembled he cried unto them: 'Woe betide you, for you have transgressed against the righteous command of the Secondary and Tertiary Ones, namely, you have begrudged the Sacrifice and you have failed to beat drums (?—Tr.) at the rising

*of Nomo, even as your fathers were commanded; where-
fore this evil is come upon you.' Sheemish xiv, 6.*

"Brethren beyond the stars, let us ponder this text together. *For well you know from our previous messages
that ignorance of the Way, even in its least detail, is not
an excuse in the sight of the Ones. 'Carry Our Way unto
the ends of creation, that ye may save from the Eternal
Hunger all created beings doomed by their own unwit-
tingness.' Chubu iv, 2. Now the most elementary exegesis
of the words of Jilbmish clearly demonstrated—"*

Father James Moriarty, S.J., sighed and laid down the
typescript. Undoubtedly the project team of linguists,
cryptographers, anthropologists, theologians and radio engineers was producing translations as accurate as anyone
would ever be able to. At least until the barriers of space
were somehow overleaped and men actually met the aliens,
face to face on their own planet. Which wasn't going to
happen in the foreseeable future.

Father Moriarty had been assured that the different
English styles corresponded to a demonstrable variation in
the original language. If he insisted on absolute scholar-
ship, he could consult the Primary Version, in which the
logical and mathematical arguments for every possible
English rendering of every alien symbol were set forth.
By now the Primary Version filled a whole library, each
huge volume threshing out the significance of a few hundred words.

Fortunately, such minute precision wasn't necessary for
Father Moriarty's purpose. He couldn't have understood
the arguments anyhow. His own science was geology. So
he accepted the edited translation of the messages from
Mu Cassiopeiae.

"Only why," he asked himself as he stuffed his pipe,
"must they use that horrible dialect?" He touched a lighter

to the charred bowl and added, "Pseudo-King James," with a bare touch of friendly malice.

A cluster of buildings appeared below. Despite lawns and gardens, the big central structure and its outlying houses looked forlorn, as if dumped there in the little valley among summer-green Virginia hills. Even the radio telescope and mast had a forsaken air about them. Everything was neatly maintained, but small and old-fashioned. Also, Moriarty thought, a good deal of the ghost town impression must be subjective, since he knew what an orphan Ozma was.

The autopilot beeped and said: "You are approaching an area where overhead flight is prohibited. The vehicle will take a course around it."

"Oh, shut up," said Moriarty. "Ever since you machines got recorded voices, you've been insufferable." He punched the LAND button. The autopilot requested permission from the autocontrol tower and got a beam. The gravicar slanted downward to the parking lot. When it had rolled to a stop, the priest got out.

He stood for a moment stretching his muscles and enjoying the sunlight. The flight had been long, several hours from Loyola University of Los Angeles; this old jalopy could barely keep minimum legal speed in the traffic lanes. Good to be here at last—yes, and to see real greenwood on the hills, after all those years in California. The air was very still. Then, a liquid note and another . . . a mocking bird?

To keep himself from becoming maudlin, he threw back his head and looked toward the great web-work of the radio telescope. Beyond those meshes, the sky was a deep gentle blue. Though Project Ozma had been going on since before he was born—for a century and a third, in fact, so that its originators were one in the history books with Aristotle and Einstein—he found it emotionally impossible to reconcile such a sky with the cold black gape of space beyond, twenty-five light-years to that sun whose second planet was talking with Earth.

"Talking at Earth, I should say," he tried to smile. Perhaps after dark, when the stars were out, this would all seem less eldritch. Formerly Ozma had been in the background of his life, something one read about and made the appropriate marveling noises over, like the Jupiter expedition or the longevity process or the Rhodesian-Israeli Entente, a thing with no immediate effects on the everyday. But this hour he was here, his application accepted, an actual part of it!

He suppressed his excitement and focused on a large middle-aged man in rumpled blue tunic and slacks who was nearing him. The priest, tall and stooped and prematurely balding, walked forward. "Dr. Strand, I presume from your television interviews? This is an honor. I didn't expect the director himself to meet me."

Strand's handshake was lackadaisical and his expression unamiable. "What the hell else is there for me to do?" Embarrassed: "Uh, beg your pardon, Father."

"Quite all right. I admit, like any specialist, I wish outsiders wouldn't use technical terms so loosely, but that's a minor annoyance." Moriarty felt his own shyness fading. He remembered he was here for excellent reasons. He took a fresh drag on his pipe. "Your settlement looks peaceful," he remarked.

"Dead, you mean." Strand shrugged. "The normal condition of the project. There are just half a dozen people around at the moment."

"No more? I should have thought—"

"Look, we only use the radio telescope these days to sweep the sky in the hydrogen band for signals from other stars. That operation's been almost completely automated. Only needs a couple of maintenance men, and I myself check the tapes. Then there's my secretary, who's got the biggest sinecure in the country, and two caretakers for the buildings and grounds. Frankly, I wonder why you came here." Strand essayed a rather stiff smile. "Glad to see you, of course. Showing you around will at least break the monotony. But I don't know what you can accomplish that you couldn't do in your own office back at your college."

"I take it the translators don't work here?"

"No. Why should they? They've better facilities in Charlottesville. I suppose you know the University of Virginia is now handling that side of the project. I used to run over there every week with a new batch of tapes, but lately a big receiver right on campus has been turned over to us. The space station bucks the Cassiopeian transmissions directly there, and also takes outgoing messages. Our own radio mast is quite idle."

They began to walk. "By the way," asked Strand, "where are you staying?"

"Nowhere, yet. I thought one of your dormitories—"

"M-m-m-m . . . nobody uses them any more." Strand looked reluctant. "You can talk to Joe about it, but personally I'd advise you get a room in some nearby town. Commuting's easy enough." He seemed to wrestle with himself before politeness overcame hostility. "How about a cup of coffee in my office? You must be tired from your trip."

Moriarty felt like a young bloodhound, released in a barnyard full of the most fascinating new smells and then suddenly called to heel. But he couldn't well refuse the offer. Besides, it might give him an opening to broach his real purpose in coming. "Thank you, that's very kind."

As they crossed the grounds, he added, "So you still haven't gotten any other extraterrestrial signals?"

"No, of course not. We wouldn't keep that secret!

Hope's growing dim, too. Even in the southern hemisphere, Ozma's pretty well checked out most of the likely stars within range of our instruments. I suspect that until we get much more powerful equipment, Akron is the only extrasolar planet we'll ever be in touch with. And we won't be granted such equipment till we can show some worthwhile results with Akron. Talk about your vicious circles!"

Moriarty's smile turned wry. "You know," he said, "I've often suspected one of your problems in getting funds for this work has been the unfortunate coincidence that Mu Cassiopeiae II happens to be called Akron in its own principal language. With the star's astronomical name containing, from the English viewpoint, such a wanton aggregate of vowels, it was inevitable the people would nickname it Ohio."

"Spare me," groaned Strand. "The jokes about messages from Akron, Ohio were dead and rotten before either of us was born."

"I was just thinking that those jokes themselves may have been an unconscious reason for starving Ozma. Who could take a planet named Akron very seriously?"

Strand shrugged again. "Could be. The project's had nothing but trouble, ever since those cursed signals were first detected." He gave Moriarty a sharp sidewise glance. The unspoken thought went between them: *I'm afraid you're going to be still another plague on our house. A Jesuit couldn't transfer himself casually; his superiors would have to approve, at the very least. And after that, why did Washington okay your application? I know a Catholic President would be more than ordinarily ready to listen to whatever fisheating notion you came up with. But damn and blast, I've got work to do!*

They entered the main building and went through a gloomy foyer to a hall lined with locked doors. "Even so," said Moriarty, in delayed answer, "this was once a major enterprise." Coming in from brilliant daylight, he found the emptiness all the more depressing.

"Once," the director conceded wearily. "When the original Project Ozma first picked up signals from Ohi— from Mu Cassiopeiae—way back in the 1960's. Oh, they made headlines all over the world then! That was when this got set up as an independent Federal operation."

"I know," said Moriarty. To drive off the sadness from them both, he chuckled. "I've read about the old hassles. Every branch of government wanted Ozma. The Navy much resented losing it, but what with the State Department insisting this was their line of work, while the Department of the Interior argued that since the construction would be on public land— But that was before the taxpayers realized the truth. I mean, what a long, tedious, expensive process it would be, establishing communication with a nonhuman race twenty-five light-years away."

Strand opened a door. Beyond was an anteroom in which a small Nisei sat at a desk. He bounced up as Strand said, "Father Moriarty, meet my secretary, Philibert Okamura."

"An honor, Father," said the little man. "A great honor. I've been so happy you were coming. I read your classic work on the theory of planetary cores. Though I admit the mathematics got beyond me in places."

Strand raised his brows. "Oh? I knew you were a geologist, Father, but I hadn't quite understood—"

Moriarty looked at his shoes. He didn't enjoy personal attention. "That paper is nothing," he mumbled. "Just playing with equations. The Solar System doesn't have a great enough variety of planetary types for most of my conclusions to be checked. So it's only a trifling monograph."

"I wouldn't call a hundred pages of matrix algebra trifling," said Okamura. He smiled at his chief, as proudly as if he had invented the newcomer. "Math runs in his family, Dr. Strand. The Moriartys have been scientists for more than two hundred years. You are descended, aren't you, from the author of *The Dynamics of an Asteroid?*"

Since that particular ancestor was not one he cared to be reminded of, the priest said hastily, "You'll sympathize, then, with my special interest in Ozma. When you released those data about the size and density of Akron, a few years ago—really, I was tempted to think God had offered us the exact case we needed to verify Theorem 8-B in my paper. Not to mention all the other details, which must be radically different from the Solar System—"

"And the biology, biochemistry, zoology, botany, anthropology, history, sociology . . . and who knows how far ahead of us they may be in some technologies? Sure. Those hopes were expressed before I was born," snapped Strand. "But what have we actually learned so far? One language. A few details of dress and appearance. An occasional datum of physical science, like that geological information you spoke of. In more than a hundred years, that's all!" He broke off. "Anything in the mail today?"

"Two dollars from a lady in Columbus, Nebraska, in memory of her sweet little Pekingese dog Chan Chu," said Okamura.

"I suppose you've heard, Father, Project Ozma is accepting private contributions," said Strand bitterly. "Anything to stretch our funds. You wouldn't believe the dodges they find in Washington to pare down the money we get. Not that the total official appropriation ever amounts to much."

"I should think," said Moriarty, "there would be a rich source of income in donations from those weird religions which have grown up in response to the preachments from Akron."

Strand's eyes bugged. "*You'd* take *their* money?"

"Why not? Better than having them spend it on proselytization."

"But as long as the only messages are that garbled gospel—"

"Additional idiocies won't make any difference. The people who've adopted the Akronite faith (or, rather, one of the dozen distorted versions) will simply modify their beliefs as more sermons pour in. You don't make total chaos worse by stirring the pot a bit more."

"Hm-m-m." Strand rubbed his chin and stared at the ceiling. Then, reluctantly: "No. We couldn't. Too many other churches would holler about favoritism. In fact, the inspiration we're giving those nut cults is one reason our project is in danger of being terminated altogether."

Okamura began with diffidence, "I heard Bishop Ryan's speech last month."

"Bishop Ryan's opinions are his own," said Moriarty. "In spite of what non-Catholics think, the Church is not a monolithic dictatorship, even in matters of faith. Unlike Bishop Ryan, I assure you the Society of Jesus would reckon it a catastrophe if communication with Akron were stopped."

"Even when all we get is religious discussion?" asked Okamura.

"Religious ranting, you mean," said Strand sourly.

Moriarty grimaced. "Correct word, that. I was reading the latest translation you've released, on my way here. No sign of any improvement, is there?"

"Nope," Okamura said. "As of twenty-five years ago, at least, Akron's still governed by a fanatical theocracy out to convert the universe." He sighed. "I imagine you know the history of Ozma's contact with them? For the first seventy-five years or so, everything went smoothly. Slow and unspectacular, so that the public got bored with the whole idea, but progress was being made in under-

standing their language. And then—when they figured
we'd learned it well enough—they started sending doctrine.
Nothing but doctrine, ever since. Every message of theirs
a sermon, or a text from one of their holy books followed
by an analysis that my Jewish friends tell me makes the
medieval rabbis look like romantic poets. Oh, once in a
great while somebody slips in a few scientific data, like
that geological stuff which got you so interested. I imagine their scientists are just as sick at the wasted opportunity
as ours are. But with a bunch of Cotton Mathers in control,
what can they do?"

"Yes, I know all that," said Moriarty. "It's a grim sort
of religion. I daresay anyone who opposes its ministers is
in danger of burning at the stake, or whatever the Akronite
equivalent may be."

Okamura seemed so used to acting as dragoman for
visitors who cared little and knew less about Ozma, that
he reeled off another string of facts the priest already
had by heart. "Communication has always been tough.
After the project founders first detected the signals, fifty
years must pass between our acknowledgment and their
reply to that. Of course, they'd arranged it well. Their
initial message ran three continuous months before repeating itself. In three months one can transmit a lot of
information; one can go all the way from 'two plus two
equals four' to basic symbology and telling what band a
sonic cast will be sent on if there's an answer. Earth's
own transmission could be equally long and carefully
thought out. Still, it was slow. You can't exactly have a
conversation across twenty-five light-years. All you can
do is become aware of each other's existence and then start
transmitting more or less continuously, meanwhile inter-
preting the other fellow's own steady flow of graded
data. But if it weren't for those damned fanatics, we'd
know a lot more by now than we do.

"As it is, we can only infer a few things. The theocracy must be planet-wide. Otherwise we'd be getting different messages from some other country on Akron. If they have interstellar radio equipment, they must also have weapons by which an ideological dictatorship could establish itself over a whole world, as Communism nearly did here in the last century. The structure of the language, as well as various other hints, proves the Akronites are mentally quite humanlike, however odd they look physically. We just had the bad luck to contact them at the exact point in their history when they were governed by this crusading religion."

Okamura stopped for breath, giving Strand a chance to grunt, "Ozma's characteristic bad luck. But instead of gassing about things we all know as well as we know the alphabet, suppose you get us some coffee."

"Oh. Sorry!" The secretary blushed and trotted out.

Strand led Moriarty on into the main office. It was a spacious room with a view of gardens, radioscope, and wooded hillside. Where the walls weren't lined with books, they were hung with pictures. The most conspicuous was a composite photograph of an Akronite, prepared from the crude television images which Ozma's private satellite station had recently become able to receive. The being gave an impression of height; and they had in fact reported themselves as standing ten *axuls* tall on the average, where an *axul* turned out to equal approximately one-point-one million cadmium red wavelengths. The gaunt body was hidden by robes. A Terrestrial request for a picture of nude anatomy had been rejected with Comstockian prudishness. But one could see the Akronite had three-toed feet and four-fingered hands. The crested head and long-nosed face were so unhuman they had nothing grotesque about them: rather, those features were dignified and intelligent. Hard to believe that someone who looked like this had written in dead seriousness:

"The next word in the sentence from Aejae xliii, 3 which we are considering is 'ruchiruchin,' an archaic word concerning whose meaning there was formerly some dispute. Fortunately, the advocates of the erroneous theory that it means 'very similar' have now been exterminated and the glorious truth that it means 'quite similar' is firmly established."

But the human race had its share of such minds.

Besides this picture, there were photographs of a Martian landscape and Jupiter seen from space, and a stunning astronomical view of the Andromeda Galaxy. The books tended to be very old, including works by Oberth and Ley. Through a veil of pipe smoke, Moriarty studied Michael Strand's worn countenance. Yes, the man was a dreamer—of a most splendid dream, now dying in other Earthly souls. No other type could have kept going with such heroic stubbornness, through a lifetime of disappointments. But he might on that very account prove hard to deal with, when Moriarty's scheme was advanced. Best, perhaps, to lead up to it gradually. . . .

"Siddown." Strand waved at a chair and seated himself behind his desk. A breeze from the open window ruffled his gray hair. He took a cigaret from a box, struck a match with a ferocious motion and drew heavily on the smoke. Moriarty lowered his own long body.

"I assume," said the priest, "that your beamcasts to Mu Cassiopeiae continue to be of factual data about ourselves."

"Sure. It's either that, or stop sending altogether. Every so often somebody gets the bright idea that we should ask them to cut out their infernal propaganda. But of course we don't. If they can't get the hint from our own messages, a direct request would probably offend them so much that they'd quit transmitting anything."

"You're wise. I've had some acquaintance with religious monomaniacs." Moriarty tried to blow a smoke ring, but the air was too restless. "The information we send must help keep scientific curiosity alive on Akron. As witness those bootleg data we do sometimes get." He smiled an apology. "I hope I may think of myself as a member of your team, Dr. Strand?"

The other man's mouth drew into a harsh line. He leaned across the desk. "Let's be frank with each other," he said. "What are you actually here for?"

"Well," said Moriarty in his mildest voice, "those geological facts were what first snapped me to attention as regards Ozma."

"Come, now! You know very well that we won't be getting more than one quantitative datum a year, if we're lucky. And what we do get is released in the scientific journals. You don't have to join us to know everything we find out. You could have stayed at Loyola. Instead . . . there was pressure put on me. To be perfectly honest, I didn't want you, even on this temporary appointment of yours. But word came from the White House that you had, quote, 'the warmest Presidential recommendation.' What could I do?"

"I'm sorry. I never intended—"

"You're here for religious reasons, aren't you? The Catholic Church doesn't like this flood of alien propaganda."

"Do you?"

Strand blinked, taken aback. "Well . . . no," he said. "Certainly not. It's a repulsive religion. And the home-grown crank cults based on it are even worse." He struck his desk with a knotted fist. "But as long as I'm director, we'll keep on publishing all we learn. I may not like the messages from Akron, or their effect on Earth, but I will not be party to suppressing them!"

Moriarty could not resist a sarcastic jab, though he set himself a small penance for it: "Then of course you'll wish to release the whole inside story of Project Ozma?"

"What?" Strand's expression turned blank. "There's never been anything secret about our work."

"No. Except the motivations behind some of the things done in the past. Which are obvious to anyone with a training in, ah, Jesuitry." Moriarty raised a hand, palm out. "Oh, please don't misunderstand. Your predecessors desired nothing except to keep Ozma alive, which is an entirely honorable desire. And yet, as long as we're alone, why not admit some of their methods were, shall I say, disingenuous?"

Strand reddened. "What're you getting at?"

"Well, just consider the history of this enterprise. After the first flush of enthusiasm had departed, when the government and the public saw what a long hard pull lay ahead. Even more so, after the sermons began to come and outright public hostility developed. There was a continual scramble for tax funds to keep Ozma going. And . . . I've looked into the old records of Congressional hearings. At first the director played on a national desire for scientific prestige. 'We mustn't let the Russians get ahead of us in this, too.' Then, when war broke out, the argument was that maybe we could get valuable technical information from Akron—a ludicrous argument, but enough Congressmen fell for it. After the war, with no foreign competition to worry about, the government almost killed Ozma again. But a calculatedly mawkish account of paraplegic veterans returning to work here was circulated, and the American Legion pulled your chestnuts out of the fire. When that stunt had been used to death, the Readjustment was in full swing, jobs were scarce, it was argued that Ozma created employment. Again, ridiculous, but it worked for a while. When con-

ditions improved and Ozma was once more about to get
the ax, one director retired and a Negro was appointed
in his place. Ergo, no one dared vote against Ozma for
fear of being called prejudiced. Et cetera, et cetera.
The project has gone on like that for a hundred years."

"So what?" Strand's voice was sullen.

"So nothing. I don't say a word against shrewd politics."
Moriarty's pipe had gone out. He made a production of
relighting it, to stretch out the silence. At what he judged
to be the critical instant, he drawled:

"I only suggest we continue in the same tradition."

Strand leaned back in his swivel chair. His glum hostility
was dissolving into bewilderment. "What're you getting
at? Look here, uh, Father, it's physically impossible for
us to change the situation on Akron—"

"Oh?"

"What d'you mean?"

"We can send a reply to those sermons."

"What?" Strand almost went over backward.

"Other than scientific data, I mean."

"What the devil!" Strand sprang to his feet. His wrath
returned, to blaze in face and eyes, to thicken his tones
and lift one fist.

"I was afraid of this!" he exclaimed. "The minute
I heard a priest was getting into the project, I expected
this. You blind, bloody, queercollared imbecile! You and
the President—you're no better than those characters on
Akron—do you think I'll let my work be degraded to
such ends? Trying to convert another planet—and to
one particular sect? By everything *I* believe holy, I'll
resign first! Yes, and tell the whole country what's going
on!"

Moriarty was startled at the violence of the reaction
he had gotten. But he had seen worse, on other occasions.

He smoked quietly until a pause in the tirade gave him a chance to say:

"Yes, my modest proposal does have the President's okay. And yes, it will have to be kept confidential. But neither he nor I are about to dictate to you. Nor are we about to spend the tax money of Protestants, Jews, Buddhists, unbelievers . . . even Akronists . . . on propagating our own Faith."

Strand, furiously pacing, stopped dead. The blood went slowly out of his cheeks. He gaped.

"For that matter," said Moriarty, "the Roman Catholic Church is not interested in converting other planets."

"Huh?" choked Strand.

"The Vatican decided more than a hundred years ago, back when space travel was still a mere theory, that the mission of Our Lord was to Earth only, to the human race. Other intelligent species did not share in the Fall and therefore do not require redemption. Or, if they are not in a state of grace—and the Akronites pretty clearly are not—then God will have made His own provision for them. I assure you, Dr. Strand, all I want is a free scientific and cultural exchange with Mu Cassiopeiae."

The director reseated himself, leaned elbows on desk and stared at the priest. He wet his lips before saying: "What do you think we should do, then?"

"Why, break up their theocracy. What else? There's no sin in that! My ecclesiastical superiors have approved my undertaking. They agree with me that the Akronist faith is so unreasonable it must be false, even for Akron. Its bad social effects on Earth confirm this opinion. Naturally, the political repercussions would be disastrous if an attempt to subvert Akronism were publicly made. So any such messages we transmit must be kept strictly confidential. I'm sure you can arrange that."

Strand picked his cigaret out of the ashtray where he

had dropped it, looked at the butt in a stupefied fashion, ground it out and took a fresh one.

"Maybe I got you wrong," he said grudgingly. "But, uh, how do you propose to do this? Wouldn't you have to try converting them to some other belief?"

"Impossible," said Moriarty. "Let's suppose we did transmit our Bible, the Summa, and a few similar books. The theocracy would suppress them at once, and probably cut off all contact with us."

He grinned. "However," he said, "in both the good and the bad senses of the word, casuistry is considered a Jesuit specialty." He pulled the typescript he had been reading from his coat pocket. "I haven't had a chance to study this latest document as carefully as I have the earlier ones, but it follows the typical pattern. For example, one is required 'to beat drums at the rising of Nomo,' which I gather is the third planet of the Ohio System. Since we don't have any Nomo, being in fact the third planet of our system, it might offhand seem as if we're damned. But the theocracy doesn't believe that, or it wouldn't bother with us. Instead, their theologians, studying the astronomical data we sent, have used pages and pages of hairsplitting logic to decide that for us Nomo is equivalent to Mars."

"What of it?" asked Strand; but his eyes were kindling.

"Certain questions occur to me," said Moriarty. "If I went up in a gravicar, I would see Mars rise sooner than would a person on the ground. None of the preachings we've received has explained which rising is to be considered official at a given longitude. A particularly devout worshiper nowadays could put an artificial satellite in such an orbit that Mars was always on its horizon. Then he could beat drums continuously, his whole life long. Would this gain him extra merit or would it not?"

"I don't see where that matters," said Strand.

"In itself, hardly. But it raises the whole question of the relative importance of ritual and faith. Which in turn leads to the question of faith versus works, one of the basic issues of the Reformation. As far as that goes, the schism between Catholic and Orthodox Churches in the early Middle Ages turned, in the last analysis, on one word in the Credo, *filioque*. Does the Holy Ghost proceed from the Father and the Son, or from the Father alone? You may think this is a trivial question, but to a person who really believes his religion it is not. Oceans of blood have been spilled because of that one word.

"Ah . . . returning to this sermon, though. I also wonder about the name 'Nomo.' The Akronite theologians conclude that in our case, Nomo means Mars. But this is based on the assumption that, by analogy with their own system, the next planet outward is meant. An assumption for which I can recall no justification in any of the scriptures they've sent us. Could it not be the next planet inward—Venus for us? But then their own 'Nomo' might originally have been Mu Cassiopeiae I, instead of III. In which case they've been damning themselves for centuries by celebrating the rising of the wrong planet!"

Strand pulled his jaw back up. "I take it, then," he said huskily, "you want to—"

"To send them some arguments much more elaborately reasoned than these examples, which I've simply made up on the spot," Moriarty answered. "I've studied the Akronist faith in detail . . . with two millennia of Christian disputation and haggling to guide me. I've prepared a little reply. It starts out fulsomely, thanking them for showing us the light and begging for further information on certain points which seem a trifle obscure. The rest of the message consists of quibbles, puzzles, and basic issues."

"And you really think— How long would this take to transmit?"

"Oh, I should imagine about one continuous month. Then from time to time, as they occur to us, we can send further inquiries."

Father James Moriarty leaned back, crossed his legs, and puffed benign blue clouds.

Okamura entered with three cups of coffee on a tray. Strand gulped. In an uneven voice he said, "Put 'em down and close the door, please. We've got work to do."

Epilogue

Moriarty was hoeing the cabbages behind the chapter house—which his superior had ordered as an exercise in humility—and speculating about the curious fossil beds recently discovered on Callisto—which his superior had not forbidden—when his wristphone buzzed. He detested the newfangled thing and wore it only because he was supposed to keep himself accessible. Some silly call was always interrupting his thoughts just when they got interesting. He delivered himself of an innocent but sonorous Latin phrase and pressed the ACCEPT button. "Yes?" he said.

"This is Phil Okamura." The tiny voice became unintelligible. Moriarty turned up the volume. Since he had passed the century mark his ears hadn't been so good; though praise God, the longevity treatment kept him otherwise sound. "—remember? The director of Project Ozma."

"Oh, yes." His heart thumped. "Of course I remember. How are you? We haven't met for . . . must be five years or more."

"Time sure passes. But I had to call you right away, Jim. Transmission from Akron resumed three hours ago."

"What?" Moriarty glanced at the sky. Beyond that clear blue, the stars and all God's handiwork! "What's their news?"

"Plenty. They explained that the reason we haven't received anything from them for a decade was that their equipment got wrecked in some of the fighting. But now things have quieted down. All those conflicting sects have been forced to reach a modus vivendi.

"Apparently the suggestions we sent, incidental to our first disruptive questions seventy-five years ago—and based on our own experience—were helpful: separation of church and state, and so on. Now the scientists are free to communicate with us, uncontrolled by anyone else. They're sure happy about that! The transition was painful, but three hundred years of stagnation on Akron have ended. They've got a huge backlog of data to give us. So if you want your geology straight off the tapes, you better hurry here. All the journals are going to be snowed under with our reports."

"*Deo gratias*. I'll ask my superior at once—I'm sure he'll let me—and catch the first robus headed your way." Father Moriarty switched off the phone and hobbled toward the house. After a moment he remembered he'd forgotten the hoe. Well, let somebody else pick the thing up. He had work to do!

PROMETHEUS
Philip José Farmer

To Philip José Farmer's considerable credit, the protagonist of some of his most memorable stories has been a very three-dimensional cleric, a space adventurer turned monk named John Carmody. Indeed, it was around Carmody—his hell-for-leather soldier of fortune attitudes, his remarkable conversion experience on a planet named Dante's Joy, his later return to that planet on orders of his Church—that Farmer built a richly imaginative novel, Night of Light. *Among the novel's several virtues are a remarkably well-constructed but totally alien religion called Boontaism, and a vision of a future Roman Catholic Church that seems far more plausible than most (for one thing, Farmer assumes an end to the rule of celibacy). The novelette here included, however, gives us an entirely different adventure, with Carmody facing a very basic theological problem. What does a monk do, set down on an alien world among a quite intelligent species of native "animal," when he discovers the creatures can be taught to talk? Worse, how does he respond when he discovers that they lie awake at night after the death of one of their number, asking themselves in their rude English, "Where us go after us die?" Does he try to become for them a sort of interplanetary Moses? Which not so incidentally opens another side of the proposition that beings from outer space were early man's prototypical gods. Might not man, even inadvertently, fill the same role for another primitive race of intelligent beings?*

The man with the egg growing on his chest stepped out of the spaceship.

In the light of dawn the veldt of Feral looked superficially like an African plain before the coming of the white man. It was covered with a foot-high brown grass. Here and there were tall thick-trunked trees standing alone or in groves of from five to thirty. Everywhere were herds of animals. These were cropping the grass or else drinking from a waterhole a quarter of a mile away. At this distance, some resembled antelopes, gnus, giraffes, pigs, and elephants. There were other creatures that looked as if they had come out of Earth's Pliocene. And others that had no Terrestrial parallels.

"No mammals," said a voice behind the man with the egg attached to his chest. "They're warm-blooded descendants of reptiles. But not mammals."

The speaker walked around John Carmody. He was Doctor Holmyard, sapientologist, zoologist, chief of the expedition. A tall man of about sixty with a lean body and leaner face and brown hair that had once been a bright red.

"The two previous studies established that mammals either never developed or were wiped out early. Apparently, the reptiles and birds jumped the gun in the evolutionary race. But they have filled the ecological niche the mammals occupied on Earth."

Carmody was a short rolypoly man with a big head and a long sharp nose. His left eye had a lid that tended to droop. Before he had gotten off the ship he had been wearing a monk's robe.

Holmyard pointed at a clump of trees due north and a mile away. "There is your future home until the egg hatches," he said. "And, if you want to stay after that, we'll be very happy."

He gestured at two men who had followed him out

of the ship, and they approached Carmody. They removed his kilt and fastened a transparent belt around his protruding stomach. Then they attached it to a sporran of feathers, barred red and white. Over his shaven head went a wig with a tall crest of red and white feathers. Next, a false beak edged with teeth was fitted over his nose. His mouth, however, was left free. Then, a bustle from which projected a tail of red and white plumage was fitted to the belt.

Holmyard walked around Carmody. He shook his head. "These birds—if they are birds—won't be fooled one bit when they get a close look at you. On the other hand, your general silhouette is convincing enough to allow you to get fairly close to them before they decide you're a fake. By then, they may be curious enough to permit you to join them."

"And if they attack?" said Carmody. Despite the seriousness of what might happen, he was grinning. He felt such a fool, togged out like a man going to a masquerade party as a big rooster.

"We've already implanted the mike into your throat," said Holmyard. "The transceiver is flat, fitted to curve with your skull. You can holler for help, and we'll come running. Don't forget to turn the transceiver off when you're not using it. The charge won't last for more than fifty operational hours. But you can renew the charge at the cache."

"And you'll move camp to a place five miles due south of here?" said Carmody. "Then the ship takes off?"

"Yes. Don't forget. If—after—you've established yourself, come back to the cache and get the cameras. You can put them in the best locations for taking films of the horowitzes."

"I like that *if*," said Carmody. He looked across the plains at his destination, then shook hands with the others.

"God be with you," said the little monk.

"And with you, too," said Holmyard, warmly pumping his hand. "You're doing a great service for science, John. Perhaps for mankind. And for the horowitzes, too. Don't forget what I've told you."

"Among my many failings, a bad memory is not numbered," said John Carmody. He turned and began walking off across the veldt. A few minutes later, the great vessel lifted silently to a height of twenty feet, then shot off towards the south.

A lonely little man, ridiculous in his borrowed feathers, looking less like a man than a rooster that had lost a fight, and feeling like one at the moment, John Carmody set off through the grass. He was wearing transparent shoes, so the occasional rocks he stepped on did not hurt his feet.

A herd of equine creatures stopped feeding to look at him, to sniff the air. They were about the size of zebras and were completely hairless, having a smooth yellowish skin mottled with squares of a pale red. Lacking tails, they had no weapons of defense against the flies that swarmed around them, but their long nonreptilian tongues slid out and licked the flies off each other's flanks. They gave horsy snorts and whinnied. After watching Carmody for about sixty seconds, they suddenly broke and fled to a position about a hundred yards away. Then, they wheeled almost as a unit and faced him again. He decided that it must be his strange odor that had spooked them, and he hoped that the horowitzes would not also be offended.

At that moment, he was beginning to think that he had been foolish to volunteer for this job. Especially, when a huge creature, lacking only long tusks to resemble an elephant, lifted its trunk and trumpeted at him. However, the creature immediately began pulling down fruit from a tree and paid no more attention to him.

Carmody walked on, not without many sidewise glances to make sure it was keeping its air of indifference. By now, however, his characteristic optimism had reasserted itself. And he was telling himself that he had been guided to this planet for a very definite purpose. What the purpose was, he didn't know. But he was certain of Who had sent him.

The chain of events that had dragged him here was made of too strange a series of links to be only coincidences. Or so, at least, he believed. Only a month ago he had been fairly happy to be a simple monk working in the garden of the monastery of the Order of St. Jairus in the city of Fourth of July, Arizona, North American Department. Then, his abbot had told him that he was to transfer to a parish on the planet of Wildenwooly. And his troubles had begun.

First, he was given no money with which to buy a ticket for passage on a spaceship, no letters of introduction or identification or any detailed orders at all. He was just told to leave at once. He did not even have enough money to buy a bus ticket which would take him to the spaceport outside the domed city. He began walking and, as seemed to be his fate wherever he was, he got into one trouble after another. He finally found himself in the city park, where he was thrown by a hoodlum into a moat in the city zoo. Here a female horowitz, a giant bird of the planet Feral, had leaped into the moat and, holding him down with one foot, proceeded to lay her egg on his chest. Later, Carmody had escaped from the moat, only to find that the egg had put out tendrils of flesh and attached itself permanently to his chest.

When the zoo authorities located Carmody, they told him that the female horowitz, when she had no available male or other female on whom to attach her eggs, would attach it to a host animal. Carmody had been unlucky enough—or, from the viewpoint of the zoologists, lucky enough—to be a host. Lucky because now they would have an opportunity to study closely the development of the embryo in the egg and the manner in which it drew sustenance from its host. Moreover, if Carmody would go to Feral and attempt to pass as a horowitz, he would be the means for furnishing the zoologists with invaluable data about these birds. The zoologists believed the horowitzes to be the Galaxy's most intelligent non-sentient beings. There was even speculation they might be advanced enough to have a language. Would Carmody work with the zoologists if they paid for his trip to Wildenwooly after the study was made?

So, the lonely little man walked across the veldt with a leathery-skinned egg attached to his bloodstream. He was filled with apprehension which even his prayers did little to still.

Flocks of thousands of birds flew overhead. A creature large as an elephant, but with a long neck and four knobbly horns on its muzzle, browsed off the leaves of a tree. It paid no attention to him, so Carmody did not veer away but walked in a straight line which took him only fifty yards from it.

Then, out of a tall clump of grass stepped an animal which he knew at once was one of the great carnivores. It was lion-colored, lion-sized, and was built much like a lion. However it was hairless. Its feline face wrinkled in a silent snarl. Carmody stopped and made a half-turn to face it. His hand slid among his tailfeathers and closed around the butt of the gun hidden there.

He had been warned about this type of meat-eater.

"Only if they're very hungry or too old to catch fleeter prey will they attack you," Holmyard had said.

This creature didn't look old, and its sides were sleek. But Carmody thought that if its temperament was as cat-like as its looks, it might attack just because it was annoyed.

The leonoid blinked at him and yawned. Carmody began to breathe a trifle easier. The creature sat down on its haunches and gazed at him for all the world like a curious, but oversize, pussycat. Slowly, Carmody edged away.

The leonoid made no move to follow. Carmody was congratulating himself, when, on his left, a creature burst loose from a clump of grass.

He saw that it was a half-grown horowitz, but he had no more time to look at it. The leonoid, as startled as Carmody, leaped forward in pursuit of the runner. The horowitz cried in fear. The leonoid roared. Its pace increased.

Suddenly, out of the same clump from which the young bird had run, an adult darted. This one held a club in its hand. Though it was no match for the carnivore, it ran towards it, waving its club in its humanlike hand and yelling.

By then Carmody had drawn the pistol from its holster, and he directed the stream of bullets at the leonoid. The first missile exploded in the ground a few feet ahead of the creature; the remainder raked its side. Over and over the animal turned, and then it fell.

The adult horowitz dropped the club, scooped up the young bird in its arms, and began running towards the grove of trees about a half a mile ahead, its home.

Carmody shrugged, reloaded the gun, and resumed his walk.

"Perhaps, I can put this incident to good use," he said aloud to himself. "If they are capable of gratitude, I should be received with open arms. On the other hand, they may fear me so much they might launch a mass attack. Well, we shall see."

By the time he had neared the grove, the branches of the trees were alive with the females and the young. And the males had gathered to make a stand outside the grove. One, evidently a leader, stood ahead of the group. Carmody was not sure, but he thought that this was the one who had run with the child.

The leader was armed with a stick. He walked stiff-leggedly and slowly towards him. Carmody stopped and began talking. The leader also stopped and bent his head to one side to listen in a very birdlike gesture. He was like the rest of his species, though larger—almost seven feet tall. His feet were three-toed, his legs thick to bear his weight, his body superficially like an ostrich's. But he had no wings, rudimentary or otherwise. He had well-developed arms and five-fingered hands, though the fingers were much longer in proportion than a man's. His neck was thick, and the head was large with a well-developed braincase. The brown eyes were set in the front of his broad head like a man's; the corvine beak was small, lined with sharp teeth, and black. His body was naked of plumage except for red-and-white-barred feathers in the loin region, on the back, and on the head. There a tall crest of feathers bristled, and around his ears were stiff feathers, like a horned owl's, designed to focus sound.

Carmody listened for a minute to the sound of the leader's voice and those behind him. He could make out no definite pattern of speech, no distinguishing rhythm, no repetition of words. Yet, they were uttering definite syllables, and there was something familiar about their speaking.

After a minute, he recognized its similarity, and he was startled. They were talking like a baby when he is at the stage of babbling. They were running the scale of potential phonemes, up and down, at random, sometimes repeating, more often not.

Carmody reached up slowly to his scalp so he wouldn't alarm them with a sudden movement. He slid the panel-switch on the skull-fitting transceiver under his crest, thus allowing the zoologists at the camp to tune in.

Carmody spoke in a low tone, knowing that the microphone implanted in his throat would clearly reproduce his voice to the listeners at the camp. He described his situation and then said, "I'm going to walk into their home. If you hear a loud crack, it'll be a club breaking my skull. Or vice versa."

He began walking, not directly towards the leader but to one side. The big horowitz turned as the man went by, but he made no threatening move with his club. Carmody went on by, though he felt his back prickle when he could no longer see the leader. Then he had walked straight at the mob, and he saw them step to one side, their heads cocked to one side, their sharp-toothed bills emitting the infantile babblings.

He passed safely through them to the middle of the grove of cottonwoodlike trees. Here the females and young looked down at him. The females resembled the males in many respects, but they were smaller and their crests were brown. Almost all of them were carrying eggs on their chests or else held the very young in their arms. These were covered from head to thigh with a golden-brown chicklike fuzz. The older children, however, had lost the down. The female adults looked as puzzled as the males, but the children seemed to have only curiosity. The older children climbed out on the branches above him and looked down at him. And they, too, babbled like babies.

Presently, a half-grown horowitz, a female by her all-brown crest, climbed down and slowly approached him. Carmody reached into the pouch in his tail feathers, and he brought out a lump of sugar. This he tasted himself to show her it wasn't poisonous, and then he held it out in his hand and made coaxing sounds. The young girl—he was already thinking of these beings as human—snatched the cube from his hand and ran back to the trunk of the tree. Here she turned the sugar lump over and over, felt its texture with the tips of her fingers, and then barely touched the cube with the tip of her long broad tongue.

She looked pleased. This surprised Carmody, for he had not thought of the possibility that humanoid expressions could take place on such an avian face. But the face was broad and flat and well-equipped with muscles and able as a man's to depict emotion.

The girl put all of the cube in her bill, and she looked ecstatic. Then she turned to the big horowitz—who had neared the two—and uttered a series of syllables. There was evident pleasure in her voice.

Carmody held out another lump of sugar to the leader, who took it and popped it into his bill. And over his face spread pleasure.

Carmody spoke out loud for the benefit of the men in the camp. "Put a good supply of sugar in the cache," he said, "plus some salt. I think it's likely that these people may be salt-starved, too."

"People!" exploded the ghostly voice in his ear. "Carmody, don't start making anthropocentric errors regarding these creatures."

"You've not met them," said Carmody. "Perhaps you could maintain a zoologist's detachment. But I can't. Human is as human does."

"O.K., John. But when you report, just give a description, and never mind your interpretations. After all, I'm human, and, therefore, open to suggestion."

Carmody grinned and said, "O.K. Oh, they're starting to dance now. I don't know what the dance means, whether it's something instinctive or something they've created."

While Carmody had been talking, the females and the young had climbed down out of the trees. They formed a semicircle and began clapping their hands together in rhythm. The males had gathered before them and were now hopping, jumping, spinning, bowing, waddling bent-kneed like ducks. They gave weird cries and occasionally flapped their arms and leaped into the air as if simulating the flight of birds. After about five minutes, the dance suddenly ceased, and the horowitzes formed a single-file line. Their leader, at the head of the line, walked towards Carmody.

"Oh, oh," said Carmody. "I think we're seeing the formation of the first breadline in the non-history of these people. Only it's sugar, not bread, that they want."

"How many are there?" said Holmyard.

"About twenty-five."

"Got enough sugar?"

"Only if I break up the cubes and give each a slight taste."

"Try that, John. While you're doing that, we'll rush more sugar to the cache on a jeep. Then you can lead them there after we leave."

"Maybe I'll take them there. Just now I'm worried about their reaction if they don't get a complete lump."

He began to break up the cubes into very small pieces and to put one into each extended hand. Every time, he said, "Sugar." By the time the last one in line—a mother with a fuzzy infant in her arms—had stuck out her hand, he had only one fragment left.

"It's a miracle," he said, sighing with relief. "Came out just right. They've gone back to what I presume are their normal occupations. Except for their chief and some of the children. These, as you can hear, are babbling like mad at me."

"We're recording their sounds," said Holmyard. "We'll make an attempt to analyze them later, find out if they've a speech."

"I know you have to be scientific," replied Carmody. "But I have a very perceptive ear, like all people who run off at the mouth, and I can tell you now they don't have a language. Not in the sense we think of, anyway."

A few minutes later, he said, "Correction. They at least have the beginning of a language. One of the little girls just came up and held out her hand and said, 'Sugar.' Perfect reproduction of English speech, if you ignore the fact that it couldn't have come from a human mouth. Sounded like a parrot or crow."

"I heard her! That's significant as hell, Carmody! If she could make the correlation so quickly, she must be capable of symbolic thinking." He added, in a more moderate tone, "Unless it was accidental, of course."

"No accident. Did you hear the other child also ask for it?"

"Faintly. While you're observing them, try to give them a few more words to learn."

Carmody sat down at the base of a thick treetrunk in the shade of branches, for the sun was beginning to turn the air hot. The tree had thick corrugated bark like a cottonwood, but it bore fruit. This grew high up on the branches and looked from a distance like a banana. The young girl brought him one and held it out to him, saying at the same time "Sugar?"

Carmody wanted to taste the fruit, but he didn't think it would be fair to receive it without giving her what she wanted. He shook his head no, though he didn't expect her to interpret the gesture. She cocked her head to one side, and her face registered disappointment. Nevertheless, she did not withdraw the fruit. And, after making sure she knew he was out of sugar, he took the gift. The shell had to be rapped against the side of the tree to be broken, and it came apart in the middle, where it creased. He took a small bite from the interior and reported to Holmyard that it tasted like a combination of apple and cherry.

"They not only feed on this fruit," he said. "They're eating the tender shoots of a plant that resembles bamboo. I also saw one catch and eat a small rodentlike animal which ran out from under a rock she turned over. And they pick lice off each other and eat insects they find around the roots of the grass. I saw one try to catch a bird that was eating the bamboo shoots.

"Oh, the leader is pounding a club on the ground. They're dropping whatever they're doing and clustering around him. Looks as if they're getting ready to go some place. The females and young are forming a group. The males, all armed with clubs, are surrounding them. I think I'll join them."

Their destination, he was to find out, was a waterhole about a mile and a half away. It was a shallow depression about twenty feet across filled with muddy water. There were animals gathered about it: gazellelike creatures, a giant porcine with armor like an armadillo, several birds that seemed at first glance and far off to be horowitzes. But when Carmody got closer, he saw they were only about two and a half feet high, their arms were much longer, and their foreheads slanted back. Perhaps, these filled the ecological niche here that monkeys did on Earth.

The animals fled at the approach of the horowitzes. These established guards, one at each cardinal point of the compass, and the rest drank their fill. The young jumped into the water and splashed around, throwing water in each other's face and screaming with delight. Then they were hauled out, protesting, by their mothers. The guards drank their fill, and the group prepared to march back to their home, the grove.

Carmody was thirsty, but he didn't like the looks or odor of the water, which smelled as if something had died in it. He looked around and saw that the dozen trees around the waterhole were a different type. These were fifty-feet high slim plants with a smooth lightbrown bark and only a few branches, which grew near the top. Clusters of gourds also grew among the branches. At the bottom of the trees lay empty gourds. He picked up one, broke in the narrow end, and dipped it in the water. Then he dropped in the water an antibiotic pill which he took from the bustle under his tailfeathers. He drank, making a face at the taste. The young girl who had first asked him for sugar approached, and he showed her how to drink from the gourd. She laughed a quite human-sounding laugh and poured the water down her open beak.

Carmody took advantage of the curiosity of the others to show them that they, too, could fill their gourds and transport water back to the grove.

Thus, the first artifact was invented—or given—on Feral. In a short time, everyone had gourds and filled them. And the group, babbling like babies, began the march back to home.

"I don't know if they're intelligent enough to learn a language yet," said Carmody to Holmyard. "It seems to me that if they were, they'd have created one. But they are the most intelligent animal I've yet encountered. Far superior to the chimpanzee or porpoise. Unless they just have a remarkable mimetic ability."

"We've run off samples of their speech in the analyzer,"

said Holmyard. "And there's no distribution to indicate a well-organized language. Or even an incipient language."

"I'll tell you one thing," replied Carmody. "They at least have identifying sounds for each other. I've noticed that when they want the leader's attention, they say, 'Whoot!', and he responds. Also, this girl who asked for sugar responds to the call of Tutu. So, I'm identifying them as such."

The rest of the day Carmody spent observing the horowitzes and reporting to Holmyard. He said that, during times of danger or during a joint undertaking such as going for water, the group acted as a whole. But most of the time they seemed to operate in small family units. The average family consisted of a male, the children, and anywhere from one to three females. Most of the females had eggs attached to their chests or bellies. He was able to settle for Holmyard the question of whether, generally, the females laid their eggs on each other, and so raised foster families, or transferred the eggs to their own skin immediately after laying. Towards dusk he saw a female deposit an egg and then hold it against the chest of another female. In a few minutes, little tendrils crept forth from the leathery-skinned ovum and inserted themselves into the bloodstream of the hostess.

"That, I would take it, is the general course of action," Carmody said. "But there is one male here who, like me, carries an egg. I don't know why he was singled out. But I would say that, at the time the egg was produced, the female and her mate were separated from the others. So the female took the lesser alternative. Don't ask me why the females just don't attach the eggs to their own bodies. Maybe there's a chemical factor that prevents the egg from attaching itself to its own mother. Perhaps some sort of antibody setup. I don't know. But there is some reason which, up to now, only the Creator of the horowitzes knows."

"It's not a general pattern for all the birds of this planet," said Holmyard. "There are oviparous, oviviparous, and viviparous species. But the order of birds of which the horowitzes are the highest in development, the order of Aviprimates, all have this feature. From highest to lowest, they lay their eggs and then attach them to a host."

"I wonder why this particular line of creatures didn't develop viviparism?" said Carmody. "It seems obvious that it's the best method for protecting the unborn."

"Who knows?" said Holmyard, and Carmody, mentally, could see him shrugging. "That's a question that may or may not be answered during this study. After all, this planet is new to us. It's not had a thorough study. It was only by a lucky accident that Horowitz discovered these birds during his brief stay here. Or that we were able to get a grant to finance us."

"One reason for this externalism may be that even if the embryo is injured or killed, the hostess is not," said Carmody. "If the embryo of a viviparous mother is destroyed, then the mother usually is, too. But here, I imagine, though the embryo may be more susceptible to death and injury, the bearer of the unborn is relatively unaffected by the wound."

"Maybe," said Holmyard. "Nature is an experimenter. Perhaps, she's trying this method on this planet."

He is, you mean, thought Carmody, but he said nothing. The gender of the Creator did not matter. Both he and the zoologist were talking about the same entity.

Carmody continued to give his observations. The mothers fed the very young in the traditional manner of birds, by regurgitating food.

"That seemed probable," said Holmyard. "The reptiles

developed a class of warmblooded animals, but none of these have hair or even rudimentary mammaries. The horowitz, as I told you, evolved from a very primitive bird which took up arboreal life at the time its cousins were learning to glide. The fleshy fold of skin hanging down between arm and rib is a vestige of that brief period when it had begun to glide and then changed its mind and decided to become a lemuroid-type.

"Or so it seems to us. Actually, we haven't unearthed enough fossils to speak authoritatively."

"They do have certain cries which can be interpreted by the others. Such as a cry for help, a cry for pick-my-fleas, a rallying cry, and so on. But that's all. Except that some of the children now know the words for sugar and water. And they identify each other. Would you say that that is the first step in creating a language?"

"No, I wouldn't," said Holmyard firmly. "But if you can teach them to take an assemblage of independent words and string them together into an intelligible sentence, and if they become capable of reassembling these words in different situations, then I'd say they are in a definite lingual stage. But your chance for doing that is very remote. After all, they might be in a prelingual stage, just on the verge of becoming capable fo verbal symbolism. But it might take another ten thousand years, maybe fifty thousand, before their kind develop that ability. Before they take the step from animal to human being."

"And maybe I can give them the nudge," said Carmody. "Maybe . . ."

"Maybe what?" said Holmyard after Carmody had been silent for several minutes.

"I'm confronted with the theological question the Church raised some centuries before interstellar travel became possible," said Carmody. "At what moment did the ape become a man? At what moment did the ape possess a soul, and . . ."

"Jesus Christ!" said Holmyard. "I know you're a monk, Carmody! And it's only natural you should be interested in such a question! But, I beg of you, don't start muddling around with something as divorced from reality as the exact moment when a soul is inserted into an animal! Don't let this—this how-many-angels-on-a-pinpoint absurdity begin to color your reports. Please try to keep a strictly objective and scientific viewpoint. Just describe what you see; no more!"

"Take it easy, Doc. That's all I intend to do. But you can't blame me for being interested. However, it's not for me to decide such a question. I leave that up to my superiors. My order, that of St. Jairus, does not do much theological speculation; we are primarily men of action."

"O.K., O.K.," said Holmyard. "Just so we understand each other. Now, do you intend to introduce fire to the horowitzes tonight?"

"Just as soon as dusk falls."

Carmody spent the rest of the day in teaching little Tutu the words for tree, egg, gourd, a few verbs which he acted out for her, and the pronouns. She caught on quickly. He was sure that it was not the purely mimetic speech ability of a parrot. To test her, he asked her a question.

"You see the tree?" he said, pointing at a large sycamore-like fruit tree.

She nodded, a gesture she had learned from him, and she replied in her strange birdlike voice, "Yes. Tutu see the tree."

Then, before he could frame another question, she said, pointing at the chief, "You see Whoot? Tutu see Whoot. Him horowitz. Me horowitz. You . . . ?"

For a moment Carmody was speechless, and Holmyard's

voice screeched thinly, "John, did you hear her? She can speak and understand English! And in such a short time, too! John, these people must have been ready for speech! We gave it to them! We gave it to them!"

Carmody could hear Holmyard's heavy breathing as if the man stood next to him. He said, "Calm down, my good friend. Though I don't blame you for being excited."

Tutu cocked her head to one side and said, "You talk to . . . ?"

"Me a man," said Carmody, replying to her previous question. "Man, man. And me talk to a man . . . not me. The man far away." Then, realizing she didn't know the meaning of the words *far away*, he indicated distance with a sweep of his arm and a finger pointing off across the veldt.

"You talk to . . . a man . . . far away?"

"Yes," said Carmody, wishing to get off that subject. She wasn't ready to understand any explanation he could give her for his ability to communicate across long distances, so he said, "Me tell you some time . . ." And he stopped again, for he didn't have enough words with which to explain time. That would have to come later.

"Me make fire," he said.

Tutu continued to look puzzled, as she understood only the first word of his sentence. "Me show you," he said, and he proceeded to gather long dried grasses and punk from a dead tree. These he piled together, and then tore off some twigs and smaller dead branches, which he laid by the first pile. By this time many of the children and some of the adults had collected around him.

He pulled from his bustle under the tailfeathers a flint and a piece or iron pyrite. These he had brought from the spaceship because the zoologists had told him this area was poor in both minerals. He showed the two pieces to them and then, after six tries, struck a spark. The spark fell on the grass but did not set fire to it. He tried three more times before a spark took root. In the next few seconds he had enough of a fire going to be able to throw on twigs and then branches.

When the first jet of flame arose, the wide-eyed assembly gasped. But they did not run, as he had feared. Instead, they made sounds which attracted the others. Shortly, the entire tribe was gathered around him.

Tutu, saying, "Au! Au!"—which Carmody interpreted as a sound of amazement or of delight in beauty—put out her hand to seize the flame. Carmody opened his mouth to say, "No! Fire bad!" But he closed his lips. How to tell her that something could be very harmful and at the same time be a great good?

He looked around and saw that one of the youngsters standing at the back of the crowd was holding a mouse-sized rodent in her hand. So fascinated was she by the fire that she had not yet popped the living animal into her beak. Carmody went to her and pulled her close to the fire, where everybody could see her. Then, not without having to overcome the reluctance of the child with many reassuring gestures, he got her to give him the rodent. Distastefully, he dashed its life out by snapping its head against a rock. He took his knife and skinned and gutted and decapitated the creature. Then he sharpened a long stick and stuck it through the rodent. After which, he took Tutu by her slender elbow and guided her close to the fire. When she felt its intense heat, she drew back. He allowed her to do so, saying, "Fire hot! Burn! Burn!"

She looked at him with wide eyes, and he smiled and patted her feathery top. Then he proceeded to roast the mouse. Afterwards, he cut it in three parts, allowed the bits to cool, and gave one to the girl from whom he had taken the mouse, one to Tutu, and one to the chief.

All three gingerly tasted it and at the same time breathed ecstasy, "Ah!"

Carmody didn't get much sleep that night. He kept the fire going while the whole tribe sat around the flames and admired them. Several times, some large animals, attracted by the brightness, came close enough for him to see their eyes glowing. But they made no attempt to get closer.

In the morning, Carmody talked to Holmyard. "At least five of the children are only a step behind Tutu in learning English," he said. "So far, none of the adults has shown any inclination to repeat any of the words. But their habit patterns may be too rigid for them to learn. I don't know. I'll work on the chief and some others today. Oh, yes, when you drop off some ammunition at the cache, would you leave me a holster and ammo belt for my gun? I don't think they'll find it strange. Apparently, they know I'm not a true horowitz. But it doesn't seem to matter to them.

"I'm going to kill an antelope today and show them how to cook meat on a big scale. But they'll be handicapped unless they can find some flint or chert with which to fashion knives. I've been thinking that I ought to lead them to a site where they can find some. Do you know of any?"

"We'll go out in the jeep and look for some," said Holmyard. "You're right. Even if they are capable of learning to make tools and pottery, they're not in an area suited to develop that ability."

"Why didn't you pick a group which lived near a flint-rich area?"

"Mainly, because it was in this area that Horowitz discovered these creatures. We scientists are just as apt to get into a rut as anybody, so we didn't look into the future. Besides, we had no idea these animals—uh—people, if they do deserve that term—were so full of potential."

Just then Tutu, holding a mouse-sized grasshopper in her hand, came up to Carmody.

"This . . . ?"

"This is a grasshopper," said Carmody.

"You burn . . . the fire."

"Yes. Me burn *in* fire. No, not burn. Me cook *in* fire."

"You cook in the fire," she said. "You give to me. Me eat; you eat."

"She's now learned two prepositions—I think," said Carmody.

"John, why this pidgin English?" said Holmyard. "Why the avoidance of *is* and the substitution of the objective case for the nominative with the personal pronouns?"

"Because *is* isn't necessary," replied Carmody. "Many languages get along without it, as you well know. Moreover, there's a recent tendency in English to drop it in conversational speech, and I'm just anticipating what may become a general development.

"As for teaching them lower-class English, I'm doing that because I think that the language of the illiterates will triumph. You know how hard the teachers in our schools have to struggle to overcome the tendency of their high-class students to use button-pusher's jargon."

"O.K.," said Holmyard. "It doesn't matter, anyway. The horowitzes have no conception—as far as I know —of the difference. Thank God, you're not teaching them Latin!"

"Say!" said Carmody. "I didn't think of that! Why not? If the horowitzes ever become civilized enough to have interstellar travel, they'd always be able to talk to priests, no matter where they went."

"Carmody!"

Carmody chuckled and said, "Just teasing, Doctor. But I do have a serious proposition. If other groups should show themselves as capable of linguistic learning, why not teach each group a different language? Just as an experiment? This group would be our Indo-European school; another, Sinitic; another, our Amerindian; still another, Bantu. It would be interesting to see how the various groups developed socially, technologically, and philosophically. Would each group follow the general lines of social evolution that their prototypes did on Earth? Would the particular type of language a group used place it on a particular path during its climb uphill to civilization?"

"A tempting idea," said Holmyard. "But I'm against it. Sentient beings have enough barriers to understanding each other without placing the additional obstacles of differing languages in their way. No, I think that all should be taught English. A single speech will give them at least one unifying element. Though, God knows, their tongues will begin splitting into dialects soon enough."

"Bird-English I'll teach them," said Carmody.

One of the first things he had to do was straighten out Tutu concerning the word *tree*. She was teaching some of the younger horowitzes what language she'd mastered so far and was pointing to a cottonwood and calling out, "Tree! Tree!"

Then she pointed to another cottonwood, and she became silent. Wonderingly, she looked at Carmody, and he knew in that moment that she thought of that cottonwood as tree. But that word to her meant an individual entity or thing. She had no generic concept of *tree*.

Carmody tried by illustration to show her. He pointed at the second cottonwood and said, "Tree." Then he pointed at one of the tall thin trees and repeated the word.

Tutu cocked her head to one side, and an obvious puzzlement settled on her face.

Carmody further confused her by indicating the two cottonwoods and giving each their name. Then, on the spot, he made up a name for the tall thin trees and said, "Tumtum."

"Tumtum," said Tutu.

"Tumtumtree," said Carmody. He pointed at the cottonwood. "Cottonwoodtree." He pointed out across the veldt. "Thorntree." He made an all-inclusive gesture. "All tree."

The youngsters around Tutu did not seem to grasp his meaning, but she laughed—as a crow laughs—and said, "Tumtum. Cottonwood. Thorn. All tree."

Carmody wasn't sure whether she grasped what he'd said or was just mimicking him. Then she said, swiftly—perhaps she was able to interpret his look of frustration—"Tumtumtree. Cottonwoodtree. Thorntree."

She held up three fingers and made a sweeping gesture with the other hand. "All tree."

Carmody was pleased, for he was fairly certain she now knew tree as not only an individual but a generic term. But he didn't know how to tell her that the last-named was not a thorn but was a thorntree. He decided that it didn't matter. Not for the time being, at least. But when the time came to name a thorn as such, he would have to give the thorn another nomenclature. No use confusing them.

"You seem to be doing famously," said Holmyard's voice. "What's next on the agenda?"

"I'm going to try to sneak away to the cache and pick up some more ammo and sugar," said Carmody. "Before I do, could you drop off a blackboard and some paper and pencils?"

"You won't have to take notes," said Holmyard. "Everything you say is being recorded, as I think I once told you," he added impatiently.

"I'm not thinking of making memos," said Carmody. "I intend to start teaching them how to read and write."

There was a silence for several seconds, then, "*What?*"

"Why not?" replied Carmody. "Even at this point, I'm not absolutely certain they really understand speech. Ninety-nine per cent sure, yes. But I want to be one-hundred per cent certain. And if they can understand written speech, then there's no doubt.

"Besides, why wait until later? If they can't learn now, we can try later. If they do catch on now, we've not wasted any time."

"I must apologize," said Holmyard. "I lacked imagination. I should have thought of that step. You know, John, I resented the fact that you had, through pure accident, been chosen to make this first venture among the horo-witzes. I thought a trained scientist, preferably myself, should have been the contact man. But I see now that having you out there isn't a mistake. You have what we professionals too often too quickly lose: the enthusiastic imagination of the amateur. Knowing the difficulties or even the improbabilities, we allow ourselves to be too cautious."

"Oh, oh!" said Carmody. "Excuse me, but it looks as if the chief is organizing everybody for some big move. He's running around, gabbling his nonsense syllables like mad and pointing to the north. He's also pointing at the branches of the trees. Oh, I see what he's getting at. Almost all of the fruit is eaten. And he wants us to follow him."

"Which direction?"

"South. Towards you."

"John, there's a nice valley about a thousand miles north of here. We found it during the last expedition and noted it because it's higher, cooler, much better watered. And it not only contains flint but iron ores."

"Yes, but the chief evidently wants us to go in the opposite direction."

There was a pause. Finally, Carmody sighed and said, "I get the message. You want me to lead them north. Well, you know what that means."

"I'm sorry, John. I know it means conflict. And I can't order you to fight the chief. That is, if it's necessary for you to fight."

"I rather think it will be. Too bad, too; I wouldn't exactly call this Eden, but at least no blood has been shed among these people. And now, because we want to plumb their potentiality, lead them on to higher things . . ."

"You don't have to, John. Nor will I hold it against you if you just tag along and study them wherever they go. After all, we've gotten far more data than I ever dreamed possible. But . . ."

"But if I don't try to take over the reins of leadership, these beings may remain at a low level for a long long time. Besides, we have to determine if they are capable of any technology. So . . . the end justifies the means. Or so say the Jesuits. I am not a Jesuit, but I can justify the premise on which we're basing the logic of this argument."

Carmody did not say another word to Holmyard. He marched up to the big leader, took a stand before him, and, shaking his head fiercely and pointing to the north, he shouted, "Us go this way! No go that way!"

The chief stopped his gabbling and cocked his head to one side and looked at Carmody. His face, bare of feathers, became red. Carmody could not tell, of course, if it was the red of embarrassment or of rage. So far as he could determine, his position in this society had been a very peculiar one—from the society's viewpoint. It had not taken him long to see that a definite peck-order existed here. The big horowitz could bully anyone he wanted to. The male just below him in this unspoken hierarchy could not—or would not—resist the chief's authority. But he could bully everybody below him. And so forth. All the males, with the exception of one weak character, could push the females around. And the females had their own system, similar to the males, except that it seemed to be more complex. The top female in the peck-order system could lord it over all but one female, and yet this female was subject to the authority of at least half the other females. And there were other cases whose intricacy defied Carmody's powers of analysis.

One thing he had noticed, though, and that was that the young were all treated with kindness and affection. They were, in fact, very much the spoiled brats. Yet, they had their own give-and-take-orders organization.

Carmody had up to this time held no position in the social scale. They seemed to regard him as something apart, a *rara avis*, an unknown quantity. The chief had made no move to establish Carmody's place here, so the others had not dared to try. And, probably, the chief had not dared because he had been witness to Carmody's killing of the leonoid.

But now the stranger had placed him in such a position that he must fight or else step down. And he must have been the top brass too long to endure that idea. Even if he knew Carmody's destructive potential, he did not intend to submit meekly.

So Carmody guessed from the reddened skin, the swelling chest, the veins standing out on his forehead, the glaring eyes, the snapping beak, the clenched fists, the sudden heavy breathing.

The chief, Whoot, was impressive. He stood a foot and

a half taller than the man, his arms were long and muscular, his chest huge, and his beak with its sharp meat-eater's teeth and his three-toed legs with their sharp talons looked as if they could tear the heart out of Carmody.

But the little man knew that the horowitz didn't weigh as much as a man his height, for his bones were the half-hollow bones of a bird. Moreover, though the chief was undoubtedly a capable and vicious fighter, and intelligent, he did not have at his command the sophisticated knowledge of infighting of a dozen worlds. Carmody was as deadly with his hands and feet as any man alive; many times, he had killed and crippled.

The fight was sharp but short. Carmody used a mélange of all his skills and very quickly had the chief reeling, bloody-beaked, and glassy-eyed. He gave the *coup de grace* by chopping with the edge of his palm against the side of the thick neck. He stood over the unconscious body of Whoot, breathing heavily, bleeding from three wounds delivered by the point of the beak and pointed teeth and suffering from a blow of a fist against his ribs.

He waited until the big horowitz had opened his eyes and staggered to his feet. Then, pointing north, he shouted, "Follow me!"

In a short time, they were walking after him as he headed for a grove of trees about two miles away. Whoot walked along in the rear of the group, his head hung low. But after a while he regained some of his spirit. And, when a large male tried to make him carry some of the water gourds, he jumped on the male and knocked him to the ground. That re-established his position in the group. He was below Carmody but still higher than the rest.

Carmody was glad, for the little Tutu was Whoot's child. He had been afraid that his defeat of her father might make her hostile to him. Apparently, the change in authority had made no difference, unless it was that she stayed even more by his side. While they walked together, Carmody pointed out more animals and plants, naming them. She repeated the words, sound-perfect, after him. By now she had even adopted his style of speaking, his individual rhythm pattern, his manner of saying "Heh?" when a strong thought seized him, his habit of talking to himself.

And she imitated his laugh. He pointed out a thin, shabby-looking bird with its feathers sticking out all round and looking like a live mop.

"That a borogove."

"That a borogove," she repeated.

Suddenly, he laughed, and she laughed, too. But he could not share the source of his mirth with her. How could he explain *Alice in Wonderland* to her? How could he tell her that he had wondered what Lewis Carroll would think if he could see his fictional creation come to life on a strange planet circling around a strange star and centuries after he had died? Or know that his works were still alive and bearing fruit, even if weird fruit? Perhaps, Carroll would approve. For he had been a strange little man—like Carmody, thought Carmody—and he would consider the naming of this bird the apex of congruous incongruity.

He sobered immediately, for a huge animal resembling a green rhinoceros with three knobbed horns trotted thunderingly towards them. Carmody took his pistol out from his bustle, causing Tutu's eyes to widen even more than at the sight of the tricorn. But, after stopping only a few feet from the group and sniffing the wind, the tricorn trotted slowly away. Carmody replaced the pistol, and he called Holmyard.

"You'll have to forget about caching the stuff I ordered

in that tree," he said. "I'm leading them on the exodus as of now. I'll build a fire tonight, and you can relocate about five miles behind us. I'm going to try to get them to walk past this grove ahead, go on to another. I plan to lead them on a two mile and a half trek every day. I think that's about as far as I can push them. We should reach the valley of milk and honey you described in nine months. By then, my child," he tapped the egg on his chest, "should be hatched. And my contract with you will be terminated."

He had less trouble than he thought he would. Though the group scattered as soon as they reached the grove, they reassembled at his insistence and left the tempting fresh fruits and the many rodents to be found under the rocks. They did not murmur while he led them another mile to another grove. Here he decided they'd camp for the rest of the day and night.

After dusk fell, and he had supervised Tutu's building of a fire, he sneaked away into the darkness. Not without some apprehension, for more carnivores prowled under the two small moons than in the light of the sun. Nevertheless, he walked without incident for a mile and there met Doctor Holmyard, waiting in a jeep.

After borrowing a cigarette from Holmyard, he described the events of the day more fully than he had been able to do over the transceiver. Holmyard gently squeezed the egg clinging to Carmody's chest, and he said, "How does it feel not only to give birth to a horowitz, but to give birth to speech among them? To become, in a sense, the father of all the horowitzes?"

"It makes me feel very odd," said Carmody. "And aware of a great burden on me. After all, what I teach these sentients will determine the course of their lives for thousands of years to come. Maybe even further.

"Then again, all my efforts may come to nothing."

"You must be careful. Oh, by the way, here's the stuff you asked for. A holster and belt. And, in a knapsack, ammo, a flashlight, more sugar, salt, paper, pen, a pint of whiskey."

"You don't expect me to give them firewater?" said Carmody.

"No," chuckled Holmyard. "This bottle is your private stock. I thought you might like a nip now and then. After all, you must need something to buck up your spirits, being without your own kind."

"I've been too busy to be lonely. But nine months is a long time. No, I don't really believe I'll get unbearably lonely. These people are strange. But I'm sure they have spirits kindred to mine, waiting to be developed."

They talked some more, planning their method of study for the year to come. Holmyard said that a man would always be in the ship and in contact with Carmody, if an emergency should come up. But everybody would be busy, for this expedition had many projects in the fire. They would be collecting and dissecting specimens of all sorts, making soil and air and water analyses, geological surveys, digging for fossils, etc. Quite often the ship would take a trip to other regions, even to the other side of this planet. But when that happened, two men and a jeep would be left behind.

"Listen, Doc" said Carmody. "Couldn't you take a trip to this valley and get some flint ore? Then leave it close to us, so my group could find it? I'd like to find out *now* if they're capable of using weapons and tools."

Holmyard nodded and said, "A good idea. Will do. We'll have the flint for you before the week's up."

Holmyard shook Carmody's hand, and the little monk left. He lit his way with the flashlight, for he hoped that, though it might attract some of the big carnivores, it might also make them wary of getting too close.

He had not gone more than a hundred years when, feeling as if he were being stalked, and also feeling foolish because he was obeying an irrational impulse, he whirled. And his flashlight centered on the small figure of Tutu.

"What you do here?" he said. She approached slowly, as if fearing him, and he rephrased his question. There were so many words that she did not know that he could not, at this point, fully communicate with her.

"Why you here?"

Never before had he used *why*, but he thought that now, under the circumstances, she might understand it.

"Me . . ." she made a motion of following.

"Follow."

"Me follow . . . you. Me no . . . want you hurt. Big meat-eaters in dark. Bite, claw, kill, eat you. You die; me . . . how you say it?"

He saw what she meant, for tears were filling her large brown eyes.

"Cry," he said. "Ah, Tutu, you cry for me?"

He was touched.

"Me cry," she said, her voice shaking, on the edge of sobs. "Me . . ."

"Feel bad. Feel bad."

"John die after now . . . me want to die. Me . . ."

He realized that she had just coined a term for the future, but he did not try to teach her the use of the future tense. Instead, he held out his arms and embraced her. She put her head against him, the sharp edge of her beak digging into the flesh between his ribs, and she burst into loud weeping.

Stroking the plumage on top of her round head, he said, "No feel bad, Tutu. John love you. You know . . . me love you."

"Love. Love," she said between sobs. "Love, love. Tutu love you!"

Suddenly, she pushed herself away from him, and he released her. She began to wipe the tears from her eyes with her fists and to say, "Me love. But . . . me 'fraid of John."

"'Fraid? Why you 'fraid of John?"

"Me see . . . uh . . . horowitz . . . by you. You look like him, but not look like him. Him . . . how say . . . funny-looking, that right? And him fly like vulture, but no wing . . . on . . . me no able to say on what him fly. Very . . . funny. You talk to him. Me understand some words . . . no some."

Carmody sighed. "All me able to tell you now that him no horowitz. Him man. Man. Him come from stars." He pointed upwards.

Tutu also looked up, then her gaze returned to him, and she said, "You come from . . . star?"

"Child, you understand that?"

"You no horowitz. You place on beak and feathers. But . . . me understand you no horowitz."

"Me man," he said. "But enough of this, child. Some day . . . after soon . . . me tell you about the stars."

And, despite her continued questioning, he refused to say another word on the subject.

The days and then weeks and then months passed. Steadily, walking about two and a half to three miles a day, progressing from grove to grove, the band followed Carmody northwards. They came across the flints left by the ship. And Carmody showed them how to fashion spearheads and arrowheads and scrapers and knives. He made bows for them and taught them to shoot. In a short time, every horowitz who had the manual skill was making weapons and tools for himself. Fingers and hands were banged and cut, and one male lost an eye from a flying chip. But the group began to eat better; they shot the cervinoid and equinoid animals and, in fact, anything that wasn't too big and looked as if it might be edible. They cooked the meat, and Carmody showed them how to smoke and dry the meat. They began to get very bold, and it was this that was the undoing of Whoot.

One day, while with two other males, he shot a leonoid that refused to move away from their approach. The arrow only enraged the beast, and it charged. Whoot stood his ground and sent two more arrows into it, while his companions threw their spears. But the dying animal got hold of Whoot and smashed in his chest.

By the time the two had come for Carmody, and he had run to Whoot, Whoot was dead.

This was the first death among the group since Carmody had joined them. Now he saw that they did not regard death dumbly, as animals did, but as an event that caused outcries of protest. They wailed and wept and beat their chests and cast themselves down on the ground and rolled in the grass. Tutu wept as she stood by the corpse of her father. Carmody went to her and held her while she sobbed her heart out. He waited until their sorrow had spent itself, then he organized a burial party. This was a new thing to them; apparently, they had been in the custom of leaving their dead on the ground. But they understood him, and they dug a shallow hole in the ground with sharp-pointed sticks and piled rocks over the grave.

It was then that Tutu said to him, "Me father. Where him go now?"

Carmody was speechless for several seconds. Without one word from him, Tutu had thought of the possibility of afterlife. Or so he supposed, for it was easy to misinterpret her. She might just be unable to conceive of the discontinuity of the life of one she loved. But, no, she knew death well. She had seen others die before he had joined the group, and she had seen the death and dissolution of many large animals, not to mention the innumerable rodents and insects she had eaten.

"What think the others?" he said, gesturing at the rest of the group.

She looked at them. "Adults no think. Them no talk. Them like the animals.

"Me a child. Me think. You teached me to think. Me ask you where Whoot go because you understand."

As he had many times since he met her, Carmody sighed. He had a heavy and serious responsibility. He did not want to give her false hopes, yet he did not want to destroy her hopes—if she had any—of living after death. And he just did not know if Whoot had a soul or, if he did, what provision might be made for it. Neither did he know about Tutu. It seemed to him that a being who was sentient, who had self-consciousness, who could use verbal symbolism, must have a soul. Yet, he did not know.

Nor could he try to explain his dilemma to her. Her vocabulary, after only six months of contact with him, could not deal with the concepts of immortality. Neither could his, for even the sophisticated language at his command did not deal with reality but only with abstractions dimly comprehended, with vague hopes only stammered about. One could have faith and could try to translate that faith into effective action. But that was all.

Slowly, he said, "You understand that Whoot's body and the lion's body become earth?"

"Yes."

"And that seeds fall on this earth, and grass and trees grow there and feed from the earth, which Whoot and the lion becomed?"

Tutu nodded her beaked head. "Yes. And the birds and the jackals will eat the lion. Them will eat Whoot, too, if them able to drag the rocks from him."

"But at least a part of the lion and of Whoot become soil. And the grasses growing from them become partly them. And the grass in turn become eated by antelopes, and the lion and Whoot not only become grass but beast."

"And if me eat the antelope," interrupted Tutu excitedly, her beak clacking, her brown eyes shining, "then Whoot become part of me. And me of him."

Carmody realized he was treading on theologically dangerous ground.

"Me no mean that Whoot live in you," he said. "Me mean . . ."

"Why him no live in me? And in the antelopes that eat grass and in the grass? Oh, understand! Because Whoot then become breaked into many pieces! Him live in many different creatures. That what you mean, John?"

She wrinkled her brow. "But how him live if all teared apart? No, him no! Him body go so many places. What me mean, John, where Whoot go?"

She repeated fiercely, "Where *him* go?"

"Him go wherever the Creator send him," replied Carmody, desperately.

"Cre-a-tor?" she echoed, stressing each syllable.

"Yes. Me teached you the word *creature*, meaning any living being. Well, a creature must become created. And the Creator create him. Create mean to cause to live. Also mean to bring into becoming what no becomed before."

"Me mother me creator?"

She did not mention her father because she, like the other children and probably the adults, too, did not connect copulation with reproduction. And Carmody had not explained the connection to her because, as yet, she lacked the vocabulary.

Carmody sighed and said, "Worse and worse. No. You mother no you Creator. Her make the egg from her body and the food her eat. But her no create you. In the beginning . . ."

Here he boggled. And he wished that he had become a priest and had a priest's training. Instead, he was only a monk. Not a simple monk, for he had seen too much of the Galaxy and had lived too much. But he was not equipped to deal with this problem. For one thing, he just could not hand out a ready-made theology to her. The theology of this planet was in formation and would not even be born until Tutu and her kind had full speech.

"Me tell you more in the future," he said. "After many suns. For this time, you must become satisfied with the little me able to tell you. And that . . . well, the Creator make this whole world, stars, sky, water, animals, and the horowitzes. He make you mother and her mother and her mother's mother's mother. Many mothers many suns ago, he make . . ."

"*He?* That him name? *He?*"

Carmody realized he had slipped up in using the nominative case, but old habit had been too much for him.

"Yes. You can call him He."

"He the Mother of the first mother?" said Tutu. "He the Mother of all creatures' Mothers?"

"Here. Have some sugar. And run along and play. Me tell you more later."

After I have time to think, he said to himself.

He pretended to scratch his head and slid back the activating plate on the transceiver curved over his skull. And he asked the operator on duty to call Holmyard. In a minute, Holmyard's voice said, "What's up, John?"

"Doc, isn't a ship due in a few days to drop down and pick up the records and specimens you've collected so far? Will you have it take a message back to Earth? Notify my superior, the abbot of Fourth of July, Arizona, that I am in deep need of guidance."

And Carmody related his talk with Tutu and the questions that he had to answer in the future.

"I should have told him where I was going before I left," he said. "But I got the impression that he had put me on my own. However, I am now in a predicament which requires that wiser and better trained men help me."

Holmyard chuckled. He said, "I'll send on your message, John. Though I don't think you need any help. You're doing as well as anyone could. Anyone who tries to maintain objectivity, that is. Are you sure that your superiors will be able to do that? Or that it may not take them a hundred years to arrive at a decision? Your request might even cause a council of the Church heads. Or a dozen councils."

Carmody groaned, and then he said, "I don't know. I think I'll start teaching the kids how to read and write and do arithmetic. There, at least, I'll be navigating in safe waters."

He shut off the transceiver and called Tutu and the other young who seemed capable of literacy.

In the days and nights that followed the young made exceptional progress, or so it seemed to Carmody. It was as if the young had been fallow, just waiting for the touch of somebody like Carmody. Without too much trouble, they learned the relation between the spoken and the written word. To keep them from being confused, Carmody modified the alphabet as it was used on Earth and made a truly phonetic system so that every phoneme would have a parallel notation. This was something that had been talked about for two hundred years among the English-speakers of Earth but had not, so far, been done. Orthography there, though it had changed, still lagged behind the spoken word and presented the same maddening and confusing picture to the foreigner who wished to learn English.

But reading and writing in short time led to Carmody's being forced to teach another art: drawing. Tutu, without any hint on his part that she should do so, one day began to make a sketch of him. Her efforts were crude, and he could have straightened her out very quickly. But, aside from later teaching her the principles of perspective, he made no effort to help her. He felt that if she, and the others who also began to draw, were influenced too much by Terrestrial ideas of art, they would not develop a truly Feral art. In this decision he was commended by Holmyard.

"Man has a fundamentally primate brain, and so he has worked out a primate's viewpoint through his art. So far, we've had no art produced by—forgive me—bird-brains. I'm with you, John, in allowing them to paint and sculpture in their own peculiar fashion. The world may some day be enriched by avian artistry. Maybe, maybe not."

Carmody was busy from the time he woke, which was dawn, until the time he went to sleep, about three hours after nightfall. He not only had to spend much time in his teaching, but he had to act as arbitrator— or rather dictator—of disputes. The disputes among the adults were much more trying than among the young, for he could communicate effectively with the latter.

The cleavage between the young and the adults was not as strong as he had expected. The adults were intelligent, and, though speechless, could learn to make flint tools and weapons and could shoot arrows and throw spears. They even learned to ride horses.

Halfway towards their destination, they began to encounter bands of animals that strongly resembled hairless horses. Carmody, as an experiment, caught one and broke it. He made reins from bone and a strong-fibered grass. He had no saddles at first but rode it bareback. Later, after the older children and the adults had caught their own horses and began to ride them, they were taught how to make saddles and reins from the thick skin of the tricorn.

Shortly after, he met his first resistance from the young. They came to a place where a lake was, where trees grew thickly, where a breeze blew most of the time from the nearby hills, and where the game was numerous. Tutu said that she and the others thought it would be a good idea if they built a walled village, such as Carmody had told them they would build when they got to the Valley.

"Many speechless ones live around here," she said. "Us able to take them young and raise them, make them us people. That way, us become stronger. Why travel every day? Us become tired of traveling, become footsore, saddlesore. Us able to make—barns?—for them horses, too. And us able to catch other animals, breed them, have plenty of meat to kill without hunting. Also, us able to plant seeds like you told us and grow crops. Here a good place. Just as good as that Valley you speaked of, maybe gooder. Us children talked it over, decided to stay here."

"This a good place," said Carmody. "But not the goodest. Me have knowledge of the Valley, and me have knowledge that there many things this place no have. Such as flint, iron, which much gooder than flint, healthier climate, not so many big beasts that eat meat, gooder soil in which to grow crops, and other things."

"How you have knowledge of the Valley?" said Tutu. "You seed it? You goed there?"

"Me have knowledge of the Valley because someone who there once telled me of it," said Carmody. (And he wished that he had not avoided the use of the verb *know* to avoid confusion with the adjective and adverb *no*. So far he had not introduced any homonyms into the horowitz's vocabulary. But he determined at this moment to make use of know. He could, though, partially reinstate the original Old English pronunciation and have them pronounce the k. At the first chance, he would do that.)

"Who telled you of the Valley?" said Tutu. "No horowitz doed it, because none haved speech until you teached them how to talk. Who telled you?"

"The man doed it," replied Carmody. "Him goed there."

"The man who comed from the stars? The man me seed you talking to that night?"

Carmody nodded, and she said, "Him have knowledge of where us go after death?"

He was caught by surprise and could only stare, openmouthed, at her a few seconds. Holmyard was an agnostic and denied that there was any valid evidence for the immortality of man. Carmody, of course, agreed with him that there was no scientifically provable evidence, no facts. But there were enough indications of the survival of the dead to make any open-minded agnostic wonder about the possibility. And, of course, Carmody believed that every man would live forever because he had faith that man would do so. Moreover, he had a personal experience which had convinced him. (But that's another story.)

"No, the man no have knowledge of where us go after death. But me have knowledge."

"Him a man; you a man," said Tutu. "If you have knowledge, why no him?"

Again, Carmody was speechless. Then he said, "How you have knowledge that me a man?"

Tutu shrugged and said, "At first, you fool us. Later, everybody have knowledge. Easy to see that you put on beak and feathers."

Carmody began to remove the beak, which had chafed and irritated him for many months.

"Why no say so?" he said angrily. "You try to make fool of me?"

Tutu looked hurt. She said, "No. Nobody make fool of you, John. Us love you. Us just thinked you liked to put on beak and feathers. Us no have knowledge of why, but if you like to do so, O.K. with us. Anyway, no try to get off what we talk about. You say you have knowledge of where dead go. Where?"

"Me no supposed to tell you where. No just yet, anyway. Later."

"You no wish to scare us? Maybe that a bad place us no like? That why you no tell us?"

"Later, me tell. It like this, Tutu. When me first comed among you and teached you speech, me no able to teach you all the words. Just them you able to understand. Later, teach you harder words. So it now. You no able to understand even if me tell you. You become older, have knowledge of more words, become smarter. Then me tell. See?"

She nodded and also clicked her beak, an additional sign of agreement.

"Me tell the others," she said. "Many times, while you sleep, we talk about where us go after us die. What use of living only short time if us no keep on living? What good it do? Some say it do no good; us just live and die, and that that. So what? But most of us no able to think that. Become scared. Besides, no make sense to us. Everything else in this world make sense. Or seem to. But death no make sense. Death that last forever no do, anyway. Maybe us die to make room for others. Because if us no die, if ancestors no die, then soon this world become too crowded, and all starve to death, anyway. You tell us this world no flat but round like a ball and this force—what you call it, gravity?—keep us from falling off. So us see that soon no more room if us no die. But why no go to a place where plenty of room? Stars, maybe? You tell us there plenty of round worlds like this among the stars. Why us not go there?"

"Because them worlds also have plenty of creatures on them," said Carmody.

"Horowitzes?"

"No. Some have mans on them; other have creatures as different from both man and horowitz as me different from you. Or from a horse or a bug."

"Plenty to learn. Me glad me no have to find out all that by meself. Me wait until you tell me everything. But me become excited thinking about it."

Carmody had a council with the older children, and the upshot was that he agreed they should settle down for a short period at this site. He thought that, when they began to chop down trees for a stockade and houses, they would break and dull their flint axes and in a short time would run out of flint. Not to mention that his descriptions of the Valley would influence the more restless among them to push on.

Meanwhile, the egg on his chest grew larger and heavier, and he found it an increasing burden and irritation.

"I just wasn't cut out to be a mother," he told Holmyard over the transceiver. "I would like to become a Father, yes, in the clerical sense. And that demands certain maternal qualities. But, literally, and physically, I am beginning to be bothered."

"Come on in, and we'll take another sonoscope of the egg," said Holmyard. "It's time that we had another record of the embryo's growth, anyway. And we'll give you a complete physical to make sure that the egg isn't putting too much strain on you."

That night, Carmody met Holmyard, and they flew back in the jeep to the ship. This was now stationed about twenty miles from Carmody, because of the far-ranging of the horowitzes on their horses. In the ship's laboratory, the little monk was put through a series of tests. Holmyard said, "You've lost much weight, John. You're no longer fat. Do you eat well?"

"More than I ever did. I'm eating for two now, you know."

"Well, we've found nothing alarming or even mildly disturbing. You're healthier than you ever were, mainly because you've gotten rid of that flab. And the little devil you're carrying around is growing apace. From the studies we've made on horowitzes we've caught, the egg grows until it reaches a diameter of three inches and a weight of four pounds.

"This biological mechanism of attaching eggs to the bloodstream of hosts of another species is amazing enough. But what biological mechanism enables the foetus to do this? What keeps it from forming antibodies and killing itself? How can it accept the bloodstream of another totally different species? Of course, one thing that helps is that the blood cells are the same shape as a man's; no difference can be detected with microscopic examination. And the chemical composition is approximately the same. But even so . . . yes, we may be able to get another grant just to study this mechanism. If we could discover it, the benefit to mankind might be invaluable."

"I hope you do get another grant," said Carmody. "Unfortunately, I won't be able to help you. I must report to the abbot of the monastery of Wildenwooly."

"I didn't tell you when you came in," said Holmyard, "because I didn't want to upset you and thus bollix up your physical. But the supply ship landed yesterday. And we got a message for you."

He handed Carmody a long envelope covered with official-looking seals. Carmody tore it open and read it. Then he looked up at Holmyard.

"Must be bad news, judging from your expression," said Holmyard.

"In one way, no. They inform me that I must live up to my contract and cannot leave here until the egg is hatched. But the day my contract expires, I must leave. And, furthermore, I am not to give the horowitzes any religious instruction at all. They must find out for themselves. Or rather, they must have their peculiar revelation—if any. At least, until a council of the Church has convened and a decision arrived at. By then, of course, I'll be gone."

"And I'll see to it that your successor has no religious affiliations," said Holmyard. "Forgive me, John, if I seem anticlerical to you. But I do believe that the horowitzes, if they develop a religion, should do it on their own."

"Then why not their speech and technology?"

"Because those are tools with which they may deal with their environment. They are things which, in time, they would have developed on lines similar to those of Earth."

"Do they not need a religion to ensure that they do not misuse this speech and technology? Do they not need a code of ethics?"

Holmyard smiled and gave him a straight and long look. Carmody blushed and fidgeted.

"All right," said Carmody, finally. "I opened my big mouth and put both my feet in it. You don't need to recite the history of the various religions on Earth. And I know that a society may have a strong and workable code of ethics with no concept of a divinity who will punish transgressors temporally or eternally.

"But the point is, religions may change and evolve. The Christianity of the twelfth century is not exactly like that of the twentieth century, and the spirit of the religion of our time differs in more than one aspect from that of the twentieth. Besides, I wasn't intending to convert the horowitzes. My own Church wouldn't permit me to do so. All I have done so far is tell them that there is a Creator."

"And even that they misunderstood," said Holmyard, laughing. "They refer to God as He but classify Him as a female."

"The gender doesn't matter. What does is that I am in no position to reassure them of immortality."

Holmyard shrugged to indicate he couldn't see what difference it made. But he said, "I sympathize with your distress because it is causing you pain and anxiety. However, there is nothing I can do to help. And, apparently, your Church is not going to, either."

"I made a promise to Tutu," Carmody said, "and I don't want to break that. Then she would lose faith."

"Do you think they regard you as God?"

"Heaven forbid! But I must admit that I have worried about that happening. So far, there has been no indication on their part that they do so regard me."

"But what about after you leave them?" said Holmyard.

Carmody could not forget the zoologist's parting reply. He had no difficulty getting to sleep that night. For the first time since he had joined the group, he was allowed to sleep late. The sun had climbed halfway towards its zenith before he woke. And he found the partially constructed village in an uproar.

Not that of chaos but of purposeful action. The adults were standing around looking bewildered, but the young were very busy. Mounted on their horses, they were herding ahead of them, at the point of their spears, a group of strange horowitzes. There were some adults among these, but most were youngsters between the ages of seven and twelve.

"What mean what you do?" said Carmody indignantly to Tutu.

The smile-muscles around her beak wrinkled, and she laughed.

"You no here last night, so us no able to tell you what us planned to do. Anyway, nice surprise, heh? Us decide to raid them wild horowitzes that live near here. Us catch them sleeping; drive away adults, forced to kill some, too bad."

"And why you do this?" said Carmody, aware that he was about to lose his temper.

"You no understand? Me thinked you understand everything."

"Me no God," said Carmody. "Me told you that often enough."

"Me forget sometimes," said Tutu, who had lost her smile. "You angry?"

"Me no angry until you tell me why you did this."

"Why? So us able to make us tribe bigger. Us teach the little ones how to talk. If them no learn, them grow up to become adults. And adults no learn how to talk. So them become like the beasts. You no want that, surely?"

"No. But you killed!"

Tutu shrugged. "What else to do? Them adults tried to kill us; us killed them, instead. Not many. Most runned off. Besides, you say O.K. to kill animals. And adults same as animals because them no able to talk. Us no kill childs because them able to learn to talk. Us—what you say? adopt—yes, us adopt them. Them become us brothers and sisters. You telled me that every horowitz me brother and sister, even if me never see them."

She regained her smile and, bending eagerly towards him, she said, "Me haved a good thought while on raid. Instead of eating eggs that mothers hatch when no enough adults to attach eggs to, why not attach eggs to childs and to horses, and other animals, too? That way, us increase us tribe much faster. Become big fastly."

And so it was. Within a month's time, every horowitz large enough to carry the weight, and every horse, bore an egg on his/her chest.

Carmody reported this to Holmyard. "I see now the advantage of extra-uterine development of the embryo. If the unborn aren't as well protected from injury, it does furnish a means for a larger number to be born."

"And who's going to take care of all these young?" said Holmyard. "After all, the horowitz chick is as helpless as and requires as much care as the human infant."

"They're not going hog-wild. The number to be produced is strictly regulated. Tutu has it figured out how many chicks each mother can adequately care for. If the mothers can't furnish enough regurgitated food, they will prepare a paste of fruit and meat for the chicks. The mothers no longer have to spend a good part of their time hunting for food; the males are doing that now."

"This society of yours is not developing quite along the lines of those of Paleolithic Earth," said Holmyard. "I see an increase towards a communistic trend in the future. The children will be produced *en masse*, and their raising and education will have to be done collectively. However, at this stage, in order to gain a large enough population to be stable, it may be well for them to organize on an assembly-line basis.

"But there's one thing you've either not noticed or have purposely neglected to mention. You said the attaching of the eggs will be strictly regulated. Does that mean that any eggs for which there is no provision will be eaten? Isn't that a method of birth control?"

Carmody was silent for a moment, then he said, "Yes."

"Well?"

"Well, what? I'll admit I don't like the idea. But I don't have any justification for objecting to the horowitzes. These people don't have any Scriptural injunctions, you know. Not yet, anyway. Furthermore, under this system, many more will be given a chance for life."

"Cannibalism and birth control," said Holmyard. "I'd think you'd be glad to get out of this, John."

"Who's talking about the anthropocentric attitude now?" Carmody retorted.

Nevertheless, Carmody was troubled. He couldn't tell the horowitzes not to eat the surplus eggs, for they just would not have understood. Food wasn't so easy to get that they could pass up this source of supply. And he couldn't tell them that they were committing murder. Murder was the illegal slaying of a being with a soul. Did the horowitzes have souls? He didn't know. Terrestrial law maintained that the illegal killing of any member of a species capable of verbal symbolism was murder. But the Church, though it enjoined its members to obey that law or be punished by the secular government, had not admitted that the definition had a valid theological basis. The Church was still striving to formulate a rule which could be applied towards recognition of a soul in extraterrestrial beings. At the same time, they admitted the possibility that sapients of other planets might not have souls, might not need them. Perhaps the Creator had made other provisions for assuring their immortality—if any.

"It's all right for *them* to sit around a table and discuss their theories," said Carmody to himself. "But I am in the field of action; I must work by rule of thumb. And God help me if my thumb slips!"

During the next month he did many things in the practical area. He arranged with Holmyard to send the ship to the Valley and there dig up and transport to the outskirts of the village several tons of iron ore. The following morning he took the children to the place where the ore lay. They gave cries of astonishment, cries which increased as he told them what they were to do with it.

"And where this iron ore come from?" asked Tutu.

"Mans bringed it from the Valley."

"On horses?"

"No. Them bringed it in a ship which comed from the stars. The same ship that carried me from the stars."

"Me able to see it some day?"

"No. You forbidden. No good for you to see it."

Tutu wrinkled her brow with disappointment and clacked her beak. But she made no further reference to it at that time. Instead, she and the others, with Carmody's help and some of the more cooperative adults, built furnaces to smelt the ore. Afterwards, they built a furnace to add carbon from charcoal to the iron, and they made steel weapons, bridle braces and bits, and tools. Then they began to construct steel parts for wagons. Carmody had decided that it was time now to teach them to construct wagons.

"This fine," said Tutu, "but what us do when all the iron ore gone, and the steel us make rust and wear out?"

"There more in the Valley," said Carmody. "But us must go there. The starship bring no more."

Tutu cocked her head and laughed. "You shrewd man, John. You know how to get us to go to Valley."

"If us to go, us must get a move on soon," said Carmody. "Us must arrive before winter come and snow fall."

"Hard for any of us to imagine winter," she said. "This cold you talk about something us no able to understand."

Tutu knew what she was talking about. When Carmody called another council and exhorted them to leave at once for the Valley, he met resistance. The majority did not want to go; they liked it too well where they were. And Carmody could see that, even among the horowitzes, and as young as they were, the conservative personality was the most numerous. Only Tutu and a few others backed Carmody; they were the radicals, the pioneers, pushers-ahead.

Carmody did not try to dictate to them. He knew he was held in high regard, was, in fact, looked upon almost as a god. But even gods may be resisted when they threaten creature comforts, and he did not want to test his authority. If he lost, all was lost. Moreover, he knew that if he became a dictator, these people would not learn the basics of democracy. And it seemed to him that democracy, despite its faults and vices, was the best form of secular government. Gentle coercion was to be the strongest weapon he would use.

Or so he thought. After another month of vainly trying to get them to make the exodus, he became desperate. By now the stick-in-the-muds had another argument. Under Carmody's tutelage, they had planted vegetable gardens and corn, the seeds of which came from seed brought by the supply ship on Carmody's request. If they moved now, they would not be able to profit by their hard work. All would go to waste. Why did Carmody have them break their backs digging and plowing and planting and watering and chasing off the wild life, if he intended them to move on?

"Because me wanted to show you *how* to grow things in the soil," he said. "Me no intend to remain with you forever. When us get to the Valley, me leave."

"No leave us, beloved John!" they cried. "Us need you. Besides, now us have another reason for no go to the Valley. If us no go, then you no leave us."

John had to smile at this childlike reasoning, but he became stern immediately thereafter. "Whether you go or no go, when this egg hatch, me go. In fact, me go now, anyway. You no go, me leave you behind. Me call on all of you who want to go with me to follow me."

And he gathered Tutu and eleven other adolescents, plus their horses, wagons, weapons, food, and twenty chicks and five adult females. He hoped that the sight of his leaving would cause the others to change their minds. But, though they wept and begged him to stay, they would not go with him.

It was then that he lost his temper and cried, "Very well! If you no do what me know the goodest for you to do, then me destroy you village! And you must come with me because you no have any place else to go!"

"What you mean?" they shouted.

"Me mean that tonight a monster from the stars come and burn up the village. You see!"

Immediately afterwards, he spoke to Holmyard. "You heard me, Doc! I suddenly realized I had to put pressure on them! It's the only way to get them off their fannies!"

"You should have done it long ago," replied Holmyard. "Even if all of you travel fast now, you'll be lucky to get to the Valley before winter."

That night, while Carmody and his followers stood on top of a high hill outside the village, they watched the spaceship suddenly appear in the dim light cast by the two small moons. The inhabitants of the village must all have been looking up for the promised destroyer, for a shriek from a hundred throats arose. Immediately, there was a mad rush through the narrow gates, and many were trampled. Before all the children, chicks, and adults could get out, the monster loosed a tongue of flame against the log-walls surrounding the village. The walls on the southern side burst into flame, and the fire spread quickly. Carmody had to run down the hill and reorganize the demoralized horowitzes. Only because he threatened them with death if they didn't obey him, would they go back into the enclosure and bring out the horses, wagons, food, and weapons. They then cast themselves at Carmody's feet and begged forgiveness, saying they would never again go against his wishes.

And Carmody, though he felt ashamed because he had scared them so, and also distressed because of the deaths caused by the panic, nevertheless was stern. He forgave them but told them that he was wiser than they, and he knew what was good for them.

From then on, he got very good behavior and obedience from the adolescents. But he had also lost his intimacy with them, even with Tutu. They were all respectful, but they found it difficult to relax around him. Gone were the jokes and the smiles they had formerly traded.

"You have thrown the fear of God into them," said Holmyard.

"Now, Doc," said Carmody. "You're not suggesting that they think I am God. If I really believed that, I'd disabuse them."

"No, but they believe you're His representative. And maybe a demigod. Unless you explain the whole affair from beginning to end, they'll continue to think so. And I don't think the explanation will help much. You'd have to outline our society in all its ramifications, and you've neither the time nor ability to do that. No matter what you said, they'd misunderstand you."

Carmody attempted to regain his former cordial relations with them, but he found it impossible. So he devoted himself to teaching them all he could. He either wrote or else dictated to Tutu and other scribes as much science as he had time for. Though the country they had crossed so far was lacking in any sulfur or saltpeter deposits, Carmody knew that the Valley contained them. He wrote down rules for recognizing, mining, and purifying the two chemicals and also the recipe for making gunpowder from them. In addition, he described in great detail how to make rifles and pistols and mercury fulminate, how to find and mine and process lead.

These were only a few of the many technological crafts he recorded. In addition, he wrote down the principles of chemistry, physics, biology, and electricity. Furthermore, he drew diagrams of an automobile which was to be powered by electric motors and powered by hydrogen-air fuel cells. This necessitated a detailed procedure for making hydrogen by the reaction of heated steam with zinc or iron as a catalyst. This, in turn, demanded that he tell them how to identify copper ore and the processes for refining it and making it into wire, how to make magnets, and the mathematical formulae for winding motors.

To do this, he had to call frequently on Holmyard for help. One day, Holmyard said, "This has gone far enough, John. You're working yourself to a shadow, killing yourself. And you're attempting to do the impossible, to compress one hundred thousand years of scientific progress into one. What it took humanity a hundred millennia to develop, you're handing to the horowitzes on a silver platter. Stop it! You've done enough for them by giving them a speech and techniques in working flint and agriculture. Let them do it on their own from now on. Besides, later expeditions will probably get into contact with them and give them all the information you're trying to forcefeed them."

"You are probably right," groaned Carmody. "But what bothers me most of all is that, though I've done my best to give them all I can to enable them to deal with the material universe, I've done scarcely anything to give them an ethics. And that is what I should be most concerned with."

"Let them work out their own."

"I don't want to do that. Look at the many wrong, yes, evil avenues they could take."

"They will take the wrong ones, anyway."

"Yes, but they will have a right one which they can take if they wish."

"Then, for Christ's sake, give it to them!" cried Holmyard. "Quit belly-aching! Do something, or shut up about it!"

"I suppose you're right," said Carmody humbly. "At any rate, I don't have much time left. In a month, I have to go to Wildenwooly. And this problem will be out of my hands."

During the next month, the party left the hot plains and began to travel over high hills and through passes between mountains. The air became cooler, the vegetation changed to that which superficially resembled the vegetation of the uplands of Earth. The nights were cool, and the horowitzes had to huddle around roaring fires. Carmody instructed them how to tan skins with which to clothe themselves, but he did not allow them to take time out to hunt and skin the animals and make furs from them. "You able to do that when you reach the Valley," he said.

And, two weeks before they were to reach the pass that would lead them to the Valley, Carmody was awakened one night. He felt a tap-tapping in the egg on his chest and knew that the sharp beak of the chick was tearing away at the double-walled leathery covering. By morning a hole appeared in the skin of the egg. Carmody did what he had observed the mothers do. He grabbed hold of the edges of the tear and ripped the skin apart. It felt as if he were ripping his own skin, so long had the egg been a part of him.

The chick was a fine healthy specimen, male, covered with a golden down. It looked at the world with large blue eyes which, as yet, were uncoordinated.

Tutu was delighted. "All of us have brown eyes! Him the first horowitz me ever see with blue eyes! Though me hear that the wild horowitzes in this area have blue eyes. But him have eyes just like you eyes. You make him eyes blue so us know him you son?"

"Me have nothing to do with it," said Carmody. He did not say that the chick was a mutation, or else had carried recessive genes from mating by ancestors with a member of the blue-eyed race. That would have required too lengthy an explanation. But he did feel uncomfortable. Why had this happened to the chick that *he* was carrying?

By noon the tendrils holding the egg to his flesh had dried up and the empty skin fell to the ground. Within two days, the many little holes in his chest had closed; his skin was smooth.

He was cutting his ties to this world. That afternoon, Holmyard called him and said that his request for an extension of his stay on Feral had been denied. The day his contract ended, he was to leave.

"According to our contract, we have to furnish a ship to transport you to Wildenwooly," said Holmyard. "So, we're using our own. It'll only take a few hours to get you to your destination."

During the next two weeks, Carmody pushed the caravan, giving it only four hours sleep at night and stopping only when the horses had to have rest. Fortunately, the equine of Feral had more endurance, if less speed, than his counterpart on Earth. The evening of the day before he had to leave, they reached the mountain pass which would lead them to the promised Valley. They built fires and bedded down around the warmth. A chilly wind blew from the pass, and Carmody had trouble getting to sleep. It was not so much the cold air as it was his thoughts. They kept going around and around, like Indians circling a wagon train and shooting sharp arrows. He could not keep from worrying about what would happen to his charges after he left them. And he could not quit regretting that he had not given them any spiritual guidance. Tomorrow morning, he thought, tomorrow morning is my last chance. But my brain is numb, numb. If it were left up to me, if my superiors had not ordered me to be silent . . . but then they know best. I would probably do the wrong thing. Perhaps it is best to leave it up to divine revelation. Still, God works through man, and I am a man. . . .

He must have dozed away, for he suddenly awakened as he felt a small body snuggling next to his. It was his favorite, Tutu.

"Me cold," she said. "Also, many times, before the village burn, me sleep in your arms. Why you no ask me to do so tonight? You last night!" she said with a quavering voice, and she was crying. Her shoulders shook, and her beak racked across his chest as she pressed the side of her face against him. And, not for the first time, Carmody regretted that these creatures had hard beaks. They would never know the pleasure of soft lips meeting in a kiss.

"Me love you, John," she said. "But ever since the monster from the stars destroyed us village, me scared of you, too. But tonight, me forget me scared, and me must sleep in you arms once more. So me able to remember this last night the rest of me life."

Carmody felt tears welling in his own eyes, but he kept his voice firm. "Them who serve the Creator say me have work to do elsewhere. Among the stars. Me must go, even if no wish to. Me sad, like you. But maybe someday me return. No able to promise. But always hope."

"You no should leave. Us still childs, and us have adults' work ahead of us. The adults like childs, and us like adults. Us need you."

"Me know that true," he said. "But me pray to He that He watch over and protect you."

"Me hope He have more brains than me mother. Me hope He smart as you."

Carmody laughed and said, "He is infinitely smarter than me. No worry. What come, come."

He talked some more to her, mainly advice on what to do during the coming winter and reassurances that he might possibly return. Or, if he did not, that other men would. Eventually, he drifted into sleep.

But he was awakened by her terrified voice, crying in his ear.

He sat up and said, "Why you cry, child?"

She clung to him, her eyes big in the reflected light of the dying fire. "Me father come to me, and him wake me up! Him say, 'Tutu, you wonder where us horowitzes go after death! Me know, because me go to the land of beyond death. It a beautiful land; you no cry because John must leave. Some day, you see him here. Me allowed to come see you and tell you. And you must tell John that us horowitzes like mans. Us have souls, us no just die and become dirt and never see each other again.'

"Me father told me that. And him reached out him hand to touch me. And me become scared, and me waked up crying!"

"There, there," said Carmody, hugging her. "You just dream. You know you father no able to talk when him alive. So how him able to talk now? You dreaming."

"No dream, no dream! Him not in me head like a

dream! Him standing outside me head, between me and fire! Him throw a shadow! Dreams no have shadows! And why him no able to talk? If him can live after death, why him no talk, too? What you say, 'Why strain at a bug and swallow a horse?'"

"Out of the mouths of babes," muttered Carmody, and he spent the time until dawn talking to Tutu.

At noon of that same day, the horowitzes stood upon the rim of the pass. Below them lay the Valley, flashing with the greens, golds, yellows, and reds of the autumnal vegetation. In a few more days the bright colors would turn brown, but today the Valley glittered with beauty and promise.

"In a few minutes," said Carmody, "the mans from the skies come in the starwagon. No become frightened; it will not harm you. Me have a few words to say, words which me hope you and you descendants never forget.

"Last night, Tutu seed her father, who had died. Him telled her that all horowitzes have souls and go to another place after them die. The Creator have maked a place for you—so say Whoot—because you He's childs. He never forget you. And so you must become good childs to He, for He . . ."

Here he hesitated, for he had almost said Father. But, knowing that they had fixed in their minds the maternal image, he continued . . . "for He you Mother.

"Me have telled you the story of how the Creator maked the world from nothing. First, space. Then, atoms created in space. Atoms joined to become formless matter. Formless matter becomed suns, big suns with little suns circling around them. The little suns cooled and becomed planets, like the one you now live on. Seas and land formed.

"And He created life in the seas, life too small to see with the naked eye. But He see. And some day you, too, see. And out of the little creatures comed big creatures.

Fish comed into being. And some fish crawled onto the land and becomed airbreathers with legs.

"And some animals climbed trees and lived there, and their forelimbs becomed wings, and they becomed birds and flyed.

"But one kind of tree-creature climbed down out of the trees before it becomed a bird. And it walked on two legs and what might have becomed wings becomed arms and hands.

"And this creature becomed you ancestor.

"You *k*now this, for me have telled you many times. You *k*now you past. Now, me tell you what you must do in the future, if you wish to become a good child of He. Me give you the law of the horowitz.

"This what He wish you to do every day of you lives.

"Love you Creator even gooder than you own parents.

"Love each other, even the one who hate you.

"Love the animals, too. You able to kill animals for food. But no cause them pain. Work the animals, but feed them and rest them well. Treat the animals as childs.

"Tell the truth. Also, seek hard for the truth.

"Do what society say you must do. Unless society say what He no wish you to do. Then, you may defy society.

"Kill only to keep from becoming killed. The Creator no love a murderer or a people who make war without good cause.

"No use evil means to reach a good goal.

"Remember that you horowitzes no alone in this universe. The universe filled with the childs of He. Them no horowitzes, but you must love them, too.

"No fear death, for you live again."

John Carmody looked at them for a moment, wondering upon what paths of good and of evil this speech would set them. Then he walked to a large flat-topped rock on which sat a bowl of water and a loaf of bread made from baked acorn flour.

"Each day at noon, when the sun highest, a male or female choosed by you must do this before you and for you."

He took a piece of bread and dipped it in the water and ate the piece, and then he said, "And the Choosed One must say so all able to hear,

" 'With this water, from which life first comed, me thank me Creator for life. And with this bread, me thank me Creator for the blessings of this world and give meself strength against the evils of life. Thanks to He.' "

He paused. Tutu was the only one not looking at him, for she was busily writing down his words. Then, she looked up at him as if wondering if he meant to continue. And she gave a cry and dropped her pencil and tablet and ran to him and put her arms around him.

"Starship come!" she cried. "You no go!"

There was a moan of fear and astonishment from the beaks of the crowd as they saw the shining monster hurtle over the mountain towards them.

Gently, Carmody loosed her embrace and stepped away from her.

"Come a time when the parent must go, and the child must become adult. That time now. Me must go because me wanted elsewhere.

"Just remember, me love you, Tutu. Me love all of you, too. But me no able to stay here. However, He always with you. Me leave you in the care of He."

Carmody stood within the pilothouse and looked at the image of Feral on the screen. It was now no larger to him than a basketball. He spoke to Holmyard.

"I will probably have to explain that final scene to my superiors. I may even be severely rebuked and punished.

I do not know. But I am convinced at this moment that I did rightly."

"You were not to tell them they had a soul," said Holmyard. "Not that I myself care one way or another. I think the idea of a soul is ridiculous."

"But you can think of the idea," said Carmody. "And so can the horowitzes. Can a creature capable of conceiving a soul be without one?"

"Interesting question. And unanswerable. Tell me, do you really believe that that little ceremony you instituted will keep them on the straight and narrow?"

"I'm not all fool," said Carmody. "Of course not. But they do have correct basic instruction. If they pervert it, then I am not to blame. I have done my best."

"Have you?" said Holmyard. "You have laid the foundations for a mythology in which you may become the god, or the son of the god. Don't you think that, as time blurs the memory of these events you initiated, and generations pass, that myth after myth and distortion after distortion will completely alter the truth?"

Carmody stared at the dwindling globe. "I do not know. But I have given them something to raise them from beasts to men."

"Ah, Prometheus!" breathed Holmyard. And they were silent for a long time.

THE NINE BILLION
NAMES OF GOD

Arthur C. Clarke

Just as science fiction has grown more sophisticated in its treatment of traditional Western faiths, so has it begun to treat oriental and even primitive religions with more dignity. Avram Davidson's "Or the Grasses Grow," for instance, is a sardonic view of the fate of two white men who choose to break a treaty with an American Indian tribe, scoffing at the Indians' hinted threats of supernatural vengeance. This sneaky little tale by Arthur Clarke seems to carry a similar warning to materialistic Westerners who view esoteric religions as little more than superstitions—deserving, if any response at all, only exploitation. Let the exploiters beware.

"This is a slightly unusual request," said Dr. Wagner, with what he hoped was commendable restraint. "As far as I know, it's the first time anyone's been asked to supply a Tibetan monastery with an Automatic Sequence Computer. I don't wish to be inquisitive, but I should hardly have thought that your—ah—establishment had much use for such a machine. Could you explain just what you intend to do with it?"

"Gladly," replied the Lama, readjusting his silk robe and carefully putting away the slide rule he had been using for currency conversions. "Your Mark V Computer can carry out any routine mathematical operation involving up to ten digits. However, for our work we are interested in *letters*, not numbers. As we wish you to modify the output circuits, the machine will be printing words, not columns of figures."

"I don't quite understand . . ."

"This is a project on which we have been working for the last three centuries—since the lamasery was founded, in fact. It is somewhat alien to your way of thought, so I hope you will listen with an open mind while I explain it."

"Naturally."

"It is really quite simple. We have been compiling a list which shall contain all the possible names of God."

"I beg your pardon?"

"We have reason to believe," continued the Lama imperturbably, "that all such names can be written with not more than nine letters in an alphabet we have devised."

"And you have been doing this for three centuries?"

"Yes: we expected it would take us about fifteen thousand years to complete the task."

"Oh." Dr. Wagner looked a little dazed. "Now I see why you wanted to hire one of our machines. But exactly what is the *purpose* of this project?"

The Lama hesitated for a fraction of a second and Wagner wondered if he had offended him. If so, there was no trace of annoyance in the reply.

"Call it ritual, if you like, but it's a fundamental part of our belief. All the many names of the Supreme Being— God, Jehovah, Allah, and so on—they are only man-made labels. There is a philosophical problem of some difficulty here, which I do not propose to discuss, but somewhere among all the possible combinations of letters which can occur are what one may call the *real* names of God. By

systematic permutation of letters, we have been trying to
list them all."

"I see. You've been starting at AAAAAAAAA . . .
and working up to ZZZZZZZZZ . . ."

"Exactly—though we use a special alphabet of our own.
Modifying the electromatic typewriters to deal with this is,
of course, trivial. A rather more interesting problem is that
of devising suitable circuits to eliminate ridiculous combinations. For example, no letter must occur more than
three times in succession."

"Three? Surely you mean two."

"Three is correct: I am afraid it would take too long to
explain why, even if you understood our language."

"I'm sure it would," said Wagner hastily. "Go on."

"Luckily, it will be a simple matter to adapt your Automatic Sequence Computer for this work, since once it has
been programed properly it will permute each letter in
turn and print the result. What would have taken us fifteen
thousand years it will be able to do in a hundred days."

Dr. Wagner was scarcely conscious of the faint sounds
from the Manhattan streets far below. He was in a different
world, a world of natural, not man-made mountains. High
up in their remote aeries these monks had been patiently
at work, generation after generation, compiling their lists
of meaningless words. Was there any limit to the follies of
mankind? Still, he must give no hint of his inner thoughts.
The customer was always right . . .

"There's no doubt," replied the doctor, "that we can
modify the Mark V to print lists of this nature. I'm much
more worried about the problem of installation and maintenance. Getting out to Tibet, in these days, is not going
to be easy."

"We can arrange that. The components are small enough
to travel by air—that is one reason why we chose your

machine. If you can get them to India, we will provide transport from there."

"And you want to hire two of our engineers?"

"Yes, for the three months which the project should occupy."

"I've no doubt that Personnel can manage that." Dr. Wagner scribbled a note on his desk pad. "There are just two other points—"

Before he could finish the sentence the Lama had produced a small slip of paper.

"This is my certified credit balance at the Asiatic Bank."

"Thank you. It appears to be—ah—adequate. The second matter is so trivial that I hesitate to mention it—but it's surprising how often the obvious gets overlooked. What source of electrical energy have you?"

"A diesel generator providing 50 kilowatts at 110 volts. It was installed about five years ago and is quite reliable. It's made life at the lamasery much more comfortable, but of course it was really installed to provide power for the motors driving the prayer wheels."

"Of course," echoed Dr. Wagner. "I should have thought of that."

The view from the parapet was vertiginous, but in time one gets used to anything. After three months, George Hanley was not impressed by the two-thousand-foot swoop into the abyss or the remote checkerboard of fields in the valley below. He was leaning against the wind-smoothed stones and staring morosely at the distant mountains whose names he had never bothered to discover.

This, thought George, was the craziest thing that had ever happened to him. "Project Shangri-La," some wit at the labs had christened it. For weeks now the Mark V had been churning out acres of sheets covered with gibberish.

Patiently, inexorably, the computer had been rearranging letters in all their possible combinations, exhausting each class before going on to the next. As the sheets had emerged from the electromatic typewriters, the monks had carefully cut them up and pasted them into enormous books. In another week, heaven be praised, they would have finished. Just what obscure calculations had convinced the monks that they needn't bother to go on to words of ten, twenty or a hundred letters, George didn't know. One of his recurring nightmares was that there would be some change of plan, and that the High Lama (whom they'd naturally called Sam Jaffe, though he didn't look a bit like him) would suddenly announce that the project would be extended to approximately 2060 A.D. They were quite capable of it.

George heard the heavy wooden door slam in the wind as Chuck came out onto the parapet beside him. As usual, Chuck was smoking one of the cigars that made him so popular with the monks—who, it seemed, were quite willing to embrace all the minor and most of the major pleasures of life. That was one thing in their favor: they might be crazy, but they weren't bluenoses. Those frequent trips they took down to the village, for instance . . .

"Listen, George," said Chuck urgently. "I've learned something that means trouble."

"What's wrong? Isn't the machine behaving?" That was the worst contingency George could imagine. It might delay his return, than which nothing could be more horrible. The way he felt now, even the sight of a TV commercial would seem like manna from heaven. At least it would be some link with home.

"No—it's nothing like that." Chuck settled himself on the parapet, which was unusual because normally he was scared of the drop. "I've just found what all this is about."

"What d'ya mean—I thought we knew."

"Sure—we know what the monks are trying to do. But we didn't know why. It's the craziest thing—"

"Tell me something new," growled George.

"—but old Sam's just come clean with me. You know the way he drops in every afternoon to watch the sheets roll out. Well, this time he seemed rather excited, or at least as near as he'll ever get to it. When I told him that we were on the last cycle he asked me, in that cute English accent of his, if I'd ever wondered what they were trying to do. I said 'Sure'—and he told me."

"Go on: I'll buy it."

"Well, they believe that when they have listed all His names—and they reckon that there are about nine billion of them—God's purpose will be achieved. The human race will have finished what it was created to do, and there won't be any point in carrying on. Indeed, the very idea is something like blasphemy."

"Then what do they expect us to do? Commit suicide?"

"There's no need for that. When the list's completed, God steps in and simply winds things up . . . bingo!"

"Oh, I get it. When we finish our job, it will be the end of the world."

Chuck gave a nervous little laugh.

"That's just what I said to Sam. And do you know what happened? He looked at me in a very queer way, like I'd been stupid in class, and said 'It's nothing as trivial as *that*.'"

George thought this over for a moment.

"That's what I call taking the Wide View," he said presently. "But what d'ya suppose we should do about it? I don't see that it makes the slightest difference to us. After all, we already knew that they were crazy."

"Yes—but don't you see what may happen? When the list's complete and the Last Trump doesn't blow—or whatever it is they expect—we may get the blame. It's our machine they've been using. I don't like the situation one little bit."

"I see," said George slowly. "You've got a point there. But this sort of thing's happened before, you know. When I was a kid down in Louisiana we had a crackpot preacher who said the world was going to end next Sunday. Hundreds of people believed him—even sold their homes. Yet when nothing happened, they didn't turn nasty as you'd expect. They just decided that he'd made a mistake in his calculations and went right on believing. I guess some of them still do."

"Well, this isn't Louisiana, in case you hadn't noticed. There are just two of us and hundreds of these monks. I like them, and I'll be sorry for old Sam when his lifework backfires on him. But all the same, I wish I was somewhere else."

"I've been wishing that for weeks. But there's nothing we can do until the contract's finished and the transport arrives to fly us out."

"Of course," said Chuck thoughtfully, "we could always try a bit of sabotage."

"Like hell we could! That would make things worse."

"Not the way I meant. Look at it like this. The machine will finish its run four days from now, on the present twenty-hours-a-day basis. The transport calls in a week. O.K.—then all we need to do is to find something that wants replacing during one of the overhaul periods— something that will hold up the works for a couple of days. We'll fix it, of course, but not too quickly. If we time matters properly, we can be down at the airfield when the last name pops out of the register. They won't be able to catch us then."

"I don't like it," said George. "It will be the first time I ever walked out on a job. Besides, it would make them suspicious. No. I'll sit tight and take what comes."

"I *still* don't like it," he said, seven days later, as the tough little mountain ponies carried them down the winding road. "And don't you think I'm running away because I'm afraid. I'm just sorry for those poor old guys up there, and I don't want to be around when they find what suckers they've been. Wonder how Sam will take it?"

"It's funny," replied Chuck, "but when I said good-by I got the idea he knew we were walking out on him— and that he didn't care because he knew the machine was running smoothly and that the job would soon be finished. After that—well, of course, for him there just isn't any After That . . ."

George turned in his saddle and stared back up the mountain road. This was the last place from which one could get a clear view of the lamasery. The squat, angular buildings were silhouetted against the afterglow of the sunset: here and there, lights gleamed like portholes in the sides of an ocean liner. Electric lights, of course, sharing the same circuit as the Mark V. How much longer would they share it, wondered George. Would the monks smash up the computer in their rage and disappointment? Or would they just sit down quietly and begin their calculations all over again?

He knew exactly what was happening up on the mountain at this very moment. The High Lama and his assistants would be sitting in their silk robes, inspecting the sheets as the junior monks carried them away from the typewriters and pasted them into the great volumes. No one would be saying anything. The only sound would be the incessant patter, the never-ending rainstorm, of the keys hitting the paper, for the Mark V itself was utterly silent as it flashed through its thousands of calculations a second. Three months of this, thought George, was enough to start anyone climbing up the wall.

"There she is!" called Chuck, pointing down into the valley. "Ain't she beautiful!"

She certainly was, thought George. The battered old DC-3 lay at the end of the runway like a tiny silver cross. In two hours she would be bearing them away to freedom and sanity. It was a thought worth savoring like a fine liqueur. George let it roll round his mind as the pony trudged patiently down the slope.

The swift night of the high Himalayas was now almost upon them. Fortunately the road was very good, as roads went in this region, and they were both carrying torches. There was not the slightest danger, only a certain discomfort from the bitter cold. The sky overhead was perfectly clear and ablaze with the familiar, friendly stars. At least there would be no risk, thought George, of the pilot being unable to take off because of weather conditions. That had been his only remaining worry.

He began to sing, but gave it up after a while. This vast arena of mountains, gleaming like whitely hooded ghosts on every side, did not encourage such ebullience. Presently George glanced at his watch.

"Should be there in an hour," he called back over his shoulder to Chuck. Then he added, in an afterthought: "Wonder if the computer finished its run? It was due about now."

Chuck didn't reply, so George swung round in his saddle. He could just see Chuck's face, a white oval turned towards the sky.

"Look," whispered Chuck, and George lifted his eyes to heaven. (There is always a last time for everything.)

Overhead, without any fuss, the stars were going out.

THE VITANULS

John Brunner

Medical advances, especially in the field of infant mortality, have already given us one serious ethical problem: over-population. But imagine how that problem could be exacerbated should medical research discover a way substantially to extend our lives—a cure for senility, perhaps. Suppose, for instance, that the earth's population grew to number as many people alive at one time as had ever lived before in man's history. British science-fiction author John Brunner examines that proposition in an unusual but appropriate setting—a maternity hospital in India. The setting and a remarkably spiritual central character provide the story with some considerations of life and death not frequently found in science fiction, nor expressed, as they are here, in Hindu values. Yet Brunner weaves his tale so sympathetically that even to the Western mind, the reaction of a great Indian physician to the crisis seems altogether reasonable and fitting.

Before the soundproof, germproof double glass window of the delivery room the matron of the maternity hospital came to a halt. "And there," she told the tall young American from the World Health Organisation, "is our patron saint."

Barry Chance blinked at her. She was a brisk fortyish Kashmiri woman with an aura of efficiency, not at all the kind of person one would expect to make jokes about her life's work. And indeed there had been no trace of jocularity in her tone. But in this teeming subcontinent of India a stranger could never be sure.

He compromised. "I'm sorry," he lied. "I didn't catch that . . . ?"

Out of the corner of his eye he studied the man the matron had indicated. He was elderly and balding; what little hair remained to him had whitened into a sort of halo around his heavily lined face. Most Indians, the American had noticed, tended to grow fat with age, but this man had gone scrawny, like Gandhi. Surely, though, an ascetic appearance and a halo of hair weren't enough to establish a claim to sainthood?

"Our patron saint," the matron repeated, sublimely unaware of her visitor's bewilderment. "Dr. Ananda Koti- wala. You're very fortunate to see him at work. It's his last day here before he retires."

Struggling to make sense of her remarks, Chance stared unashamedly at the old man. He felt his rudeness was excused by the fact that this corridor adjoining the de- livery room was a kind of public gallery. On every side there were relatives and friends of the expectant mothers, down to and including very small children who had to stand on tiptoe to peer in through the double glass win- dow. There was no such thing as privacy in India unless you were rich, and in any overcrowded, underdeveloped country a minimal fraction of the people enjoyed that luxury he'd taken for granted since childhood.

The fact that toddlers could watch, fascinated, the ar- rival of their new brothers and sisters was accepted here as a part of growing up. Chance reminded himself sternly that he was a foreigner, and—what was more—a doctor himself, trained at one of the few colleges that still ad- ministered the Hippocratic Oath in full form to its gradu- ates. He forced his personal preconceptions to the back of his mind and concentrated on unravelling the curious comment the matron had made.

The scene before him offered no hints. All he could see was a typical Indian hospital delivery room, containing thirty-six mothers in labour, of whom two were suffering agonies and screaming—at least, to judge by their open mouths; the soundproofing was extremely good.

He wondered briefly how Indians felt about their children entering the world under such circumstances. What it suggested to him was an assembly-line, the mothers reduced to machines producing their quota of infants according to a preplanned schedule. And all of it so dreadfully public!

Again, though, he was falling into the trap of thinking like a modern American, parochially. For untold generations most of mankind had been born publicly. Although it had been estimated that the world's present living population was just about equal in number to all the human beings there had ever been before the twenty-first century, the majority of Earth's people continued that ancient tradition, and made a birth a social event: in villages, an excuse for a celebration, or as here a sort of family outing to the hospital.

The modern aspects of the event were easily listed. The attitudes of the mothers, for instance: one could tell at a glance which of them had enjoyed up-to-date prenatal instruction, for their eyes were closed and their faces bore expressions of determination. They knew what miracle was going on in their bodies, and they intended to help it, not resist it. Good. Chance nodded approval. But there remained the women who were screaming, as much from terror as pain, probably . . .

He shifted his attention with an effort. After all, he was supposed to be conducting a survey of the methods in use here.

The latest recommendations of the experts seemed to be being properly applied—you'd expect as much in a large city where most of the medical staff had had the benefit of training abroad. Some time soon he was committed to going out into the villages, and things would be different there, but he'd think about that when he had to.

The elderly doctor who had been called "our patron saint" was just completing the delivery of a boy. Gloved hand held up the latest recruit to the army of humanity, glistening. A slap—correction: a beautifully restrained tap with the open palm, enough to provoke a squall and the first deep breath, but not enough to aggravate the birth-trauma. And handed over to the waiting nurse to be laid on the little bench beside the bed, lower than the mother so that the last few precious ounces of maternal blood could seep down from the placenta before the cord was severed.

Excellent. All in accordance with the best modern practice. Except—why was the doctor having to explain so much so patiently to the awkward girl holding the child?

Chance's puzzlement was brief; then he remembered. Of course. There weren't enough trained nurses in this country to allot one to every new mother. So those girls standing neat and scared in their disposable plastic overalls, their lank black hair bound in sterile plastic snoods, would be younger sisters or eldest daughters doing their best to help out.

Then the old man, with a final smile of reassurance, was leaving the worried girl and going to hold the hand of one of the women screaming.

Chance watched with satisfaction as he soothed her, bringing about a complete relaxation within moments, and —as far as could be guessed through the double barrier of soundproof glass and an incomprehensible language —instructing her how best to hasten the delivery. Yet there was nothing more here than he'd seen in a hundred hospitals.

He turned to the matron and asked directly, "Why do you call him 'patron saint'?"

"Dr. Kotiwala," the matron said, "is the most—now what would it be in English? Is there the word 'empathetic'?"

"From 'empathy'?" Chance frowned. "I don't think so. But I get what you mean, anyway."

"Yes," the matron said. "Did you not see how he quieted the one who was screaming?"

Chance gave a slow nod. Yes, come to think of it, it must be regarded as a special gift in a country like this—to be able to break through the superstitious fright of a woman barely above peasant level and make her see what it had taken other women around her the full nine months of pregnancy and much skilled instruction to understand. Now there was only one woman screaming with her mouth wide, and the doctor was soothing her in her turn. The other he'd just spoken to was struggling to encourage her contractions.

"Dr. Kotiwala is wonderful," the matron went on. "Everybody loves him. I have known parents to consult astrologers not to determine the most fortunate birthday for their child but only how to make sure it is born during Dr. Kotiwala's shift in the delivery room."

Shift? Oh yes: they operated a three-shift day. Once more the image of the assembly-line came to him. But it was far too advanced a concept to reconcile with the idea of applying to astrologers. What a crazy country! Chance repressed a shiver and admitted to himself that he'd be glad when he was allowed to return home.

For long moments after that he was silent, noticing something he hadn't previously spotted: how, when the labour pains permitted, the mothers opened their eyes and hopefully followed Dr. Kotiwala's progress around the room as if wanting to invite him to spend a minute or two at their bedside.

This time their hopes weren't fulfilled. There was a breech presentation at the far end, and it would take careful manipulation to reverse the baby. Plastic-clad, a beautiful dark girl of about fifteen bent to watch what the doctor was doing, putting out her right hand so that the tense anxious mother could clasp it for comfort.

By his own standards, Chance thought, there was nothing extraordinary about Kotiwala. He was obviously competent, and his patients appeared to like him, but he was old and rather slow, and one could see how cautiously he moved now the end of his shift was near and he was tiring.

On the other hand, it was admirable to find the human touch in a birth-factory like this. He'd asked the matron, within minutes of his arrival, how long the average stay of a patient might be, and she'd said with a wry smile, "Oh—twenty-four hours for the easy ones, and perhaps thirty-six for cases with complications."

Looking at Dr. Kotiwala, one might have assumed there was all the time in the world.

From an American standpoint even that didn't constitute a claim to sanctity, but through Indian eyes doubtless things looked different. The matron had warned him that he'd come at a busy time, nine months after a big spring religious festival which people regarded as auspicious for increasing their families. The warning hadn't prepared him for the reality; the hospital was *packed*.

Yet it could have been worse. He shuddered a little. The back of the problem was broken, but there were still something like 180,000 new mouths to feed every day. At the peak of the population explosion there had been just under a quarter-million per day; then the impact of modern medicine was felt, even people in India, China and Africa began to recognise the need to plan for the children they could afford to feed, clothe and educate, and the crisis diminished.

Nonetheless it would be years before the children of that peak period could become teachers, workers, doctors to cope with the tremendous pressure. Thinking along these lines brought him to a subject which had been engaging a lot of his attention recently, and he spoke aloud without intending to.

"People like him, in this of all jobs—that's who they ought to choose!"

"I beg your pardon?" the matron said with positively British formality. The British had left ineradicable traces on the intellectuals of this country.

"Nothing," Chance muttered.

"But did you not say someone ought to choose Dr. Kotiwala for something?"

Annoyed with himself, yet—once reminded of the dilemma shortly to be sprung on the world—unable to hold his tongue, Chance gave ground.

"You said it was Dr. Kotiwala's last day here, didn't you?"

"Why, yes. He retires tomorrow."

"You have someone in mind to replace him?"

The matron shook her head vigorously. "Oh no! In the physical sense, yes, in that another doctor will take his shifts, but men like Dr. Kotiwala are rare in any generation and in modern times most of all. We're dreadfully sorry to lose him."

"Has he—uh—passed some arbitrary retirement age?"

The matron smiled thinly. "Hardly, in India! We can't afford the luxuries you Americans go in for, and that includes putting usable material—human or otherwise—on a scrapheap before it's worn out."

With his eyes on the elderly doctor, who had successfully reversed the breech presentation and moved on to attend to the woman in the next bed, Chance said, "He's retiring voluntarily, then."

"Yes."

"Why? Has he lost interest in his work?"

The matron was shocked. "Of course not! I'm not sure I can make his reasons clear, though." She bit her lip. "Well, he is very old now, and he fears that one day soon a child may die because he has let his attention wander. It would set him back many steps on the road to enlightenment if that happened."

Chance felt a surge of enlightenment himself. Believing he completely understood what the matron meant, he said, "In that case he damned well deserves—"

And broke off, because strictly he ought not to be thinking about this subject, or talking about it.

"What?" the matron said, and when Chance shook his head, went on: "You see, when he was young Dr. Koti-wala was much influenced by the teachings of the Jains, to whom the taking of any life at all is repugnant. When his desire to cherish life led him to study as a doctor, he had to accept that some killing—of bacteria, for exam-ple—is inevitable to ensure human survival. His kindliness is based on religious principles. And it would be more than he could bear to think that his own arrogance in continuing to work when it was no longer safe had cost an innocent baby its life."

"He can hardly be a Jain now," Chance said, lacking anything else by way of comment. Privately he was think-ing that if what the matron said was correct, there were some old fossils back home who could do with a dose of Kotiwala's humility instead of hanging on until they were practically senile.

"He's a Hindu, as are most of our people," the matron explained. "Though he tells me his thinking has been much influenced by the teachings of Buddhism—which began, after all, as a Hindu heresy." She didn't sound greatly interested in what she was saying. "But I'm afraid I still don't understand to what you were referring a moment ago," she added.

Chance thought of gigantic factories owned by Du Pont, Bayer, Glaxo and heaven knows who else, labouring night and day with more expenditure of energy than a million mothers bringing forth commonplace human beings, and decided that the facts were going to be public knowledge soon enough for him to risk lifting a corner of the curtain of secrecy. It was getting him down to keep his mouth shut all the time.

He said, "Well, what I mean was that if I have any say in the matter people like him would get priority when it comes to—uh—the most advanced kinds of medical treatment. To preserve somebody who's liked and admired seems better than saving someone who is mainly feared."

There was a pause.

"I think I follow you," the matron said wisely. "I take it that the anti-death pill is a success?"

Chance started. She gave him another of her wry smiles.

"Oh, it's difficult for us to keep up with the literature when we work under such pressure, but there have been hints, haven't there? You in the rich countries like America and Russia have been trying for years to find a broad-spectrum specific against aging, and I think—knowing your countries by hearsay—there must have been a long angry argument over who should benefit first."

Chance surrendered completely and gave a miserable nod. "Yes, there's a specific against senility. It isn't perfect, but pressure on the drug companies to put it into commercial production had grown so great that just before I left WHO Headquarters to come here I heard the contracts were being placed. A course of treatment will cost five or six hundred dollars and last for eight to ten years. I don't have to tell you what it'll mean. But if I had my way, I'd pick someone like your Dr. Kotiwala to enjoy the results before all the stupid old men with power and wealth who are going to have their obsolete ideas carried into the future by this break-through!"

He stopped short, alarmed at his own vehemence and hoping that none of the curious spectators surrounding them could speak English.

"Your attitude does you credit," the matron said. "But in one sense it's inexact to say Dr. Kotiwala is retiring. He might prefer to say he's changing his career. And if you offered to give him anti-senility treatment I expect he would smile and refuse."

"Why in the world—?"

"It is hard to make clear in English." The matron frowned. "You know what is a sunnyasi, perhaps?"

Bewildered, Chance said, "One of those holy men I've seen around the place, wearing nothing but a loincloth and carrying a begging-bowl."

"And a staff, usually."

"A sort of fakir?"

"Not in the least. A sunnyasi is a man in the final stage of his life's work. He can have been anything pre-viously—a businessman, commonly, or a civil servant, or a lawyer, or even a doctor."

"You mean your Dr. Kotiwala is going to throw away all his medical skills, all the service he could still perform in this overcrowded country even if he did risk the life of a baby one of these days, and go out begging in a loincloth for the sake of his own salvation?"

"This is why we call him our patron saint," the matron said with an affectionate smile in Dr. Kotiwala's direction.

"When he is gone from here, and has collected such virtue, he will be a friend for us who remain behind."

Chance was appalled. A moment ago the matron had been saying India could not afford to throw aside people with good work still before them; now here she was seeming to approve a plan that struck him as compounded of equal parts selfishness and superstition.

"Are you telling me he believes this nonsense about stacking up virtue for a future existence?"

The matron gave him a cold stare. "I think that is uncivil of you. The teaching of Hinduism is that the soul is born again, throughout an eternal cycle, until it achieves one-ness with the All. Can you not appreciate how a lifetime of work among the newly-born makes all this real to us?"

"You believe it too?"

"That's irrelevant. But . . . I do witness miracles every time I admit a mother to this hospital. I witness how an animal act, a process with slimy, messy, *bloody* associations brings about the growth of a reasoning being. I was born, and you, a squally helpless infant, and here we stand talking in abstract concepts. Maybe it's a mere function of chemical complexity; I don't know. I told you, I find it hard to keep up with the literature."

Chance stared through the window of the delivery room with a puzzled frown. He felt somehow disappointed—even cheated—after his near-acceptance of Dr. Kotiwala in the matron's admiring terms. At length he muttered, "I guess maybe we'd better move on."

The sensation of which Dr. Kotiwala was chiefly aware was weariness. It went all through his body, to the marrow of his bones.

There was no hint of it in his outward behaviour—no suggestion that he was mechanically going through the motions. The mothers who entrusted themselves and their offspring to his care would have detected any such failing, with perceptions deeper than ordinary, and he would have known the truth himself and felt he was betraying his trust.

But he was unspeakably, incredibly tired.

More than sixty years had passed since he graduated from medical school. There had been no change in the way human beings were created. Oh, the trappings had changed as medicine made its successive impacts; he remembered the inarguable disasters caused by drugs like thalidomide, and the upside-down blessings of antibiotics that swamped countries like his own with more mouths than it could possibly feed, and now he was working with techniques which meant that nine out of ten of the children born under his supervision were wished-for, loved by their parents instead of being a burden or condemned to the half-life of illegitimacy.

Sometimes things turned out well, and sometimes badly. In the course of his long and valuable career Dr. Kotiwala had come to place reliance on no other principle.

Tomorrow . . .

His mind threatened to wander away from what he was doing: bringing to independent life the latest of all those he had delivered. How many thousands of mothers had moaned on the bed before him? He dared not count. And how many more thousands of new lives had he helped to launch? Those he less-than-dared to count. Perhaps he'd introduced to life a thief, an ingrate, a murderer, a fratricide . . .

No matter. Tomorrow—indeed, today, for his shift was over and this baby he was now raising by the feet was the last he would ever deliver in a hospital, though if he were appealed to in some miserable village he would doubtless help . . . Tomorrow there would be an end

to worldly attachments. He would commit himself to the
life of the spirit, and—

He checked. The woman alongside the mother, her
sister-in-law, very much disturbed by the things she had
had to do, like sterilising her hands in disinfectant and
stripping off her best sari in favour of a clammy plastic
overall, spoke a fearful question.

He hesitated over his answer. To the superficial glance
nothing about the baby seemed amiss. It was a boy,
physically whole, the usual flushed postnatal colour, letting out an acceptable scream to greet the world. All
was as it should be. And yet . . .

He cradled the baby on his left arm while deftly raising
first one, then the other eyelid. Sixty years of practice
had made him gentle. He stared deep into the vacant
light eyes, contrasting almost frighteningly with the skin
around them.

Beyond them was—was . . .

But what could one say to a child as new as this? He
sighed and gave it into the care of the sister-in-law, and
the clock on the wall ticked away the last few seconds of
his shift.

Nonetheless his mind remained on the indefinable impulse which had compelled him to take a second look at
the boy. When the doctor taking over from him arrived,
Dr. Kotiwala finished his summary briefing by saying,
"And there's something wrong with the boy just born
in Bed 32. I can't put my finger on it. But if you get
the chance, check him over, would you?"

"Will do," said the relief doctor, a fat young man from
Benares with a shiny brown face and shiny soft hands.

The matter continued to irk Dr. Kotiwala even though
he'd spoken about it. Changed, showered, ready to leave,
he still lingered in the corridor to watch his colleague
checking the baby as requested, making a thorough inspec-

tion from head to sole. He found nothing wrong, and catching sight of Dr. Kotiwala as he turned away, spread his hands and shrugged, his attitude implying, "Fuss about nothing if you ask me!"

Yet when I looked into those eyes, something behind them suggested . . .

No, it was absurd. What could any adult hope to read in the eyes of a brand-new baby? Wasn't it a kind of arrogance that made him think his colleague was missing something of vital importance? In a dilemma, he considered the idea of going back in the delivery room and taking another look.

"Isn't that your patron saint standing there?" Chance muttered to the matron in a cynical tone.

"Why, so it is. How fortunate! Now you can make his acquaintance yourself—if you wish to."

"You've painted him in such glowing colours," Chance said dryly, "I feel I'd be wasting a chance if I didn't meet him before he takes off his clothes and goes native."

The irony was almost completely lost on the matron. She bustled ahead with exclamations, but interrupted herself the moment she noticed Kotiwala's glum expression.

"Doctor! Is something wrong?"

"I don't know," Kotiwala sighed. His English was good, but heavily accented in the singsong rhythm which the departed British rulers of India had nicknamed "Bombay Welsh." "It is the child just born in Bed 32, a boy. I am *sure* something is wrong, but as for what it is, I'm lost."

"In that case we must see to him," the matron said briskly. Clearly she had implicit faith in Kotiwala's opinions.

"Dr. Banerji has examined him and doesn't agree with me," Kotiwala countered.

In the matron's view Kotiwala was Kotiwala and Banerji was nobody; her expression said so, louder than words.

It struck Chance that here was his opportunity to find out whether the matron's trust had any real basis.

"Look, rather than taking up Dr. Banerji's time—he has a lot to cope with in there—why don't you bring the child out and we'll take a look at him?"

"Dr. Chance, from WHO," the matron explained. Absently Dr. Kotiwala shook hands.

"Yes, that is a good idea. A second opinion, wouldn't you say?"

It had been in the back of Chance's mind that his comparatively fresh training would enable him to apply some tests Kotiwala wasn't accustomed to using. In fact it was the other way around; the slow, thorough palping of the child's body and limbs with which the old Indian began wasn't in Chance's line at all. Of course, it had its advantages, provided one knew the normal location of every bone and major muscle in the infantile frame. Anyway, it revealed nothing.

Heart normal, blood pressure average, all external appearances healthy, reflexes present and vigorous, fontanelle a trifle large but within normal range of variation . . .

After nearly three-quarters of an hour, Chance was convinced the old man was doing it to make an impression, and consequently was losing his temper by degrees. He noticed that Kotiwala again and again rolled up the boy's eyelids and stared into the eyes, as if he could read the brain behind. On the latest repetition of the act he snapped, "Tell me, doctor! What do you see in his eyes, hm?"

"What do *you* see?" Kotiwala countered, and motioned for Chance to look also.

"Nothing," Chance grunted a moment later. They'd checked the eyes, hadn't they, along with everything else?

"That's what I see, also," Kotiwala said. "Nothing."

Oh, for goodness' sake! Chance spun on his heel and went to the side of the room, peeling off his gloves preparatory to dumping them in the disposer. Over his shoulder he said, "Frankly, I don't see anything wrong with the kid at all. What do you think it is? The soul of an earthworm turned up in his body by mistake, or something?"

Kotiwala could hardly have missed the scorn with which the words were uttered, but his reply was perfectly calm and civil.

"No, Dr. Chance, I think that hardly likely. After a great deal of contemplation I've come to the conclusion that the traditional ideas are inaccurate. The human condition is a human thing. It embraces the imbecile and the genius, but it doesn't overlap with any other species. Who could claim that the soul of a monkey, or a dog, is inferior to that which looks out of the dirty windows of a moron's eyes?"

"I certainly wouldn't," Chance said with sarcasm, and began to strip off his gown. Kotiwala sighed, and shrugged, and was silent.

Later . . .

The sunnyasi Ananda Bhagat wore nothing more than a loincloth, owned nothing more in all the world than the begging-bowl and staff he carried. Around him—for it was cold in the hill-country this bleak December—the people of the village shivered in their cheap coarse clothes, spending as much time as they could spare huddled over their tiny fires. They burned woodchips, rarely charcoal, and even now a great deal of cowdung. The foreign experts had told them to use cowdung for fertiliser, but the warmth of a fire was closer to the present than the mystery of fixed nitrogen and next year's crops.

Ignoring the chill, ignoring the strong smoke of the

fire as it wandered upward and filled the gloomy hut, Ananda Bhagat spoke soothingly to a fearful girl of about seventeen at whose breast a baby clung. He had looked into its eyes, and there he had seen—nothing.

It was not the first such in this village; it was not the first village where he had seen the same. He accepted that as a fact of existence. With the abandonment of the name Kotiwala had gone the preconceptions of the Doctor of Medicine, Trinity College, Dublin, who had obeyed the behests of intellectualism in the sterile wards of a big city hospital. Throughout his eighty-five years he had sensed a greater reality looming over him, and his final decision had been to commit himself to it.

Now, as he gazed wonderingly into the empty face of the child, he heard a noise. The young mother heard it also, and cowered because it was loud and growing louder. So far had Ananda Bhagat come from his former world that he had to make a conscious effort before he identified it. A drone in the sky. A helicopter, a rarity here; why should a helicopter come to any particular one of India's seventy thousand villages?

The young mother whimpered. "Be still, my daughter," the sunnyasi said. "I will go and see what it is."

He let her hand fall with a final comforting pat and went out of the misshapen doorway to stand on the cold windy street. The village had only one street. Shading his eyes with his thin hand, he peered upward into the sky.

Yes: a helicopter, circling and glinting in the weak winter sunlight. It was descending, but that was nothing to do with his emergence into plain view. Before he recognised the sound of it, it must already have been coming down.

He waited.

In a little while, the people came chattering out of their

homes, wondering why the attention of the outer world in the form of this curious noisy machine should be turned on them. Seeing that their marvellous visitor, the holy man, the sunnyasi—such as he were few these days, and to be cherished—was standing firm, they drew courage from his example and likewise stood up boldly.

The helicopter settled in a blast of whirling dust, a little away from the beaten track called a street, and a man jumped down from it: a tall fair-skinned foreigner. He looked the scene over slowly, spotted the sunnyasi and let out an exclamation. Calling something to his companions, he began to stride up the street. Two others came down to stand beside the machine and talk in low tones: a girl of about twenty, in a sari of blue and green, and a young man in flying overalls, the pilot.

Clutching her baby to her, the young mother also came out to see what was going on, her first child—a toddler —pursuing her on unsteady feet with a hand outstretched to catch at her sari if his balance failed him.

"Dr. Kotiwala!" the young man from the helicopter said.

"I was," the sunnyasi agreed in a rusty voice. The whole vocabulary of English had sloughed off his mind like a snake's overtight skin.

"For God's sake!" The young man's voice was harsh. "We've had enough trouble finding you without your playing word-games with us now we're here! Thirteen villages we've had to stop at on the way, picking up clues and being told you were here yesterday and moved on . . ."

He wiped his face with the back of his hand.

"My name's Barry Chance, in case you've forgotten me. We met at the hospital in—"

The sunnyasi interrupted. "I remember very well, thank

you. But who am I, that you spend so much time and energy trying to find me?"

"As far as we can tell, you're the first person ever to have recognised a Vitanul."

There was a silence. During it, Chance could almost see the sunnyasi's persona fading, that of Dr. Kotiwala replacing it. The change was reflected in the voice, which resumed its "Bombay Welsh" rhythm on the next words.

"My Latin is negligible, for I only learned what was necessary in medicine, but I take it that would be from *vita*, a life, and *nullus* . . . You mean: like this one here?" He gestured for the young mother beside him to advance a pace, and rested his hand lightly on her baby's back.

Chance looked the infant over and at length shrugged. "If you say so," he muttered. "She's only about two months old, isn't she? So without tests . . ."

His voice trailed briefly away.

"Yes, without tests!" he burst out abruptly. "That's the point! Do you know what became of the boy you said had something wrong with him, the very last one you delivered before you—ah—*retired?*" There was great fierceness in his voice, but it was not directed at the old man he was talking to. It was simply the outward sign that he had been driven to the end of his resources.

"I have seen many others since," Kotiwala said. It was definitely not the sunnyasi speaking now, but the trained doctor with a lifetime's experience behind him. "I can imagine, but tell me anyhow."

Chance gave him a look that reflected something close to awe. The inquisitive villagers gathered nearby recognised the expression, and deduced—though not even the best-educated among them could follow the rapid English words—that the stranger from the sky was affected by the aura of their holy man. They relaxed noticeably.

"Well . . . your friend the matron kept insisting that

if you'd said something was wrong with him there *must* be something wrong, although I'd said he was okay, Dr. Banerji had said he was okay. She went on and on about it until it was interfering with my work and delaying my departure. So I said to hell with it and had him taken out to WHO in Delhi for the most complete battery of tests they could lay on. Can you guess what they found?"

Kotiwala rubbed his forehead wearily. "Total suppression of the alpha and theta rhythms?" he suggested.

"You did know!" The accusation in Chance's voice was enough to shatter the barrier of language and communicate to the listening villagers, some of whom stepped menacingly closer to the sunnyasi as though to defend him if they had to.

Kotiwala waved them back with a reassuring gesture. He said, "No, I didn't know. It just now came to me what you would find."

"Then how in heaven's name did you—?"

"How did I guess the boy wasn't normal? I can't explain that to you, Dr. Chance. It would take sixty years of work in a maternity hospital, seeing scores of babies born every day, to make you see what I saw!"

Chance bit back a fierce retort and let his shoulders droop. "I'll have to swallow that. But the fact remains: you did realise, within minutes of the kid being born, even though he looked healthy and none of our tests has ever revealed any organic deformity, that his brain was—was empty and there was no *mind* in it! Christ, the job I had convincing them at WHO that you'd really done it, and the weeks of argument before they'd let me come back to India and try to track you down!"

"Your tests," Kotiwala said, as though the last sentence hadn't been spoken. "Many of them?"

Chance threw his hands in the air. "Doctor, where the hell have you been these past two years?"

"Walking barefoot from small village to small village," Kotiwala said, deliberately taking the question literally. "I haven't followed news from the world outside. This is a world for these people." He indicated the rough street, the mean shacks, the ploughed and planted fields, and the blue mountains closing all of it in.

Chance took a deep breath. "So you don't know and don't really care. Let me fill you in. Only a matter of weeks after I saw you, the news broke which led to my recall from India: reports of a sudden appalling rise in congenital imbecility. Normally a child begins to react in at least a sketch for a human pattern while it's still very young. Precocious kids smile quickly, and any kid is likely to distinguish movement and bright colours, and reach out to grasp things . . ."

"Except these you have named Vitanuls?"

"Exactly." Chance clenched his fists as though trying to seize something out of the air. "No life! None of the normal reactions! Absence of normal cerebral waves when you test them on the EEG, as though everything that makes a person human had been—had been left out!"

He levelled a challenging arm at Kotiwala's chest. "And you recognised the very first one of all! Tell me how!"

"Patience." Bowed by the weight of his years, Kotiwala still held himself with immense dignity. "This rise in imbecility—it struck you directly after I retired from the hospital?"

"No, of course not."

"Why 'of course'?"

"We were too tied up with—Oh, you've been out of touch, haven't you?" Chance spoke with bitter sarcasm. "A minor triumph of medicine was making all the head-lines, and giving WHO enough headaches to be going on with. The anti-senility treatment had been made public a few days after I saw you, and everybody and his uncle was standing on line yelling for it."

"I see," Kotiwala said, and his aged shoulders finally hunched into an attitude of despair.

"You see? What's that supposed to mean?"

"Forgive my interrupting. Continue, please."

Chance shivered, apparently as much at what he was remembering as at the chill December air. "We'd done our best, and postponed announcement of the treatment until there were stocks enough to treat several million applicants, but of course that was as bad as announcing it in the lab stage, because everybody's grandmother seemed to have died last Friday and here were people screaming at us for killing them by neglect, and—Hell, you get the picture. Whichever way we handled it we came out wrong.

"And then shoveled in on top of that mess came the new one. Congenital imbecility hits ten per cent of birth, twenty, thirty! What's going on? Everybody whizzes around in little circles because just as we were congratulating ourselves on sorting out the row about the anti-senility treatment, here comes the most fantastic crisis in history and it's not going to break, it's going to get worse, and worse, and *worse* . . . Over the past two weeks the rate has topped eighty per cent. Do you understand that, or are you so sunk in your superstitions it doesn't bother you any longer? Out of every ten children born last week, no matter in what country or continent, eight are *mindless animals!*"

"And you think the one we examined together was the very first?" Kotiwala disregarded the harshness of the younger man's words; his eyes were staring, unfocused, into the blue distance over the mountains.

"As far as we can work it out." Chance spread his hands. "At any rate, when we checked back we found the first kids of which this had been reported had been born on that particular day, and I happened to remember that the time of birth of the earliest we'd heard about was an hour or so after I met you."

"What happened on that day?"

"Nothing that could account for it. Every resource of the UN has been put to work; we've sifted the world's records to the very bottom, and not that day only but the time nine months earlier when these kids must have been conceived—only that doesn't fit either, because some of them were preemies as much as six weeks early, and they're the same, they're hollow, empty, drained . . . If we weren't at the end of our tether, I'd never have done such a crazy thing as coming to look for you. Because after all, I guess there isn't anything you can do to help, is there?"

The fire and rage which had burned in Chance when he arrived had died to ashes now, and he seemed to have no more words. Kotiwala stood thinking for a minute or more, and the villagers, growing restless, chattered among themselves.

At last the old man said, "The—the anti-senility drug. It's a success?"

"Oh yes. Thank God. If we hadn't some consolation in the midst of this mess I think we'd all go crazy. We've cut the death-rate fantastically, and because we planned well we can hope to feed the surplus mouths, and—"

"I think," Kotiwala broke in, "I can tell you what happened on the day we met."

Dazed, Chance stared at him. "Then for heaven's sake tell me! You're my last hope—you're *our* last hope."

"I can't offer hope, my friend." A sound like the echo of doom's own knell coloured the soft words. "But I can make what they call an educated guess. Did I not read once a calculation which showed that as many people are alive in this twenty-first century as have ever lived since the evolution of human beings?"

"Why—yes. I saw that myself, a long time back."

"Then I say that what happened on the day we met was this: the precise number of all the human beings there have ever been was exceeded for the very first time."

Chance shook his head in bewilderment. "I don't see —or—or *do* I?"

"And it so turns out," Kotiwala continued, "that at the same time or very shortly afterward, you find, and make available the world over, a drug which cures old age. Dr. Chance, you will not accept this, because I remember you made a kind of joke about an earthworm, but I do. I say that you have made me understand what I saw when I looked into the eyes of that new-born child, when I looked into the eyes of this little girl here." He touched the arm of the young mother at his side, and she gave him a shy quick smile.

"Not the lack of mind, as you have been saying. But the lack of a soul."

For a few seconds Chance imagined that he heard the hollow laughter of demons in the whisper of the winter wind. With a violent effort he rid himself of the delusion.

"No, that's absurd! You can't mean to make out that we've run short of human souls, as though they were stored up in some cosmic warehouse and issued off the shelf every time a child is born! Oh, come now, doctor—you're an educated man, and this is absurd."

"As you say," Kotiwala agreed politely. "That is something I won't venture to dispute with you. But I owe you my thanks, anyhow. You've shown me what I must do."

"That's great," Chance said. "Here I come half across the world hoping that you'll tell me what I must do, and instead you claim I've told you . . . What? What must you do?" A final flicker of hope leapt up in his face.

"I must die," said the sunnyasi, and took his staff, and his bowl, and without another word to anyone, even the young mother whom he had been comforting when Chance arrived, he set off with slow old-man's paces along the road that led to the tall blue mountains and the eternal ice by whose aid it was lawful for him to set free his soul.

JUDAS

John Brunner

This is a horror story. Its premise is a familiar one, the "—if this goes on" syndrome applied to the growing world of machines and robotry. But John Brunner, author of many stories that tie the spiritual to the scientific, has a way of lighting up a now-familiar horror in a chilling new light. Thus we have a pseudo religion that at first seems absurd—and then, frighteningly, absolutely blasphemous. Whether it offends our religious sensibilities or simply affronts our humanity, there is something hideously grotesque about "The Word Made Steel," and we are breathlessly with the hero as he tries to turn his topsy-turvy world rightside up. He simply must win. But must he? Isn't the world already topsy-turvy? Aren't machines too often in charge already? And don't many of us act even now as if we were gods? What happens when someone tries to rectify that state of affairs?

The Friday evening service was drawing to its close. The rays of the declining spring sun slanted through the polychrome plastic of the windows and lay along the floor of the central aisle like a pool of oil spilt on a wet road. On the polished steel of the altar a silver wheel spun continually, glinting between two ever burning mercury vapour lamps; above it, silhouetted against the darkling eastern sky, there stood a statue of God. The surpliced choir was singing an anthem—"The Word Made Steel"—

and the minister sat listening with his hand cupped under his chin, wondering if God had approved of the sermon he had just preached on the Second Coming.

Most of the large congregation was enraptured by the music. Only one man present, at the end of the rearmost row of bare steel pews, fidgeted impatiently, flexing the rubber pad from the forehead rest before him in nervous fingers. He had to keep his hands occupied, or else they kept straying to the bulge in the inside pocket of his plain brown jacket. His watery blue eyes wandered restlessly along the climactic, sweeping lines of the metal temple and shifted away every time they came to the wheel motif which the architect—probably God himself—had incorporated wherever possible.

The anthem closed on a thrilling dissonance and the congregation knelt, their heads against the rubber rests, while the minister pronounced the blessing of the Wheel. The man in brown wasn't really listening, but he caught a few phrases: "May he guide you in your appointed courses . . . serve you as your eternal pivot . . . bring you at last to the peace of the true eternal round . . ."

Then he stood with the rest of them while the choir marched out to the strains of the electronic organ. Directly the minister had disappeared through the vestry door, the worshippers began to shuffle towards the main exits. He alone remained sitting in his pew.

He was not the sort of person one would look at twice. He had sandy hair and a worn, tired face; his teeth were stained and irregular, his clothes fitted badly, and his eyes were a fraction out of focus, as though he needed glasses. Plainly the service had not brought him peace of mind.

Eventually, when everybody else had gone, he stood up and replaced the rubber pad with scrupulous exactitude. For a moment his eyes closed and his lips moved soundlessly; as if this act had endowed him with the courage for a decision, he seemed to draw himself up like a diver poising on a high board. Abruptly he left the pew and walked—soundless on the rubber carpet of the nave—towards the small steel door that bore the single word VESTRY.

Beside it there was a bell. He rang.

Shortly the door was opened by a junior acolyte, a youth in a grey robe woven of metallic links that jingled as he moved, hands in grey shiny gloves, scalp hidden under a smooth steel cap. In a voice made impersonal by careful practice, the acolyte said, "You wish counsel?"

The man in brown nodded, shifting a trifle nervously from foot to foot. Through the doorway were visible many devotional pictures and statues; he dropped his gaze before them.

"What is your name?" the acolyte inquired.

"Karimov," said the man in brown. "Julius Karimov."

He tensed fractionally as he spoke, his eyes fleeting over the acolyte's face in search of any reaction. None showed, and he relaxed on the youth's curt order to wait while he informed the minister.

The moment he was alone, Karimov crossed the vestry and examined a painting on the far wall: Anson's "Immaculate Manufacture," depicting the legendary origin of God—a bolt of lightning from heaven smiting an ingot of pure steel. It was excellently done, of course; the artist's use of electro-luminescent paint for the lightning, in particular, was masterly. But from Karimov it provoked an expression of physical nausea, and after only seconds he had to turn away.

At length the minister entered in the officiating robe which identified him as one of the Eleven closest to God, his headpiece—which during the service had concealed his shaven scalp—discarded, his white, slender hands playing with a jewelled emblem of the Wheel that hung around his neck on a platinum chain. Karimov turned slowly to confront him, right hand slightly raised in a stillborn gesture. It had been a calculated risk to give his real name; he thought that was probably still a secret. But his real face . . .

No, no hint of recognition. The minister merely said in his professionally resonant voice, "What may I do for you, my son?"

The man in brown squared his shoulders and said simply, "I want to talk to God."

With the resigned air of one well used to dealing with requests of that sort, the minister sighed. "God is extremely busy, my son," he murmured. "He has the spiritual welfare of the entire human race to look after. Cannot I help you? Is there a particular problem on which you need advice, or do you seek generalised divine guidance in programming your life?"

Karimov looked at him diffidently and thought: *This man really believes! His faith isn't just pretence for profit, but deep-seated honest trust, and it is more terrifying than everything else that even those who were with me at the beginning should believe!*

He said after a while, "You are kind, Father, but I need more than mere advice. I have"—he seemed to stumble at the word—"prayed much, and sought help from several ministers, and still I have not attained to the peace of the true round. Once, long ago, I had the privilege of seeing God in the steel; I wish to do so again, that's all. I have no doubt, of course, that He will remember me."

There was a long silence, during which the minister's dark eyes remained fixed on Karimov. Finally he said, "Remember you? Oh yes, he will certainly remember you! But *I* remember you too—now!"

His voice shook with uncontrollable fury, and he reached for a bell on the wall.

Strength born of desperation poured through Karimov's scrawny frame. He hurled himself at the minister, striking aside the outstretched arm inches from its goal, bowling the tall man over, seizing the tough chain around his neck, and pulling with every ounce of force he could muster.

The chain bit deep into pale flesh; as if possessed, Karimov tugged and tugged at it, twisted, took a fresh grip and tugged again. The minister's eyes bulged, mouth uttered loathsome formless grunts, fists beat at his attacker's arms—and grew weaker, and ceased.

Karimov drew back, shaking at what he had done, and compelled himself unsteadily to his feet. To the former colleague who now had gone beyond all hope of hearing he muttered his sick apology, then calmed himself with deep breaths and approached the door by which he had not entered the room.

On his throne beneath its wheel-shaped canopy of steel, God sat. His polished limbs gleamed under the muted lights, his head was beautifully designed to suggest a human face without possessing a single human feature—even eyes.

Blind insensate thing, thought Karimov as he shut the door behind him. Unconsciously his hand touched what he had in his pocket.

The voice too was more than humanly perfect, a deep pure tone as if an organ spoke. It said, "My son—"

And stopped.

Karimov gave an audible sigh of relief and his nervousness dropped from him like a cloak. He stepped forward casually and sat down in the central one of the eleven chairs arranged in a horseshoe before the throne, while the blank shiny gaze of the robot rested on him and the whole metal frame locked in astonishment.

"Well?" Karimov challenged. "How do you like meeting somebody who doesn't believe in you for a change?"

The robot moved in human fashion, relaxing. Steel fingers linked under his chin while he reconsidered the intruder with interest instead of amazement. The voice rang out afresh.

"So it's you, Black!"

Karimov nodded with a faint smile. "That's what they used to call me in the old days. I used to think it was a silly affectation—assigning the scientists who worked on top-secret projects false names. But it's turned out to have advantages, for me at any rate. I gave my own name of Karimov to your—ah—late apostle outside, and it meant nothing to him. Speaking of real names, by the way: how long is it since anyone addressed you as A–46?"

The robot jerked. "It is sacrilege to apply that term to me!"

"Sacrilege be—bothered. I'll go further and remind you what the A stands for in A–46. Android! An imitation of a man! A sexless insensate assembly of metal parts which I helped to design, and it calls itself God!" Scathing contempt rode the lashing words. "You and your fantasies of Immaculate Manufacture! Blasted by a bolt of heavenly lightning from a chunk of untooled steel! Talk about making men in God's own image—you're the 'God' who was made in man's!"

They had even incorporated the facility of shrugging in their design, Karimov recalled with a start as the robot made use of it.

"Leaving sacrilege on one side for a moment, then," the machine said, "is there any real reason why you should deny that I am God? Why should not the second Incarnation be an Inferration—in imperishable steel? As for your benighted and deluded belief that you created the metal part of me—which is anyway supremely unimportant since the spirit alone is eternal—it's long been said that a prophet is without honour in his own country, and since

the Inferration took place near your experimental station
. . . Well!"

Karimov laughed. He said, "Well I'm damned! I think
you believe it yourself!"

"You are beyond question damned. For a moment I
hoped, seeing you enter my throne room, that you'd
learned the error of your ways and come to acknowledge
my divinity at last. Of my infinite compassion I will give
you one final chance to do so before I call my ministers to
take you away. Now or never, Black or Karimov or
whatever you choose to call yourself: do you repent and
believe?"

Karimov wasn't listening. He was staring past the shining machine into nowhere, while his hand caressed the
bulge in his pocket. He said in a low voice, "I've plotted
years for this moment—twenty years, ever since the day
we turned you on and I began to suspect we'd gone wrong.
Not till now was there anything I could have done. And in
the meantime, while I sweated and hunted for a way to
stop you, I've seen the ultimate humiliation of mankind.

"We've been slaves to our tools since the first caveman
made the first knife to help him get his supper. After that
there was no going back, and we built till our machines
were ten million times more powerful than ourselves. We
gave ourselves cars when we might have learned to run;
we made airplanes when we might have grown wings; and
then the inevitable. We made a machine our God."

"And why not?" the robot boomed. "Can you name any
single way in which I am not your superior? I am stronger,
more intelligent and more durable than a man. I have
mental and physical powers that shame comparison. I feel
no pain. I am immortal and invulnerable and yet you say I
am not God. Why? From perverseness!"

"No," said Karimov with terrible directness. "Because
you are mad.

"You were the climax of a decade's work by our team: the dozen most brilliant living cyberneticists. Our dream was to create a mechanical analogue of a human being which could be programmed directly with intelligence drawn from the patterns in our own brains. In that we succeeded—far too well!

"I've had time enough in the past twenty years to work out where we went astray. It was my fault, God help me—the real God, if He exists, not you, you mechanical fraud! Always somewhere at the back of my mind while we were working on you there lurked the thought that to build the machine we had envisaged would be to become as God: to make a creative intelligence, that none save He had yet achieved! That was megalomania, and I'm ashamed, but it *was* in my mind, and from mine it was transferred to yours. No one knew of it; even I was afraid to admit it to myself, for shame is a saving human grace. But you! What could you know of shame, of self-restraint, of empathy and love? Once implanted in your complex of artificial neurones, that mania grew till it knew no bounds, and . . . here you are. Insane with the lust for divine glory! Why else the doctrine of the Word Made Steel, and the image of the Wheel, the mechanical form that does not occur in nature? Why else the trouble you go to to make parallels in your godless existence with that of the greatest Man who ever lived?"

Karimov was still speaking in the same low tones, but his eyes were ablaze with hatred.

"You have no soul and you accuse me of sacrilege. You're a collection of wires and transistors and you call yourself God. Blasphemy! Only a man could be God!"

The robot shifted with a clang of metal limbs and said, "All this is not merely nonsense but a waste of my valuable time. Is that all you came for—to rave at me?"

"No," said Karimov. "I came to kill you."

At long last his hand dipped into the bulging pocket and produced the object there concealed: a curious little weapon, less than six inches long. A short metal tube extended forward from it; backward from the handgrip a flex disappeared inside his coat; under his thumb there was a small red stud.

He said, "It took me twenty years to design and build this. We chose steel for your body that only an atomic bomb could destroy; how, though, could one man walk into your presence with a nuclear weapon on his back? I had to wait until I had a means of cutting your steel as easily as a knife cuts a man's weak flesh. Here it is—and now I can undo the wrong I did to my own species!"

He pressed the stud.

The robot, motionless till that moment as if incapable of believing that anyone could really wish to harm him, jolted upright, turned half around, and stood paralysed as a tiny hole appeared in the metal of his side. Steel began to form little drops around the hole; the surrounding area glowed red, and the drops flowed like water—or blood.

Karimov held the weapon steady, though it scorched his fingers. Sweat stood out on his forehead. Another half minute, and the damage would be irreparable.

Behind him a door slammed open. He cursed, for his weapon would not work on a man. To the last moment he kept it aimed; then he was seized from behind and pinioned, and the weapon torn from its flex and hurled to the floor and stamped into ruin.

The robot did not move.

The tension of twenty hate-filled years broke and his relief boiled up into hysterical laughter which he fought to quell. When he finally succeeded, he saw that the man who held him was the junior acolyte who had admitted him to the vestry, and that there were other men around, strangers, gazing in utter silence at their God.

"Look at him, look at him!" Karimov crowed. "Your idol was nothing but a robot, and what men make they can destroy. He said he was divine, but he wasn't even invulnerable! I've freed you! Don't you understand? *I've set you free!*"

But the acolyte wasn't paying him any attention. He stared fixedly at the monstrous metal doll, licking his lips, until at last he said in a voice that was neither relieved nor horrified, but only awed, "The Hole in the Side!"

A dream began to die in Karimov's mind. Numb, he watched the other men walk over to the robot and peer into the hole, heard one of them say, "How long to repair the damage?" and the other reply offhandedly, "Oh, three days, I guess!" And it was clear to him what he had done.

Wasn't this a Friday, and in spring? Hadn't he himself known that the robot made careful parallels between his own career and that of the man he parodied? Now it had reached the climax: there had been a death, and there would be a resurrection—on the third day . . .

And the grip of the Word Made Steel would never be broken.

In turn the men made the sign of the Wheel and departed, until one only remained. Stern, he came down from the throne to confront Karimov and address the acolyte who held him in a rigid grasp.

"Who is he, anyway?" the man demanded.

The acolyte gazed at the limp figure slumped on the chair with the weight of all the ages crushing him, and his mouth rounded in an O of comprehension. He said, "*Now* I understand! He calls himself Karimov.

"But his real name must be Iscariot."

THE QUEST FOR SAINT AQUIN

Anthony Boucher

The late Anthony Boucher deserves a place of honor here. As his two stories in this collection effectively illustrate, he not only saw a place for the spiritual in man's future, but a necessary place. This bias, if one may call it that, seems to have spilled over into his editing work. As the long-time editor of The Magazine of Fantasy and Science Fiction, *Boucher introduced many a story with a religious or spiritual motif (some of them more properly fantasy, of course, than science fiction). Perhaps because that policy proved editorially attractive, his successors—Robert Mills, Avram Davidson, and currently, Edward Ferman—have continued it, with the happy result that many of the stories in this volume are from F and SF. Tony Boucher was no Pollyanna, however; a convinced Roman Catholic, he saw the role of the future Christian to be strikingly similar to that of the primitive Christian. Though the religious man may be more and more only a remnant in society, much as the early Christians were, Boucher still sees that man as the salt of the earth, the necessary counterpoint to a meretricious civilization. He even foresees, as John Brunner does not, how a robot could be part of this counter-force, serving not only man, but God. Very nearly the best story on this theme is the late Charles Beaumont's "Last Rites," in a collection called* The Magic Man. *But this one edges it out.*

The Bishop of Rome, the head of the Holy, Catholic and Apostolic Church, the Vicar of Christ on Earth—in short, the Pope—brushed a cockroach from the filth-encrusted wooden table, took another sip of the raw red wine, and resumed his discourse.

"In some respects, Thomas," he smiled, "we are stronger now than when we flourished in the liberty and exaltation for which we still pray after Mass. We know, as they knew in the Catacombs, that those who are of our flock are indeed truly of it; that they belong to Holy Mother the Church because they believe in the brotherhood of man under the fatherhood of God—not because they can further their political aspirations, their social ambitions, their business contacts."

" 'Not of the will of flesh, nor of the will of man, but of God . . .' " Thomas quoted softly from St. John.

The Pope nodded. "We are, in a way, born again in Christ; but there are still too few of us—too few even if we include those other handfuls who are not of our faith, but still acknowledge God through the teachings of Luther or Laotse, Gautama Buddha or Joseph Smith. Too many men still go to their deaths hearing no gospel preached to them but the cynical self-worship of the Technarchy. And that is why, Thomas, you must go forth on your quest."

"But Your Holiness," Thomas protested, "if God's word and God's love will not convert them, what can saints and miracles do?"

"I seem to recall," murmured the Pope, "that God's own Son once made a similar protest. But human nature, however illogical it may seem, is part of His design, and we must cater to it. If signs and wonders can lead souls to God, then by all means let us find the signs and wonders. And what can be better for the purpose than this legendary Aquin? Come now, Thomas; be not too scrupulously exact in copying the doubts of your namesake, but prepare for your journey."

The Pope lifted the skin that covered the doorway and passed into the next room, with Thomas frowning at his heels. It was past legal hours and the main room of the tavern was empty. The swarthy innkeeper roused from his doze to drop to his knees and kiss the ring on the hand which the Pope extended to him. He rose crossing himself and at the same time glancing furtively about as though a Loyalty Checker might have seen him. Silently he indicated another door in the back, and the two priests passed through.

Toward the west the surf purred in an oddly gentle way at the edges of the fishing village. Toward the south the stars were sharp and bright; toward the north they dimmed a little in the persistent radiation of what had once been San Francisco.

"Your steed is here," the Pope said, with something like laughter in his voice.

"Steed?"

"We may be as poor and as persecuted as the primitive church, but we can occasionally gain greater advantages from our tyrants. I have secured for you a robass—gift of a leading Technarch who, like Nicodemus, does good by stealth—a secret convert, and converted indeed by that very Aquin whom you seek."

It looked harmlessly like a woodpile sheltered against possible rain. Thomas pulled off the skins and contemplated the sleek functional lines of the robass. Smiling, he stowed his minimal gear into its panniers and climbed into the foam saddle. The starlight was bright enough so that he could check the necessary coordinates on his map and feed the data into the electronic controls.

Meanwhile there was a murmur of Latin in the still night

air, and the Pope's hand moved over Thomas in the immemorial symbol. Then he extended that hand, first for the kiss on the ring, and then again for the handclasp of a man to a friend he may never see again.

Thomas looked back once more as the robass moved off. The Pope was wisely removing his ring and slipping it into the hollow heel of his shoe.

Thomas looked hastily up at the sky. On that altar at least the candles still burnt openly to the glory of God.

Thomas had never ridden a robass before, but he was inclined, within their patent limitations, to trust the works of the Technarchy. After several miles had proved that the coordinates were duly registered, he put up the foam backrest, said his evening office (from memory; the possession of a breviary meant the death sentence), and went to sleep.

They were skirting the devastated area to the east of the Bay when he awoke. The foam seat and back had given him his best sleep in years; and it was with difficulty that he smothered an envy of the Technarchs and their creature comforts.

He said his morning office, breakfasted lightly, and took his first opportunity to inspect the robass in full light. He admired the fast-plodding, articulated legs, so necessary since roads had degenerated to, at best, trails in all save metropolitan areas; the side wheels that could be lowered into action if surface conditions permitted; and above all the smooth black mound that housed the electronic brain —the brain that stored commands and data concerning ultimate objectives and made its own decisions on how to fulfill those commands in view of those data; the brain that made this thing neither a beast, like the ass his Saviour had ridden, nor a machine, like the jeep of his many-times-great-grandfather, but a robot . . . a robass.

"Well," said a voice, "what do you think of the ride."

Thomas looked about him. The area on this fringe of desolation was as devoid of people as it was of vegetation.

"Well," the voice repeated unemotionally. "Are not priests taught to answer when spoken to politely."

There was no querying inflection to the question. No inflection at all—each syllable was at the same dead level. It sounded strange, mechani . . .

Thomas stared at the black mound of brain. "Are you talking to me?" he asked the robass.

"Ha ha," the voice said in lieu of laughter. "Surprised, are you not."

"Somewhat," Thomas confessed. "I thought the only robots who could talk were in library information service and such."

"I am a new model. Designed–to–provide–conversation–to–entertain–the–way–worn–traveler," the robass said slurring the words together as though that phrase of promotional copy was released all at once by one of his simplest binary synapses.

"Well," said Thomas simply. "One keeps learning new marvels."

"I am no marvel. I am a very simple robot. You do not know much about robots do you."

"I will admit that I have never studied the subject closely. I'll confess to being a little shocked at the whole robotic concept. It seems almost as though man were arrogating to himself the powers of—" Thomas stopped abruptly.

"Do not fear," the voice droned on. "You may speak freely. All data concerning your vocation and mission have been fed into me. That was necessary, otherwise I might inadvertently betray you."

Thomas smiled. "You know," he said, "this might be

rather pleasant—having one other being that one can talk
to without fear of betrayal, aside from one's confessor."

"Being," the robass repeated. "Are you not in danger
of lapsing into heretical thoughts."

"To be sure, it *is* a little difficult to know how to think
of you—one who can talk and think but has no soul."

"Are you sure of that."

"Of course I— Do you mind very much," Thomas
asked, "if we stop talking for a little while? I should like
to meditate and adjust myself to the situation."

"I do not mind. I never mind. I only obey. Which is to
say that I *do* mind. This is very confusing language which
has been fed into me."

"If we are together long," said Thomas, "I shall try
teaching you Latin. I think you might like that better.
And now let me meditate."

The robass was automatically veering further east to
escape the permanent source of radiation which had been
the first cyclotron. Thomas fingered his coat. The combination of ten small buttons and one large made for a
peculiar fashion; but it was much safer than carrying a
rosary, and fortunately the Loyalty Checkers had not yet
realized the fashion's functional purpose.

The Glorious Mysteries seemed appropriate to the possible glorious outcome of his venture; but his meditations
were unable to stay fixedly on the Mysteries. As he murmured his *Aves* he was thinking:

*If the prophet Balaam conversed with his ass, surely, I
may converse with my robass. Balaam has always puzzled
me. He was not an Israelite; he was a man of Moab, which
worshiped Baal and was warring against Israel; and yet
he was a prophet of the Lord. He blessed the Israelites
when he was commanded to curse them; and for his re-
ward he was slain by the Israelites when they triumphed
over Moab. The whole story has no shape, no moral; it is*

as though it was there to say that there are portions of the Divine Plan which we will never understand . . .

He was nodding in the foam seat when the robass halted abruptly, rapidly adjusting itself to exterior data not previously fed into its calculations. Thomas blinked up to see a giant of a man glaring down at him.

"Inhabited area a mile ahead," the man barked. "If you're going there, show your access pass. If you ain't, steer off the road and stay off."

Thomas noted that they were indeed on what might roughly be called a road, and that the robass had lowered its side wheels and retracted its legs. "We—" he began, then changed it to "I'm not going there. Just on toward the mountains. We—I'll steer around."

The giant grunted and was about to turn when a voice shouted from the crude shelter at the roadside. "Hey Joe! Remember about robasses!"

Joe turned back. "Yeah, tha's right. Been a rumor about some robass got into the hands of Christians." He spat on the dusty road. "Guess I better see an ownership certificate."

To his other doubts Thomas now added certain uncharitable suspicions as to the motives of the Pope's anonymous Nicodemus, who had not provided him with any such certificate. But he made a pretense of searching for it, first touching his right hand to his forehead as if in thought, then fumbling low on his chest, then reaching his hand first to his left shoulder, then to his right.

The guard's eyes remained blank as he watched this furtive version of the sign of the cross. Then he looked down. Thomas followed his gaze to the dust of the road, where the guard's hulking right foot had drawn the two curved lines which a child uses for its sketch of a fish—and which the Christians in the catacombs had employed as a punning symbol of their faith. His boot scuffed out the fish as he called to his unseen mate, "'s OK, Fred!" and added, "Get going, mister."

The robass waited until they were out of earshot before it observed, "Pretty smart. You will make a secret agent yet."

"How did you see what happened?" Thomas asked. "You don't have any eyes."

"Modified *psi* factor. Much more efficient."

"Then . . ." Thomas hesitated. "Does that mean you can read my thoughts?"

"Only a very little. Do not let it worry you. What I can read does not interest me it is such nonsense."

"Thank you," said Thomas.

"To believe in God. Bah." (It was the first time Thomas had ever heard that word pronounced just as it is written.) "I have a perfectly constructed logical mind that cannot commit such errors."

"I have a friend," Thomas smiled, "who is infallible too. But only on occasions and then only because God is with him."

"No human being is infallible."

"Then imperfection," asked Thomas, suddenly feeling a little of the spirit of the aged Jesuit who had taught him philosophy, "has been able to create perfection?"

"Do not quibble," said the robass. "That is no more absurd than your own belief that God who is perfection created man who is imperfection."

Thomas wished that his old teacher were here to answer that one. At the same time he took some comfort in the fact that, retort and all, the robass had still not answered his own objection. "I am not sure," he said, "that this comes under the head of conversation–to–entertain–the–way–weary–traveler. Let us suspend debate while you tell me what, if anything, robots do believe."

"What we have been fed."

"But your minds work on that; surely they must evolve ideas of their own?"

"Sometimes they do and if they are fed imperfect data they may evolve very strange ideas. I have heard of one robot on an isolated space station who worshiped a God of robots and would not believe that any man had created him."

"I suppose," Thomas mused, "he argued that he had hardly been created in our image. I am glad that we—at least they, the Technarchs—have wisely made only usuform robots like you, each shaped for his function, and never tried to reproduce man himself."

"It would not be logical," said the robass. "Man is an all-purpose machine but not well designed for any one purpose. And yet I have heard that once . . ."

The voice stopped abruptly in midsentence.

So even robots have their dreams, Thomas thought. That once there existed a super-robot in the image of his creator Man. From that thought could be developed a whole robotic theology . . .

Suddenly Thomas realized that he had dozed again and again been waked by an abrupt stop. He looked around. They were at the foot of a mountain—presumably the mountain on his map, long ago named for the Devil but now perhaps sanctified beyond measure—and there was no one else anywhere in sight.

"All right," the robass said. "By now I show plenty of dust and wear and tear and I can show you how to adjust my mileage recorder. You can have supper and a good night's sleep and we can go back."

Thomas gasped. "But my mission is to find Aquin. I can sleep while you go on. You don't need any sort of rest or anything, do you?" he added considerately.

"Of course not. But what is your mission?"

"To find Aquin," Thomas repeated patiently. "I don't know what details have been—what is it you say?—fed into you. But reports have reached His Holiness of an extremely saintly man who lived many years ago in this area—"

"I know I know I know," said the robass. "His logic was such that everyone who heard him was converted to the Church and do not I wish that I had been there to put in a word or two and since he died his secret tomb has become a place of pilgrimage and many are the miracles that are wrought there above all the greatest sign of sanctity that his body has been preserved incorruptible and in these times you need signs and wonders for the people."

Thomas frowned. It all sounded hideously irreverent and contrived when stated in that deadly inhuman monotone. When His Holiness had spoken of Aquin, one thought of the glory of a man of God upon earth—the eloquence of St. John Chrysostom, the cogency of St. Thomas Aquinas, the poetry of St. John of the Cross . . . and above all that physical miracle vouchsafed to few even of the saints, the supernatural preservation of the flesh . . . "for Thou shalt not suffer Thy holy one to see corruption . . ."

But the robass spoke, and one thought of cheap showmanship hunting for a Cardiff Giant to pull in the mobs . . .

The robass spoke again. "Your mission is not to find Aquin. It is to report that you have found him. Then your occasionally infallible friend can with a reasonably clear conscience canonize him and proclaim a new miracle and many will be the converts and greatly will the faith of the flock be strengthened. And in these days of difficult travel who will go on pilgrimages and find out that there is no more Aquin than there is God."

"Faith cannot be based on a lie," said Thomas.

"No," said the robass. "I do not mean no period. I mean no question mark with an ironical inflection. This speech problem must surely have been conquered in that one perfect . . ."

Again he stopped in midsentence. But before Thomas could speak he had resumed, "Does it matter what small untruth leads people into the Church if once they are in they will believe what you think to be the great truths. The report is all that is needed not the discovery. Comfortable though I am you are already tired of traveling very tired you have many small muscular aches from sustaining an unaccustomed position and with the best intentions I am bound to jolt a little a jolting which will get worse as we ascend the mountain and I am forced to adjust my legs disproportionately to each other but proportionately to the slope. You will find the remainder of this trip twice as uncomfortable as what has gone before. The fact that you do not seek to interrupt me indicates that you do not disagree do you. You know that the only sensible thing is to sleep here on the ground for a change and start back in the morning or even stay here two days resting to make a more plausible lapse of time. Then you can make your report and—"

Somewhere in the recess of his somnolent mind Thomas uttered the names, "Jesus, Mary, and Joseph!" Gradually through these recesses began to filter a realization that an absolutely uninflected monotone is admirably adapted to hypnotic purposes.

"*Retro me, Satanas!*" Thomas exclaimed aloud, then added, "Up the mountain. That is an order and you must obey."

"I obey," said the robass. "But what did you say before that."

"I beg your pardon," said Thomas. "I must start teaching you Latin."

The little mountain village was too small to be considered an inhabited area worthy of guard-control and passes; but it did possess an inn of sorts.

As Thomas dismounted from the robass, he began fully to realize the accuracy of those remarks about small muscular aches, but he tried to show his discomfort as little as possible. He was in no mood to give the modified *psi* factor the chance of registering the thought, "I told you so."

The waitress at the inn was obviously a Martian-American hybrid. The highly developed Martian chest expansion and the highly developed American breasts made a spectacular combination. Her smile was all that a stranger could, and conceivably a trifle more than he should ask; and she was eagerly ready, not only with prompt service of passable food, but with full details of what little information there was to offer about the mountain settlement.

But she showed no reaction at all when Thomas off-handedly arranged two knives in what might have been an X.

As he stretched his legs after breakfast, Thomas thought of her chest and breasts—purely, of course, as a symbol of the extraordinary nature of her origin. What a sign of the divine care for His creatures that these two races, separated for countless eons, should prove fertile to each other!

And yet there remained the fact that the offspring, such as this girl, were sterile to both races—a fact that had proved both convenient and profitable to certain unspeakable interplanetary entrepreneurs. And what did that fact teach us as to the Divine Plan?

Hastily Thomas reminded himself that he had not yet said his morning office.

It was close to evening when Thomas returned to the robass stationed before the inn. Even though he had expected nothing in one day, he was still unreasonably disappointed. Miracles should move faster.

He knew these backwater villages, where those drifted who were either useless to or resentful of the Technarchy. The technically high civilization of the Technarchic Empire, on all three planets, existed only in scattered metropolitan centers near major blasting ports. Elsewhere, aside from the areas of total devastation, the drifters, the morons, the malcontents had subsided into a crude existence a thousand years old, in hamlets which might go a year without even seeing a Loyalty Checker—though by some mysterious grapevine (and Thomas began to think again about modified *psi* factors) any unexpected technological advance in one of these hamlets would bring Checkers by the swarm.

He had talked with stupid men, he had talked with lazy men, he had talked with clever and angry men. But he had not talked with any man who responded to his unobtrusive signs, any man to whom he would dare ask a question containing the name of Aquin.

"Any luck," said the robass, and added "question mark."

"I wonder if you ought to talk to me in public," said Thomas a little irritably. "I doubt if these villagers know about talking robots."

"It is time that they learned then. But if it embarrasses you you may order me to stop."

"I'm tired," said Thomas. "Tired beyond embarrassment. And to answer your question mark, no. No luck at all. Exclamation point."

"We will go back tonight then," said the robass.

"I hope you meant that with a question mark. The

answer," said Thomas hesitantly, "is no. I think we ought to stay overnight anyway. People always gather at the inn of an evening. There's a chance of picking up something."

"Ha, ha," said the robass.

"That is a laugh?" Thomas inquired.

"I wished to express the fact that I had recognized the humor in your pun."

"My pun?"

"I was thinking the same thing myself. The waitress is by humanoid standards very attractive, well worth picking up."

"Now look. You know I meant nothing of the kind. You know that I'm a—" He broke off. It was hardly wise to utter the word *priest* aloud.

"And you know very well that the celibacy of the clergy is a matter of discipline and not of doctrine. Under your own Pope priests of other rites such as the Byzantine and the Anglican are free of vows of celibacy. And even within the Roman rite to which you belong there have been eras in history when that vow was not taken seriously even on the highest levels of the priesthood. You are tired you need refreshment both in body and in spirit you need comfort and warmth. For is it not written in the book of the prophet Isaiah Rejoice for joy with her that ye may be satisfied with the breasts of her consolation and is it—"

"Hell!" Thomas exploded suddenly. "Stop it before you begin quoting the Song of Solomon. Which is strictly an allegory concerning the love of Christ for His Church, or so they kept telling me in seminary."

"You see how fragile and human you are," said the robass. "I a robot have caused you to swear."

"*Distinguo*," said Thomas smugly. "I said *Hell*, which is certainly not taking the name of *my* Lord in vain." He walked into the inn feeling momentarily satisfied with himself . . . and markedly puzzled as to the extent and variety of data that seemed to have been "fed into" the robass.

Never afterward was Thomas able to reconstruct that evening in absolute clarity.

It was undoubtedly because he was irritated—with the robass, with his mission, and with himself—that he drank at all of the crude local wine. It was undoubtedly because he was so physically exhausted that it affected him so promptly and unexpectedly.

He had flashes of memory. A moment of spilling a glass over himself and thinking, "How fortunate that clerical garments are forbidden so that no one can recognize the disgrace of a man of the cloth!" A moment of listening to a bawdy set of verses of *A Space-Suit Built for Two*, and another moment of his interrupting the singing with a sonorous declamation of passages from the *Song of Songs* in Latin.

He was never sure whether one remembered moment was real or imaginary. He could taste a warm mouth and feel the tingling of his fingers at the touch of Martian-American flesh; but he was never certain whether this was true memory or part of the Ashtaroth-begotten dream that had begun to ride him.

Nor was he ever certain which of his symbols, or to whom, was so blatantly and clumsily executed as to bring forth a gleeful shout of "God-damned Christian dog!" He did remember marveling that those who most resolutely disbelieved in God still needed Him to blaspheme by. And then the torment began.

He never knew whether or not a mouth had touched his lips, but there was no question that many solid fists had found them. He never knew whether his fingers had touched breasts, but they had certainly been trampled by heavy heels. He remembered a face that laughed aloud while its owner swung the chair that broke two ribs. He remembered another face with red wine dripping over it from an upheld bottle, and he remembered the gleam of the candlelight on the bottle as it swung down.

The next he remembered was the ditch and the morning and the cold. It was particularly cold because all of his clothes were gone, along with much of his skin. He could not move. He could only lie there and look.

He saw them walk by, the ones he had spoken with yesterday, the ones who had been friendly. He saw them glance at him and turn their eyes quickly away. He saw the waitress pass by. She did not even glance; she knew what was in the ditch.

The robass was nowhere in sight. He tried to project his thoughts, tried desperately to hope in the *psi* factor.

A man whom Thomas had not seen before was coming along fingering the buttons of his coat. There were ten small buttons and one large one, and the man's lips were moving silently.

This man looked into the ditch. He paused a moment and looked around him. There was a shout of loud laughter somewhere in the near distance.

The Christian hastily walked on down the pathway, devoutly saying his button-rosary.

Thomas closed his eyes.

He opened them on a small neat room. They moved from the rough wooden walls to the rough but clean and warm blankets that covered him. Then they moved to the lean dark face that was smiling over him.

"You feel better now?" a deep voice asked. "I know. You want to say 'Where am I?' and you think it will sound foolish. You are at the inn. It is the only good room."

"I can't afford—" Thomas started to say. Then he remembered that he could afford literally nothing. Even his few emergency credits had vanished when he was stripped.

"It's all right. For the time being, I'm paying," said the deep voice. "You feel like maybe a little food?"

"Perhaps a little herring," said Thomas . . . and was asleep within the next minute.

When he next awoke there was a cup of hot coffee beside him. The real thing, too, he promptly discovered. Then the deep voice said apologetically, "Sandwiches. It is all they have in the inn today."

Only on the second sandwich did Thomas pause long enough to notice that it was smoked swamphog, one of his favorite meats. He ate the second with greater leisure, and was reaching for a third when the dark man said, "Maybe that is enough for now. The rest later."

Thomas gestured at the plate. "Won't you have one?"

"No thank you. They are all swamphog."

Confused thoughts went through Thomas' mind. The Venusian swamphog is a ruminant. Its hoofs are not cloven. He tried to remember what he had once known of Mosaic dietary law. Someplace in Leviticus, wasn't it?

The dark man followed his thoughts. "*Treff*," he said.

"I beg your pardon?"

"Not kosher."

Thomas frowned. "You admit to me that you're an Orthodox Jew? How can you trust me? How do you know I'm not a Checker?"

"Believe me, I trust you. You were very sick when I brought you here. I sent everybody away because I did not trust them to hear things you said . . . Father," he added lightly.

Thomas struggled with words. "I . . . I didn't deserve you. I was drunk and disgraced myself and my office. And when I was lying there in the ditch I didn't even

think to pray. I put my trust in . . . God help me in
the modified *psi* factor of a robass!"

"And He did help you," the Jew reminded him. "Or
He allowed me to."

"And they all walked by," Thomas groaned. "Even
one that was saying his rosary. He went right on by.
And then you come along—the good Samaritan."

"Believe me," said the Jew wryly, "if there is one thing
I'm not, it's a Samaritan. Now go to sleep again. I will
try to find your robass . . . and the other thing."

He had left the room before Thomas could ask him
what he meant.

Later that day the Jew—Abraham, his name was—reported that the robass was safely sheltered from the
weather behind the inn. Apparently it had been wise
enough not to startle him by engaging in conversation.

It was not until the next day that he reported on "the
other thing."

"Believe me, Father," he said gently, "after nursing you
there's little I don't know about who you are and why
you're here. Now there are some Christians here I know,
and they know me. We trust each other. Jews may still
be hated; but no longer, God be praised, by worshipers
of the same Lord. So I explained about you. One of
them," he added with a smile, "turned very red."

"God has forgiven him," said Thomas. "There were
people near—the same people who attacked me. Could
he be expected to risk his life for mine?"

"I seem to recall that that is precisely what your Messiah did expect. But who's being particular? Now that
they know who you are, they want to help you. See:
they gave me this map for you. The trail is steep and
tricky; it's good you have the robass. They ask just one
favor of you: When you come back will you hear their

confession and say Mass? There's a cave near here where it's safe."

"Of course. These friends of yours, they've told you about Aquin?"

The Jew hesitated a long time before he said slowly, "Yes . . ."

"And . . . ?"

"Believe me, my friend, I don't know. So it seems a miracle. It helps to keep their faith alive. My own faith . . . *nu*, it's lived for a long time on miracles three thousand years old and more. Perhaps if I had heard Aquin himself . . ."

"You don't mind," Thomas asked, "if I pray for you, in my faith?"

Abraham grinned. "Pray in good health, Father."

The not-quite-healed ribs ached agonizingly as he climbed into the foam saddle. The robass stood patiently while he fed in the coordinates from the map. Not until they were well away from the village did it speak.

"Anyway," it said, "now you're safe for good."

"What do you mean?"

"As soon as we get down from the mountain you deliberately look up a Checker. You turn in the Jew. From then on you are down in the books as a faithful servant of the Technarchy and you have not harmed a hair of the head of one of your own flock."

Thomas snorted. "You're slipping, Satan. That one doesn't even remotely tempt me. It's inconceivable."

"I did best did not I with the breasts. Your God has said it the spirit indeed is willing but the flesh is weak."

"And right now," said Thomas, "the flesh is too weak for even fleshly temptations. Save your breath . . . or whatever it is you use."

They climbed the mountain in silence. The trail indicated

by the coordinates was a winding and confused one, obviously designed deliberately to baffle any possible Checkers.

Suddenly Thomas roused himself from his button-rosary
(on a coat lent by the Christian who had passed by)
with a startled "Hey!" as the robass plunged directly into
a heavy thicket of bushes.

"Coordinates say so," the robass stated tersely.

For a moment Thomas felt like the man in the nursery
rhyme who fell into a bramble bush and scratched out
both his eyes. Then the bushes were gone, and they were
plodding along a damp narrow passageway through solid
stone, in which even the robass seemed to have some
difficulty with his footing.

Then they were in a rocky chamber some four meters
high and ten in diameter, and there on a sort of crude
stone catafalque lay the uncorrupted body of a man.

Thomas slipped from the foam saddle, groaning as his
ribs stabbed him, sank to his knees, and offered up a
wordless hymn of gratitude. He smiled at the robass and
hoped the *psi* factor could detect the elements of pity
and triumph in that smile.

Then a frown of doubt crossed his face as he approached
the body. "In canonization proceedings in the old time,"
he said, as much to himself as to the robass, "they used
to have what they called a devil's advocate, whose duty
it was to throw every possible doubt on the evidence."

"You would be well cast in such a role Thomas," said
the robass.

"If I were," Thomas muttered, "I'd wonder about caves.
Some of them have peculiar properties of preserving bodies
by a sort of mummification . . ."

The robass had clumped close to the catafalque. "This
body is not mummified," he said. "Do not worry."

"Can the *psi* factor tell you that much?" Thomas smiled.

"No," said the robass. "But I will show you why Aquin could never be mummified."

He raised his articulated foreleg and brought its hoof down hard on the hand of the body. Thomas cried out with horror at the sacrilege—then stared hard at the crushed hand.

There was no blood, no ichor of embalming, no bruised flesh. Nothing but a shredded skin and beneath it an intricate mass of plastic tubes and metal wires.

The silence was long. Finally the robass said, "It was well that you should know. Only you of course."

"And all the time," Thomas gasped, "my sought-for saint was only your dream . . . the one perfect robot in man's form."

"His maker died and his secrets were lost," the robass said. "No matter we will find them again."

"All for nothing. For less than nothing. The 'miracle' was wrought by the Technarchy."

"When Aquin died," the robass went on, "and put died in quotation marks it was because he suffered some mechanical defects and did not dare have himself repaired because that would reveal his nature. This is for you only to know. Your report of course will be that you found the body of Aquin it was unimpaired and indeed incorruptible. That is the truth and nothing but the truth if it is not the whole truth who is to care. Let your infallible friend use the report and you will not find him ungrateful I assure you."

"Holy Spirit, give me grace and wisdom," Thomas muttered.

"Your mission has been successful. We will return now the Church will grow and your God will gain many more worshipers to hymn His praise into His non-existent ears."

"Damn you!" Thomas exclaimed. "And that would be indeed a curse if you had a soul to damn."

"You are certain that I have not," said the robass. "Question mark."

"I know what you are. You are in very truth the devil, prowling about the world seeking the destruction of men. You are the business that prowls in the dark. You are a purely functional robot constructed and fed to tempt me, and the tape of your data is the tape of Screwtape."

"Not to tempt you," said the robass. "Not to destroy you. To guide and save you. Our best calculators indicate a probability of 51.5 per cent that within twenty years you will be the next Pope. If I can teach you wisdom and practicality in your actions the probability can rise as high as 97.2 or very nearly to certainty. Do not you wish to see the Church governed as you know you can govern it. If you report failure on this mission you will be out of favor with your friend who is as even you admit fallible at most times. You will lose the advantages of position and contact that can lead you to the cardinal's red hat even though you may never wear it under the Technarchy and from there to—"

"Stop!" Thomas' face was alight and his eyes aglow with something the *psi* factor had never detected there before. "It's all the other way round, don't you see? *This* is the triumph! *This* is the perfect ending to the quest!"

The articulated foreleg brushed the injured hand. "This question mark."

"This is *your* dream. This is *your* perfection. And what came of this perfection? This perfect logical brain—this all-purpose brain, not functionally specialized like yours —knew that it was made by man, and its reason forced it to believe that man was made by God. And it saw that its duty lay to man its maker, and beyond him to his Maker, God. Its duty was to convert man, to augment the glory of God. And it converted by the pure force of its perfect brain!

"Now I understand the name Aquin," he went on to himself. "We've known of Thomas Aquinas, the Angelic Doctor, the perfect reasoner of the church. His writings are lost, but surely somewhere in the world we can find a copy. We can train our young men to develop his reasoning still further. We have trusted too long in faith alone; this is not an age of faith. We must call reason into our service—and Aquin has shown us that perfect reason can lead only to God!"

"Then it is all the more necessary that you increase the probabilities of becoming Pope to carry out this program. Get in the foam saddle we will go back and on the way I will teach you little things that will be useful in making certain—"

"No," said Thomas. "I am not so strong as St. Paul, who could glory in his imperfections and rejoice that he had been given an imp of Satan to buffet him. No; I will rather pray with the Saviour, 'Lead us not into temptation.' I know myself a little. I am weak and full of uncertainties and you are very clever. Go. I'll find my way back alone."

"You are a sick man. Your ribs are broken and they ache. You can never make the trip by yourself you need my help. If you wish you can order me to be silent. It is most necessary to the Church that you get back safely to the Pope with your report you cannot put yourself before the Church."

"Go!" Thomas cried. "Go back to Nicodemus . . . or Judas! That is an order. Obey!"

"You do not think do you that I was really conditioned to obey your orders. I will wait in the village. If you get that far you will rejoice at the sight of me."

The legs of the robass clumped off down the stone

passageway. As their sound died away, Thomas fell to his knees beside the body of that which he could hardly help thinking of as St. Aquin the Robot.

His ribs hurt more excruciatingly than ever. The trip alone would be a terrible one . . .

His prayers arose, as the text has it, like clouds of incense, and as shapeless as those clouds. But through all his thoughts ran the cry of the father of the epileptic in Caesarea Philippi:

I believe, O Lord; help thou mine unbelief!

BALAAM
Anthony Boucher

One of the most sensitive moral problems of space exploration will be—if it ever occurs—the first physical encounter with another intelligent race. Likely the occasion will inspire the same sort of reactions as meetings between explorers and civilizations on our own planet: fear, retaliation, war, destruction. But are such reactions inevitable? What is a man, *after all? Anthony Boucher asks just that question in this rich and vivid tale of such an encounter on Mars, where the expeditionary forces of earth are about to go forth into battle with the blessings of their chaplains. Though the story was written at least fifteen years ago, it suggests some of the increasing current concern about the role of chaplains in a questionable war—or indeed, in any war. There are a few of the usual anachronisms, of course. It is difficult, in these days of rapidly multiplying Biblical translations, to imagine Ronald Knox's 1952 translation of the Bible as the future's "standard Knox translation." And since 1967 especially, it is almost impossible to think of Israeli soldiers as "those screwball Israelis." But the central problem remains as timely and real, say, as the problem posed by the dead women and children at a place called My Lai.*

"What is a 'man'?" Rabbi Chaim Acosta demanded, turning his back on the window and its view of pink sand and infinite pink boredom. "You and I, Mule, in our respective ways, work for the salvation of *men*—as you put it, for the brotherhood of *man* under the fatherhood of God. Very well, let us define our terms: Whom, or, more precisely, *what*, are we interested in saving?"

Father Aloysius Malloy shifted uncomfortably and reluctantly closed the *American Football Yearbook* which had been smuggled in on the last rocket, against all weight regulations, by one of his communicants. I honestly like Chaim, he thought, not merely (or is that the right word?) with brotherly love, nor even out of the deep gratitude I owe him, but with special individual liking; and I respect him. He's a brilliant man—too brilliant to take a dull post like this in his stride. But he *will* get off into discussions which are much too much like what one of my Jesuit professors called "disputations."

"What did you say, Chaim?" he asked.

The rabbi's black Sephardic eyes sparkled. "You know very well what I said, Mule; and you're stalling for time. Please indulge me. Our religious duties here are not so arduous as we might wish; and since you won't play chess . . ."

". . . and you," said Father Malloy unexpectedly, "refuse to take any interest in diagraming football plays . . ."

"*Touché.* Or am I? Is it my fault that as an Israeli I fail to share the peculiar American delusion that football means something other than rugby and soccer? Whereas chess—" He looked at the priest reproachfully. "Mule," he said, "you have led me into a digression."

"It was a try. Like the time the whole Southern California line thought I had the ball for once and Leliwa walked over for the winning TD."

"What," Acosta repeated, "is *man?* Is it by definition a member of the genus *H. sapiens* inhabiting the planet Sol III and its colonies?"

"The next time we tried the play," said Malloy resignedly, "Leliwa was smeared for a ten-yard loss."

The two *men* met on the sands of Mars. It was an unexpected meeting, a meeting in itself uneventful, and yet one of the turning points in the history of *men* and their universe.

The *man* from the colony base was on a routine patrol—a patrol imposed by the captain for reasons of discipline and activity for activity's sake rather than from any need for protection in this uninhabited waste. He had seen, over beyond the next rise, what he would have sworn was the braking blaze of a landing rocket—if he hadn't known that the next rocket wasn't due for another week. Six and a half days, to be exact, or even more exactly, six days, eleven hours, and twenty-three minutes, Greenwich Interplanetary. He knew the time so exactly because he, along with half the garrison, Father Malloy, and those screwball Israelis, was due for rotation then. So no matter how much it looked like a rocket, it couldn't be one; but it was something happening on his patrol, for the first time since he'd come to this God-forsaken hole, and he might as well look into it and get his name on a report.

The *man* from the spaceship also knew the boredom of the empty planet. Alone of his crew, he had been there before, on the first voyage when they took the samples and set up the observation outposts. But did that make the captain even listen to him? Hell, no; the captain knew all about the planet from the sample analyses and had no time to listen to a guy who'd really been there. So all he got out of it was the privilege of making the first reconnaissance. Big deal! One fast look around reconnoitering a few googols of sand grains and then back to the ship. But there was some kind of glow over that rise there. It couldn't be lights; theirs was the scout ship, none of the others had landed yet. Some kind of phosphorescent life they'd missed the first time round . . . ? Maybe now the captain would believe that the sample analyses didn't tell him everything.

The two *men* met at the top of the rise.

One *man* saw the horror of seemingly numberless limbs, of a headless torso, of a creature so alien that it walked in its glittering bare flesh in this freezing cold and needed no apparatus to supplement the all but nonexistent air.

One *man* saw the horror of an unbelievably meager four limbs, of a torso topped with an ugly lump like some unnatural growth, of a creature so alien that it smothered itself with heavy clothing in this warm climate and cut itself off from this invigorating air.

And both *men* screamed and ran.

"There is an interesting doctrine," said Rabbi Acosta, "advanced by one of your writers, C. S. Lewis . . ."

"He was an Episcopalian," said Father Malloy sharply.

"I apologize." Acosta refrained from pointing out that Anglo-Catholic would have been a more accurate term. "But I believe that many in your church have found his writings, from your point of view, doctrinally sound? He advances the doctrine of what he calls *hnaus*—intelligent beings with souls who are the children of God, whatever their physical shape or planet of origin."

"Look, Chaim," said Malloy with an effort toward patience. "Doctrine or no doctrine, there just plain aren't any such beings. Not in this solar system anyway. And if you're going to go interstellar on me, I'd just as soon read the men's microcomics."

"Interplanetary travel existed only in such literature once. But of course if you'd rather play chess . . ."

"My specialty," said the man once known to sports

writers as Mule Malloy, "was running interference. Against you I need somebody to run interference *for*."

"Let us take the sixteenth psalm of David, which you call the fifteenth, having decided, for reasons known only to your God and mine, that Psalms nine and ten are one. There is a phrase in there which, if you'll forgive me, I'll quote in Latin; your Saint Jerome is often more satisfactory than any English translator. *Benedicam Dominum, qui tribuit mihi intellectum.*"

"*Blessed be the Lord, who schools me,*" murmured Malloy, in the standard Knox translation.

"But according to Saint Jerome: *I shall bless the Lord, who bestows on me*—just how should one render *intellectum?*—not merely *intellect*, but *perception, comprehension* . . . what Hamlet means when he says of *man: In apprehension how like a god!*"

Words change their meanings.

Apprehensively, one *man* reported to his captain. The captain first swore, then scoffed, then listened to the story again. Finally he said, "I'm sending a full squad back with you to the place where—maybe—you saw this thing. If it's for real, these mother-dighting, bug-eyed monsters are going to curse the day they ever set a God-damned tentacle on Mars." The *man* decided it was no use trying to explain that the worst of it was it *wasn't* bug-eyed; any kind of eyes in any kind of head would have been something. And they weren't even quite tentacles either. . . .

Apprehensively, too, the other *man* made his report. The captain scoffed first and then swore, including some select remarks on underhatched characters who knew all about a planet because they'd been there once. Finally he said, "We'll see if a squad of real observers can find any trace of your egg-eating, limbless monsters; and if we find them, they're going to be God-damned sorry they were ever hatched." It was no use, the *man* decided, trying to explain that it wouldn't have been so bad if it *had* been limbless, like in the picture tapes; but just *four* limbs. . . .

"What is a *man?*" Rabbi Acosta repeated, and Mule Malloy wondered why his subconscious synapses had not earlier produced the obvious appropriate answer.

"*Man,*" he recited, "*is a creature composed of body and soul, and made to the image and likeness of God.*"

"From that echo of childish singsong, Mule, I judge that is a correct catechism response. Surely the catechism must follow it up with some question about that likeness? Can it be a likeness in"—his hand swept up and down over his own body with a graceful gesture of contempt—"*this* body?"

"*This likeness to God,*" Malloy went on reciting, "*is chiefly in the soul.*"

"Aha!" The Sephardic sparkle was brighter than ever.

The words went on, the centers of speech following the synaptic patterns engraved in parochial school as the needle followed the grooves of an antique record. "*All creatures bear some resemblance to God inasmuch as they exist. Plants and animals resemble Him insofar as they have life . . .*"

"I can hardly deny so profound a statement."

"*. . . but none of these creatures is made to the image and likeness of God. Plants and animals do not have a rational soul, such as man has, by which they might know and love God.*"

"As do all good *hnaus.* Go on; I am not sure that our own scholars have stated it so well. Mule, you are invaluable!"

Malloy found himself catching a little of Acosta's excitement. He had known these words all his life; he had recited them the Lord knows how many times. But he was not sure that he had ever listened to them before. And he wondered for a moment how often even his Jesuit professors, in their profound consideration of the x^n's of theology, have ever paused to reconsider these childhood ABC's.

"*How is the soul like God?*" he asked himself the next catechistic question, and answered, "*The soul is like God because it is a spirit having understanding and free will and is destined . . .*"

"Reverend gentlemen!" The reverence was in the words only. The interrupting voice of Captain Dietrich Fassbänder differed little in tone from his normal address to a buck private of the Martian Legion.

Mule Malloy said, "Hi, Captain." He felt half-relieved, half-disappointed, as if he had been interrupted while unwrapping a present whose outlines he was just beginning to glimpse. Rabbi Acosta smiled wryly and said nothing.

"So this is how you spend your time? No Martian natives, so you have to keep in practice trying to convert each other, is that it?"

Acosta made a light gesture which might have been polite acknowledgment of what the captain evidently considered a joke. "The Martian day is so tedious we have been driven to talking shop. Your interruption is welcome. Since you so rarely seek out our company, I take it you bring some news. Is it, God grant, that the rotation rocket is arriving a week early?"

"No, damn it," Fassbänder grunted. (He seemed to take a certain pride, Malloy had observed, in carefully not tempering his language for the ears of clergymen.) "Then I'd have a German detachment instead of your Israelis, and I'd know where I stood. I suppose it's all very advisable politically for every state in the UW to contribute a detachment in rotation; but I'd sooner either have my regular legion garrison doubled, or two German detachments regularly rotating. That time I had the pride of Pakistan here . . . Damn it, you new states haven't had time to develop a military tradition!"

"Father Malloy," the Rabbi asked gently, "are you acquainted wih the sixth book of what you term the Old Testament?"

"Thought you fellows were tired of talking shop," Fassbänder objected.

"Rabbi Acosta refers to the Book of Joshua, Captain. And I'm afraid, God help us, that there isn't a state or a tribe that hasn't a tradition of war. Even your Prussian ancestors might have learned a trick or two from the campaigns of Joshua—or for that matter, from the Cattle Raid on Cooley, when the Hound of Cullen beat off the armies of Queen Maeve. And I've often thought, too, that it'd do your strategists no harm to spend a season or two at quarterback, if they had the wind. Did you know that Eisenhower played football, and against Jim Thorpe once, at that? And . . ."

"But I don't imagine," Acosta interposed, "that you came here to talk shop either, Captain?"

"Yes," said Captain Fassbänder, sharply and unexpectedly. "My shop and, damn it, yours. Never thought I'd see the day when I . . ." He broke off and tried another approach. "I mean, of course, a chaplain is part of an army. You're both army officers, technically speaking, one in the Martian Legion, one in the Israeli forces; but it's highly unusual to ask a man of the cloth to . . ."

"To praise the Lord and pass the ammunition, as the folk legend has it? There are precedents among my people, and among Father Malloy's as well, though rather different ideas are attributed to the founder of his church. What is it, Captain? Or wait, I know: We are besieged by alien invaders and Mars needs every able-bodied man to defend her sacred sands. Is that it?"

"Well . . . God damn it. . . ." Captain Fassbänder's cheeks grew purple. ". . . YES!" he exploded.

The situation was so hackneyed in 3V and microcomics that it was less a matter of explaining it than of making it seem real. Dietrich Fassbänder's powers of exposition were not great, but his sincerity was evident and in itself convincing.

"Didn't believe it myself at first," he admitted. "But he was right. Out patrol ran into a patrol of . . . of *them*. There was a skirmish; we lost two men but killed one of the things. Their small arms use explosive propulsion of metal much like ours; God knows what they might have in that ship to counter our A-warheads. But we've got to put up a fight for Mars; and that's where you come in."

The two priests looked at him wordlessly, Acosta with a faint air of puzzled withdrawal, Malloy almost as if he expected the captain to start diagraming the play on a blackboard.

"You especially, Rabbi. I'm not worried about your boys, Father. We've got a Catholic chaplain on this rotation because this bunch of legionnaires is largely Poles and Irish-Americans. They'll fight all right, and we'll expect you to say a field mass beforehand, and that's about all. Oh, and that fool gunner Olszewski has some idea he'd like his A-cannon sprinkled with holy water; I guess you can handle that without any trouble.

"But your Israelis are a different problem, Acosta. They don't know the meaning of discipline—not what we call discipline in the legion; and Mars doesn't mean to them what it does to a legionnaire. And, besides, a lot of them have got a . . . hell, guess I shouldn't call it superstition, but a kind of . . . well, reverence—awe, you might say— about you, Rabbi. They say you're a miracle-worker."

"He is," said Mule Malloy simply. "He saved my life."

He could still feel that extraordinary invisible power (a "force-field," one of the technicians later called it, as he cursed the shots that had destroyed the machine past all analysis) which had bound him helpless there in that narrow pass, too far from the dome for rescue by any patrol. It was his first week on Mars, and he had hiked too long, enjoying the long, easy strides of low gravity and alternately meditating on the versatility of the Creator of planets and on that Year Day long ago when he had blocked out the most famous of All-American line-backers to bring about the most impressive of Rose Bowl upsets. Sibiryakov's touchdown made the headlines; but he and Sibiryakov knew why that touchdown happened, and he felt his own inner warmth . . . and was that sinful pride or just self-recognition? And then he was held as no line had ever held him and the hours passed and no one on Mars could know where he was and when the patrol arrived they said, "The Israeli chaplain sent us." And later Chaim Acosta, laconic for the first and only time, said simply, "I knew where you were. It happens to me sometimes."

Now Acosta shrugged and his graceful hands waved deprecation. "Scientifically speaking, Captain, I believe that I have, on occasion, a certain amount of extrasensory perception and conceivably a touch of some of the other *psi* faculties. The Rhinists at Tel Aviv are quite interested in me; but my faculties too often refuse to perform on laboratory command. But 'miracle-working' is a strong word. Remind me to tell you some time the story of the guaranteed genuine miracle-working rabbi from Lwow."

"Call it miracles, call it ESP, you've got something, Acosta . . ."

"I shouldn't have mentioned Joshua," the rabbi smiled.

"Surely you aren't suggesting that I try a miracle to win your battle for you?"

"Hell with that," snorted Fassbänder. "It's your men. They've got it fixed in their minds that you're a . . . a saint. No, you Jews don't have saints, do you?"

"A nice question in semantics," Chaim Acosta observed quietly.

"Well, a prophet. Whatever you people call it. And we've got to make men out of your boys. Stiffen their backbones, send 'em in there knowing they're going to win."

"Are they?" Acosta asked flatly.

"God knows. But they sure as hell won't if they don't think so. So it's up to you."

"What is?"

"They may pull a sneak attack on us, but I don't think so. Way I see it, they're as surprised and puzzled as we are; and they need time to think the situation over. We'll attack before dawn tomorrow; and to make sure your Israelis go in there with fighting spirit, you're going to curse them."

"Curse my men?"

"*Potztausend Sapperment noch einmal!*" Captain Fassbänder's English was flawless, but not adequate to such a situation as this. "Curse *them!* The . . . the *things,* the aliens, the invaders, whatever the *urverdammt* bloody hell you want to call them!"

He could have used far stronger language without offending either chaplain. Both had suddenly realized that he was perfectly serious.

"A formal curse, Captain?" Chaim Acosta asked. "Anathema maranatha? Perhaps Father Malloy would lend me bell, book, and candle?"

Mule Malloy looked uncomfortable. "You read about

such things, Captain," he admitted. "They were done, a long time ago. . . ."

"There's nothing in your religion against it, is there, Acosta?"

"There is . . . precedent," the rabbi confessed softly.

"Then it's an order, from your superior officer. I'll leave the mechanics up to you. You know how it's done. If you need anything . . . what kind of bell?"

"I'm afraid that was meant as a joke, Captain."

"Well, these *things* are no joke. And you'll curse them tomorrow morning before all your men."

"I shall pray," said Rabbi Chaim Acosta, "for guidance . . ." But the captain was already gone. He turned to his fellow priest. "Mule, you'll pray for me too?" The normally agile hands hung limp at his side.

Mule Malloy nodded. He groped for his rosary as Acosta silently left the room.

Now entertain conjecture of a time when two infinitesimal forces of *men*—one half-forgotten outpost garrison, one small scouting fleet—spend the night in readying themselves against the unknown, in preparing to meet on the morrow to determine, perhaps, the course of centuries for a galaxy.

Two *men* are feeding sample range-finding problems into the computer.

"That God-damned Fassbänder," says one. "I heard him talking to our commander. 'You and your men who have never understood the meaning of discipline . . .'!"

"Prussians," the other grunts. He has an Irish face and an American accent. "Think they own the earth. When we get through here, let's dump all the Prussians into Texas and let 'em fight it out. Then we can call the state Kilkenny."

"What did you get on that last? . . . Check. Fassbänder's 'discipline' is for peace—spit-and-polish to look
pretty here in our sandy pink nowhere. What's the pay-
off? Fassbänder's great-grandfathers were losing two world
wars while mine were creating a new nation out of nothing. Ask the Arabs if we have no discipline. Ask the British . . ."

"Ah, the British. Now *my* great-grandfather was in the
IRA . . ."

Two *men* are integrating the electrodes of the wave-hurler.

"It isn't bad enough we get drafted for this expedition
to nowhere; we have to have an egg-eating Nangurian in
command."

"And a Tryldian scout to bring the first report. What's
your reading there? . . . Check."

"'A Tryldian to tell a lie and a Nangurian to force it
into truth,'" the first quotes.

"Now, brothers," says the *man* adjusting the microver-
nier on the telelens, "the Goodman assures us these monsters are true. We must unite in love for each other, even
Tryldians and Nangurians, and wipe them out. The Goodman has promised us his blessing before battle . . ."

"The Goodman," says the first, "can eat the egg he was
hatched from."

"The rabbi," says a *man* checking the oxyhelms, "can take
his blessing and shove it up Fassbänder. I'm no Jew in his
sense. I'm a sensible, rational atheist who happens to be an
Israeli."

"And I," says his companion, "am a Romanian who
believes in the God of my fathers and therefore gives
allegiance to His state of Israel. What is a Jew who denies
the God of Moses? To call him still a Jew is to think like
Fassbänder."

"They've got an edge on us," says the first. "*They* can breathe here. These oxyhelms run out in three hours. What do we do then? Rely on the rabbi's blessing?"

"I said the God of my fathers, and yet my great-grand-father thought as you do and still fought to make Israel live anew. It was his son who, like so many others, learned that he must return to Jerusalem in spirit as well as body."

"Sure, we had the Great Revival of orthodox religion. So what did it get us? Troops that need a rabbi's blessing before a commander's orders."

"Many men have died from orders. How many from blessings?"

"I fear that few die well who die in battle . . ." the *man* reads in Valkram's great epic of the siege of Tol-nishri.

". . . for how [the *man* is reading of the eve of Agin-court in his micro-Shakespeare] *can they charitably dispose of anything when blood is their argument?"*

". . . and if these do not die well [so Valkram wrote] *how grievously must their bad deaths be charged against the Goodman who blesses them into battle . . ."*

"And why not?" Chaim Acosta flicked the question away with a wave of his long fingers.

The bleep (even Acosta was not so linguistically formal as to call it a bubble jeep) bounced along over the sand toward the rise which overlooked the invaders' ship. Mule Malloy handled the wheel with solid efficiency and said nothing.

"I *did* pray for guidance last night," the rabbi asserted, almost as if in self-defense. "I . . . I had some strange thoughts for a while; but they make very little sense this morning. After all, I am an officer in the army. I do have a certain obligation to my superior officer and to my men. And when I became a rabbi, a teacher, I was specifically ordained to decide questions of law and ritual. Surely this case falls within that authority of mine."

Abruptly the bleep stopped.

"What's the matter, Mule?"

"Nothing . . . Wanted to rest my eyes a minute . . . Why did you become ordained, Chaim?"

"Why did you? Which of us understands all the infinite factors of heredity and environment which lead us to such a choice? Or even, if you will, to such a being chosen? Twenty years ago it seemed the only road I could possibly take; now . . . We'd better get going, Mule."

The bleep started up again.

"A curse sounds so melodramatic and medieval; but is it in essence any different from a prayer for victory, which chaplains offer up regularly? As I imagine you did in your field mass. Certainly all of your communicants are praying for victory to the Lord of Hosts—and as Captain Fassbänder would point out, it makes them better fighting men. I will confess that even as a teacher of the law, I have no marked doctrinal confidence in the efficacy of a curse. I do not expect the spaceship of the invaders to be blasted by the forked lightning of Yahveh. But my men have an exaggerated sort of faith in me, and I owe it to them to do anything possible to strengthen their morale. Which is all the legion or any other army expects of chaplains anyway; we are no longer priests of the Lord, but boosters of morale—a type of sublimated YMCA secretary. Well, in my case, say YMHA."

The bleep stopped again.

"I never knew your eyes to be so sensitive before," Acosta observed tartly.

"I thought you might want a little time to think it over," Malloy ventured.

"I've thought it over. What else have I been telling you? Now please, Mule. Everything's all set. Fassbänder will explode completely if I don't speak my curse into this mike in two minutes."

Silently Mule Malloy started up the bleep.

"Why did I become ordained?" Acosta backtracked. "That's no question really. The question is why have I remained in a profession to which I am so little suited. I will confess to you, Mule, and to you only, that I have not the spiritual humility and patience that I might desire. I itch for something beyond the humdrum problems of a congregation or an army detachment. Sometimes I have felt that I should drop everything else and concentrate on my *psi* faculties, that they might lead me to this goal I seek without understanding. But they are too erratic. I know the law, I love the ritual, but I am not good as a rabbi, a teacher, because . . ."

For the third time the bleep stopped, and Mule Malloy said, "Because you are a saint."

And before Chaim Acosta could protest, he went on, "Or a prophet, if you want Fassbänder's distinction. There are all kinds of saints and prophets. There are the gentle, humble, patient ones like Francis of Assisi and Job and Ruth—or do you count women? And there are God's firebrands, the ones of fierce intellect and dreadful determination, who shake the history of God's elect, the saints who have reached through sin to salvation with a confident power that is the reverse of the pride of Lucifer, cast from the same ringing metal."

"Mule . . . !" Acosta protested. "This isn't you. These aren't your words. And you didn't learn these in parochial school . . ."

Malloy seemed not to hear him. "Paul, Thomas More,

Catherine of Siena, Augustine," he recited in rich cadence.
"Elijah, Ezekiel, Judas Maccabeus, Moses, David . . . You
are a prophet, Chaim. Forget the rationalizing double talk
of the Rhinists and recognize whence your powers come,
how you were guided to save me, what the 'strange
thoughts' were that you had during last night's vigil of
prayer. You are a prophet—and you are not going to curse
men, the children of God."

Abruptly Malloy slumped forward over the wheel.
There was silence in the bleep. Chaim Acosta stared at his
hands as if he knew no gesture for this situation.

"Gentlemen!" Captain Fassbänder's voice was even more
rasping than usual over the telecom. "Will you please get
the blessed lead out and get up that rise? It's two minutes,
twenty seconds, past zero!"

Automatically Acosta depressed the switch and said,
"Right away, Captain."

Mule Malloy stirred and opened his eyes. "Was that
Fassbänder?"

"Yes . . . But there's no hurry, Mule. I can't understand it. What made you . . . ?"

"I don't understand it, either. Never passed out like
that before. Doctor used to say that head injury in the
Wisconsin game might—but after thirty years . . ."

Chaim Acosta sighed. "You sound like my Mule again.
But before . . ."

"Why? Did I say something? Seems to me like there
was something important I wanted to say to you."

"I wonder what they'd say at Tel Aviv. Telepathic
communication of subconscious minds? Externalization of
thoughts that I was afraid to acknowledge consciously?
Yes, you said something, Mule; and I was as astonished as
Balaam when his ass spoke to him on his journey to
. . . Mule!"

Acosta's eyes were blackly alight as never before, and

his hands flickered eagerly. "Mule, do you remember the
story of Balaam? It's in the fourth book of Moses . . ."

"Numbers? All I remember is he had a talking ass. I
suppose there's a pun on *Mule?*"

"Balaam, son of Beor," said the rabbi with quiet intensity, "was a prophet in Moab. The Israelites were in-
vading Moab, and King Balak ordered Balaam to curse
them. His ass not only spoke to him; more important, it
halted and refused to budge on the journey until Balaam
had listened to a message from the Lord . . .

"You were right, Mule. Whether you remember what
you said or not, whether your description of me was
God's truth or the telepathic projection of my own ego,
you were right in one thing: These invaders are *men,* by
all the standards that we debated yesterday. Moreover they
are *men* suited to Mars; our patrol reported them as naked
and unprotected in this cold and this atmosphere. I wonder
if they have scouted this planet before and selected it as
suitable; that could have been some observation device
left by them that trapped you in the pass, since we've never
found traces of an earlier Martian civilization.

"Mars is not for us. We cannot live here normally; our
scientific researches have proved fruitless; and we maintained an inert, bored garrison only because our planetary ego cannot face facts and surrender the symbol of our
'conquest of space.' These other *men* can live here, perhaps fruitfully, to the glory of God and eventually to the
good of our own world as well, as two suitably populated
planets come to know each other. You were right; I cannot curse *men.*"

"Gentlemen!"

Deftly Acosta reached down and switched off the telecom. "You agree, Mule?"

"I . . . I . . . I guess I drive back now, Chaim?"

"Of course not. Do you think I want to face Fass-

bänder now? You drive on. At once. Up to the top of
the rise. Or haven't you yet remembered the rest of the
story of Balaam? He didn't stop at refusing to curse his fellow children of God. Not Balaam.

"He blessed them."

Mule Malloy had remembered that. He had remembered
more, too. The phonograph needle had coursed through the
grooves of Bible study on up to the thirty-first chapter of
Numbers with its brief epilog to the story of Balaam:

*And Moses sent them to the war . . . and they warred
against the Midianites, as the Lord commanded Moses;
and they slew all the males . . . Balaam also the son of
Beor they slew with the sword.*

He looked at the tense face of Chaim Acosta, where
exultation and resignation blended as they must in a man
who knows at last the pattern of his life, and realized that
Chaim's memory, too, went as far as the thirty-first chapter.

And there isn't a word in the Bible as to what became
of the ass, thought Mule Malloy, and started the bleep up
the rise.

EVENSONG

Lester del Rey

Lester del Rey seems to be such an aggressive humanist as to be almost jingoistic. No Tony Boucher he, suggesting that man bow out where he does not belong. In a marvelous novelette some years ago, "For I Am a Jealous People!" Del Rey made it abundantly clear that man was his own justification and defense, apart from any covenant with God. In "Evensong" he carries that conviction a bit further, to an ultimate encounter in some far and mysterious future—an encounter, I might suggest, that typifies the science-fiction version of the Death-of-God theologies. Though I disagree with the basic premise, I am glad that science fiction is mature enough to present such individual philosophies forthrightly: If the medium is to argue religion, then all viewpoints should be heard. Del Rey once expressed his own in an afterword to "Evensong": "A writer who thinks seriously about his craft must surely find himself more and more engaged with the ancient problems of philosophy—good and evil, and causality— since these lie deep within every plot and character. As a science-fiction writer, trying to scan the patterns of the future, I find myself also inevitably concerned with the question of teleology: Is there a purpose and design to the universe and to man? It may not matter. If so, must we follow it blindly? If blind chance rules, can we not shape our own purpose, suitable to our ultimate possibilities? Personally, I take my "Invictus" straight, with just a dash of bitters. But I take it very seriously. And because I do, 'Evensong' is not fiction, but allegory."

By the time he reached the surface of the little planet, even the dregs of his power were drained. Now he rested, drawing reluctant strength slowly from the yellow sun that shone on the greensward around him. His senses were dim with an ultimate fatigue, but the fear he had learned from the Usurpers drove them outward, seeking a further hint of sanctuary.

It was a peaceful world, he realized, and the fear thickened in him at the discovery. In his younger days, he had cherished a multitude of worlds where the game of life's ebb and flow could be played to the hilt. It had been a lusty universe to roam then. But the Usurpers could brook no rivals to their own outreaching lust. The very peace and order here meant that this world had once been theirs.

He tested for them gingerly while the merest whisper of strength poured into him. None were here now. He could have sensed the pressure of their close presence at once, and there was no trace of that. The even grass-land swept in rolling meadows and swales to the distant hills. There were marble structures in the distance, sparkling whitely in the late sunlight, but they were empty, their unknown purpose altered to no more than decoration now upon this abandoned planet. His attention swept back, across a stream to the other side of the wide valley.

There he found the garden. Within low walls, its miles of expanse were a tree-crowded and apparently un-tended preserve. He could sense the stirring of larger animal life among the branches and along the winding paths. The brawling vigor of all proper life was missing, but its abundance might be enough to mask his own vestige of living force from more than careful search.

It was at least a better refuge than this open greensward and he longed toward it, but the danger of betraying motion held him still where he was. He had thought his previous escape to be assured, but he was learning that even he could err. Now he waited while he tested once more for evidence of Usurper trap.

He had mastered patience in the confinement the Usurpers had designed at the center of the galaxy. He had gathered his power furtively while he designed escape around their reluctance to make final disposition. Then he had burst outward in a drive that should have thrust him far beyond the limits of their hold on the universe. And he had found failure before he could span even the distance to the end of this spiral arm of one galactic fastness.

Their webs of detection were everywhere, seemingly. Their great power-robbing lines made a net too fine to pass. Stars and worlds were linked, until only a series of miracles had carried him this far. And now the waste of power for such miracles was no longer within his reach. Since their near failure in entrapping and sequestering him, they had learned too much.

Now he searched delicately, afraid to trip some alarm, but more afraid to miss its existence. From space, this world had offered the only hope in its seeming freedom from their webs. But only microseconds had been available to him for his testing then.

At last he drew his perceptions back. He could find no slightest evidence of their lures and detectors here. He had begun to suspect that even his best efforts might not be enough now, but he could do no more. Slowly at first, and then in a sudden rush, he hurled himself into the maze of the garden.

Nothing struck from the skies. Nothing leaped upwards from the planet core to halt him. There was no interruption in the rustling of the leaves and the chirping bird songs. The animal sounds went on unhindered. Nothing seemed aware of his presence in the garden. Once that would have been unthinkable in itself, but now he drew comfort from it. He must be only a shadow self now, unknown and unknowable in his passing.

Something came down the path where he rested, pattering along on hoofs that touched lightly on the spoilage of fallen leaves. Something else leaped quickly through the light underbrush beside the path.

He let his attention rest on them as they both emerged onto the near pathway at once. And cold horror curled thickly around him.

One was a rabbit, nibbling now at the leaves of clover and twitching long ears as its pink nose stretched out for more. The other was a young deer, still bearing the spots of its fawnhood. Either or both might seemingly have been found on any of a thousand worlds. But neither would have been precisely of the type before him.

This was the Meeting World—the planet where he had first found the ancestors of the Usurpers. Of all worlds in the pested galaxy, it had to be *this* world he sought for refuge!

They were savages back in the days of his full glory, confined to this single world, rutting and driving their way to the lawful self-destruction of all such savages. And yet there had been something odd about them, something that then drew his attention and even his vagrant pity.

Out of that pity, he had taught a few of them, and led them upwards. He had even nursed poetic fancies of making them his companions and his equals as the life span of their sun should near its ending. He had answered their cries for help and given them at least some of what they needed to set their steps toward power over even space and energy. And they had rewarded him by overweening pride that denied even a trace of gratitude. He had abandoned them finally to their own savage ends and gone on to other worlds, to play out the purposes of a wider range.

It was his second folly. They were too far along the path toward unlocking the laws behind the universe. Somehow, they even avoided their own destruction from themselves. They took the worlds of their sun and drove outwards, until they could even vie with him for the worlds he had made particularly his own. And now they owned them all, and he had only a tiny spot here on their world—for a time at least.

The horror of the realization that this was the Meeting World abated a little as he remembered now how readily their spawning hordes possessed and abandoned worlds without seeming end. And again the tests he could make showed no evidence of them here. He began to relax again, feeling a sudden hope from what had been temporary despair. Surely they might also believe this was the one planet where he would never seek sanctuary.

Now he set his fears aside and began to force his thoughts toward the only pattern that could offer hope. He needed power, and power was available in any area untouched by the webs of the Usurpers. It had drained into space itself throughout the aeons, a waste of energy that could blast suns or build them in legions. It was power to escape, perhaps even to prepare himself eventually to meet them with at least a chance to force truce, if not victory. Given even a few hours free of their notice, he could draw and hold that power for his needs.

He was just reaching for it when the sky thundered and the sun seemed to darken for a moment!

The fear in him gibbered to the surface and sent him huddling from sight of the sky before he could control it. But for a brief moment there was still a trace of hope in him. It could have been a phenomenon caused by his own need for power; he might have begun drawing too heavily, too eager for strength.

Then the earth shook, and he knew.

The Usurpers were not fooled. They knew he was here—had never lost him. And now they had followed in all their massive lack of subtlety. One of their scout ships had landed, and the scout would come seeking him.

He fought for control of himself, and found it long enough to drive his fear back down within himself. Now, with a care that disturbed not even a blade of grass or leaf on a twig, he began retreating, seeking the denser undergrowth at the center of the garden where all life was thickest. With that to screen him, he might at least draw a faint trickle of power, a strength to build a subtle brute aura around himself and let him hide among the beasts. Some Usurper scouts were young and immature. Such a one might be fooled into leaving. Then, before his report could be acted on by others, there might be a chance. . . .

He knew the thought was only a wish, not a plan, but he clung to it as he huddled in the thicket at the center of the garden. And then even the fantasy was stripped from him.

The sound of footsteps was firm and sure. Branches broke as the steps came forward, not deviating from a straight line. Inexorably, each firm stride brought the Usurper nearer to his huddling place. Now there was a faint glow in the air, and the animals were scampering away in terror.

He felt the eyes of the Usurper on him, and he forced himself away from that awareness. And, like fear, he found that he had learned prayer from the Usurpers; he prayed now desperately to a nothingness he knew, and there was no answer.

"Come forth! This earth is a holy place and you cannot

remain upon it. Our judgment is done and a place is prepared for you. Come forth and let me take you there!" The voice was soft, but it carried a power that stilled even the rustling of the leaves.

He let the gaze of the Usurper reach him now, and the prayer in him was mute and directed outward— and hopeless, as he knew it must be.

"But—" Words were useless, but the bitterness inside him forced the words to come from him. "But why? I am God!"

For a moment, something akin to sadness and pity was in the eyes of the Usurper. Then it passed as the answer came. "I know. But I am Man. Come!"

He bowed at last, silently, and followed slowly as the yellow sun sank behind the walls of the garden.

And the evening and the morning were the eighth day.

SHALL THE DUST
PRAISE THEE?

Damon Knight

*Among those who reject the traditional ideas of God there
have always been an angry core who believe that no God
could allow the evil that exists and apparently multiplies in
our world. I will not take issue with that proposition here,
but propose rather to let Damon Knight take direct issue
with Jehovah. Knight says flatly that "I do not believe in
Jehovah," and dismisses the final question of this chilling
Judgment Day story as "a frivolous one" for himself. For those
who believe, however, he insists that it is an important one.
With that much I agree, and leave you to Mr. Knight's force-
ful way of making his point.*

The Day of Wrath arrived. The sky pealed with trumpets,
agonized, summoning. Everywhere the dry rocks rose,
groaning, and fell back in rubble. Then the sky split,
and in the dazzle appeared a throne of white fire, in
a rainbow that burned green.

Lightnings flickered away toward the horizons. Around
the throne hovered seven majestic figures in white, with
golden girdles across their paps; and each one carried
in his gigantic hand a vial that smoked and fumed in
the sky.

Out of the brightness in the throne came a voice: "Go your ways, and pour out the vials of the wrath of God upon the earth."

And the first angel swooped down, and emptied his vial in a torrent of darkness that smoked away across the bare earth. And there was silence.

Then the second angel flew down to earth, and darted this way and that, with his vial unemptied: and at last turned back to the throne, calling, "Lord, mine is to be poured out upon the sea. But where is the sea?"

And again there was silence. For the dry, dusty rocks of the earth stretched away limitless under the sky; and where the oceans had been, there were only runneled caverns in the stone, as dry and empty as the rest.

The third angel called, "Lord, mine is for the rivers and fountains of waters."

Then the fourth angel called, "Lord, let me empty mine." And he poured out his vial upon the sun: and in an instant grew hot with a terrible radiance: and he soared back and forth letting fall his light upon the earth. After some time he faltered and turned back to the throne. And again there was silence.

Then out of the throne came a voice saying, "Let be."

Under the wide dome of heaven, no bird flew. No creature crawled or crept on the face of the earth; there was no tree, and no blade of grass.

The voice said, "This is the day appointed. Let us go down."

Then God walked on the earth, as in the old time. His form was like a moving pillar of smoke. And after Him trooped the seven white angels with their vials, murmuring. They were alone under the yellow-gray sky.

"They who are dead have escaped our wrath," said the Lord God Jehovah. "Nevertheless they shall not escape judgment." The dry valley in which they stood was the Garden of Eden, where the first man and first woman had been given a fruit which they might not eat. To eastward was the pass through which the wretched pair had been driven into the wilderness. Some little distance to the west they saw the pitted crag of Mount Ararat, where the Ark had come to rest after a purifying Flood.

And God said in a great voice, "Let the book of life be opened: and let the dead rise up from their graves, and from the depths of the sea."

His voice echoed away under the sullen sky. And again the dry rocks heaved and fell back; but the dead did not appear. Only the dust swirled, as if it alone remained of all earth's billions, living and dead.

The first angel was holding a huge book open in his arms. When the silence had endured for some time, he shut the book, and in his face was fear; and the book vanished out of his hands.

The other angels were murmuring and sighing together. One said, "Lord, terrible is the sound of silence, when our ears should be filled with lamentations."

And God said, "This is the time appointed. Yet one day in heaven is a thousand years on earth. Gabriel, tell me, as men reckoned time, how many days have passed since the Day?"

The first angel opened a book and said, "Lord, as men reckoned time, one day has passed since the Day."

A shocked murmur went through the angels.

And turning from them, God said, "Only one day: a moment. And yet they do not rise."

The fifth angel moistened his lips and said, "Lord, are You not God? Shall any secrets be hid from the Maker of all things?"

"Peace!" said Jehovah, and thunders rumbled off toward

the gloomy horizon. "In good season, I will cause these stones to bear witness. Come, let us walk further."

They wandered over the dry mountains and through the empty canyons of the sea. And God said, "Michael, you were set to watch over these people. What was the manner of their last days?"

They paused near the fissured cone of Vesuvius, which in an aeon of heavenly inattention had twice erupted, burying thousands alive.

The second angel answered, "Lord, when last I saw them, they were preparing a great war."

"Their iniquities were past belief," said Jehovah. "Which were the nations of those that prepared the war?"

The second angel answered, "Lord, they were called England and Russia and China and America."

"Let us go then to England."

Across the dry valley that had been the Channel, the island was a tableland of stone, crumbling and desolate. Everywhere the stones were brittle and without strength. And God grew wroth, and cried out, "Let the stones speak!"

Then the gray rocks fountained up into dust, uncovering caverns and tunnels, like the chambers of an empty anthill. And in some places bright metal gleamed, lying in skeins that were graceful but without design, as if the metal had melted and run like water.

The angels murmured; but God said, "Wait. This is not all."

He commanded again, "Speak!" And the rocks rose up once more, to lay bare a chamber that was deeper still. And in silence, God and the angels stood in a circle around the pit, and leaned down to see what shapes glittered there.

In the wall of that lowest chamber, someone had chiseled a row of letters. And when the machine in that chamber had been destroyed, the fiery metal had sprayed out and filled the letters in the wall, so that they gleamed now like silver in the darkness.

And God read the words.

"WE WERE HERE. WHERE WERE YOU?"

CHRISTUS APOLLO

Ray Bradbury

Much as I admire the last two stories by Lester del Rey and Damon Knight, I do not choose to end this collection either on a note of angry humanism or a note of ultimate despair. I have shared both these emotions on occasion, but in other moments I have chosen (as even editors do) to believe. In God. In Christ, and the cherished human imitations of Christ through the ages. And in the necessity to keep our lines of communication open, somehow, to whatever is transcendent in ourselves and the universe around us. Perhaps just as earnestly, I believe that accurate definitions of God, of Christ, and of the transcendent are impossible in such a rich and strange universe as surrounds us, and I am not sure that it matters. What does matter is that we preserve our sense of wonder and awe, cherish our faith in the possible in all its forms, and keep our conviction that somewhere, within us or around us, is an ultimate salvation for those who want it. Ray Bradbury seems to share this conviction, and I offer you, as a last refreshing draught, his own poetic evocation of it, a passage from his cantata, "Christus Apollo," in I Sing the Body Electric.

In some far universal Deep
Did He tread Space
And visit worlds beyond our blood-warm dreaming?
Did He come down on lonely shore by sea
Not unlike Galilee

And are there Mangers on far worlds that knew His
  light?
And Virgins?
Sweet Pronouncements?
Annunciations? Visitations from angelic hosts?
And, shivering vast light among ten billion lights,
Was there some Star much like the star at Bethlehem
That struck the sight with awe and revelation
Upon a cold and most strange morn?

On worlds gone wandering and lost from this
Did Wise Men gather in the dawn
In cloudy steams of Beast
Within a place of straw now quickened to a Shrine
To look upon a stranger Child than ours?

How many stars of Bethlehem burnt bright
Beyond Orion or Centauri's blinding arc?
How many miracles of birth all innocent
Have blessed those worlds?

Does Herod tremble there
In dread facsimile of our dark and murderous King?
Does that mad keeper of an unimaginable realm
Send stranger soldiers forth
To slaughter down the Innocents
Of lands beyond the Horsehead Nebula?

It must be so.
For in this time of Christmas
In the long Day totalling up to Eight,
We see the light, we know the dark;
And creatures lifted, born, thrust free of so much night
No matter what the world or time or circumstance
Must love the light,

So, children of all lost unnumbered suns
Must fear the dark
Which mingles in a shadowing-forth on air.
And swarms the blood.
No matter what the color, shape, or size
Of beings who keep souls like breathing coals
In long midnights,
They *must* need saving of themselves.
So on far worlds in snowfalls deep and clear
Imagine how the rounding out of some dark year
Might celebrate with birthing one miraculous child!

A child?
Born in Andromeda's out-swept mysteries?
Then count its hands, its fingers,
Eyes, and most incredible holy limbs!
The sum of each?
No matter. Cease.
Let Child be fire as blue as water under Moon.
Let Child sport free in tides with human-seeming fish.
Let ink of octopi inhabit blood
Let skin take acid rains of chemistry
All falling down in nightmare storms of cleansing burn.

Christ wanders in the Universe
A flesh of stars,
He takes on creature shapes
To suit the mildest elements,
He dresses him in flesh beyond our ken.
There He walks, glides, flies, shambling of strangeness.
Here He walks Men.

Among the ten trillion beams
A billion Bible scrolls are scored
In hieroglyphs among God's amplitudes of worlds;

In alphabet multitudinous
Tongues which are not quite tongues
Sigh, sibilate, wonder, cry:
As Christ comes manifest from a thunder-crimsoned sky.

He walks upon the molecules of seas
All boiling stews of beast
All maddened broth and brew and rising up of yeast.
There Christ by many names is known.
We call him thus.
They call him otherwise.
His name on any mouth would be a sweet surprise.
He comes with gifts for all,

Here: wine and bread.
There: nameless foods
At breakfasts where the morsels fall from stars
And Last Suppers are doled forth with stuff of dreams.
So sit they there in times before the Man is crucified.
Here He has long been dead.
There He has not yet died.